Also by Tom Turner

Charlie Crawford Mysteries

New York Homicide (Prequel Novella)

Palm Beach Nasty

Palm Beach Poison

Palm Beach Deadly

Palm Beach Bones

Palm Beach Pretenders

Palm Beach Predator

Palm Beach Broke

Palm Beach Bedlam

Palm Beach Blues

Palm Beach Taboo

Palm Beach Piranha

Nick Janzek Charleston Mysteries

Killing Time in Charleston

Charleston Buzz Kill

Charleston Noir

Savannah Sleuth Sisters Murder Mysteries

The Savannah Madam

Savannah Road Kill

Broken House

Dead in the Water

Copyright © 2022 by Tom Turner. All rights reserved.
Published by Tribeca Press
This book is a work of fiction.
Similarities to actual events, places, persons or other entities are coincidental.
www.tomturnerbooks.com
ISBN: 9798802025994

PALM BEACH PIRANHA

CHARLIE CRAWFORD PALM BEACH MYSTERIES BOOK 11

TOM TURNER

TRIBECA PRESS

JOIN TOM'S AUTHOR NEWSLETTER

Get the latest news on Tom's upcoming novels when you sign up for his free author newsletter at **tomturnerbooks.com/news**

CHAPTER ONE

One handcuff was tight around Garrett Janney's left wrist, the other hung loosely around Laurie Reback's right wrist. They were sitting on a sofa facing Chet Egan, who wore cargo shorts, well-worn sandals, and a garish Hawaiian shirt adorned with flamingos, pineapples, and surfboards.

The three were in the guest house of Janney's home at 1231 North Ocean Boulevard in Palm Beach, a huge, 35,000-square-foot French Normandy-style mansion with 240 feet of ocean frontage. It had seven bedrooms and eight full baths— the master had two— and nine half baths, which even the owner felt was overkill. When Janney bought it five years earlier, the listing broker—Rose Clarke— referred to it as an "entertainer's dream," which wasn't hyperbole. It had a 36-seat home theater, a wine cellar, a fitness center, bowling alley, and a barber shop, as if its residents or guests couldn't be bothered to have their locks shorn at just any old salon. It also had the requisite infinity-edge pool, summer kitchen, and outdoor loggia.

Garrett Janney, 84, had outlived his first wife and divorced his second two. He lived in the residence alone and eschewed butlers, maids, housekeepers, and all other standard fare Palm Beach servants. Mainly because he was cheap. But he did have a cleaning crew of Nicaraguan women who bustled around the house every Friday and dusted, vacuumed, polished, scrubbed, scoured, and changed and ironed the old man's sheets. For those services, the wizened skinflint paid them two hundred dollars, total, which worked out to one dollar for every 175 square feet of cleaning.

Laurie Reback, Chet Egan's girlfriend, was handcuffed to Garrett Janney so he couldn't get away. As if the old guy would try to make a run for it.

Janney squinted up at Egan. "How about if I just write you a check for a million dollars, then you get lost and leave me in peace."

"No such luck, old timer," Egan said, "a million bucks doesn't go very far in the south of France or Monte Carlo."

Janney thought for a second. "Well, maybe you should lower your sights a little. Say, Aruba or Cancun."

Egan shook his head. "You got a good sense of humor for a guy closing in on a hundred."

"Please. I'm only eighty-four."

"Only." Egan chuckled.

Laurie cocked her head to one side. "I went to Aruba once. It wasn't so great. But now that I think about it, mighta been Antigua."

Egan squinted at Janney. "Okay, my man, it's time to get this show on the road."

"What the hell's that s'posed to mean?" Janney asked, struggling to come across as flinty and unflappable. He had long white hair, a hawk nose, and gnarly nails—think Howard Hughes toward the end— with eyebrows that hung down over his eyes. Some men brushed their hair out of their eyes, Janney brushed his eyebrows out of them. He was stoop-shouldered: if you measured him top to bottom, he'd be about five-eight, but if you straightened him out, he'd be closer to six-two. Janney's last wife, thirty years younger than him, had once tied his white hair into a ponytail when he was napping, just as a lark. A bored-housewife kind of thing, right before they went out to a dinner party. Janney hadn't even been aware of his new hairstyle until a much younger female dinner partner complimented him on how "chill" he looked. He just nodded and thanked her, having no idea what the word meant or what she was referring to.

Egan stretched out in the chintz club chair facing Janney and Laurie. "Here's the plan, just so you're up to speed. My girlfriend and I are gonna relieve you of a small portion of your fortune. But, since you got so much, you're never gonna miss it. So, what that means is, we're gonna be your houseguests here until we get what we're after. Might take a few days, maybe more. Then we'll leave and you'll be no worse for wear."

Janney thought for a moment. "My final offer... two million dollars."

"Rejected. Listen, man, you could offer me ten million, but I wouldn't take it," Egan said. "I just read an article in the Glossy"—the *Palm Beach Daily Reporter*, the town's gossip sheet—"said there are forty-three billionaires in Palm Beach, and you were eighteenth on the list. Eight point five billion, to be exact."

"Don't believe anything you read in that rag," Janney said. "Know what I call it?"

"No, what do you call it?" Egan asked.

"*The Palm Beach Daily Bullshitter.*"

Egan glanced at Laurie and laughed. "Well, that's not very nice. Maybe it's not *The New York Times*, but it's good for keeping us common folk plugged in on who our local billionaires are and how much they're worth."

Laurie chuckled. "Not to mention who attended the latest charity ball."

"Exactly. Lowborn mutts like us wanna know stuff like that."

"So, what are you going to do?" Janney asked.

"No, it's what *you're* going to do," Egan said. "You're gonna buy a sixty-million-dollar island in the Exuma Islands and a big, old fancy boat."

"What the hell are you talking about?" Janney said with a frown. "I have no interest in going to some scrubby little island in the Caribbean or buying a boat—big, fancy or otherwise—'cause I get seasick."

"Well, that's perfect, 'cause you ain't goin' nowhere, my friend," Egan said. "Not 'til we got a big ol' bag of cash and are halfway down the road to Easy Street."

CHAPTER TWO

It was the first time in five years that Crawford had heard from his ex-wife Jill. She called early one Saturday morning. It read UNKNOWN on his cell-phone screen.

"Hello?"

"Charlie?" said the woman's muted voice.

"Yes. Who's this?"

"God, you don't even recognize my voice."

Then he did. "Oh, Jill… hey, how are you?"

"I've been better."

"What's wrong?"

"I made two big mistakes in life. Divorcing you and marrying Giles."

How in God's name do you respond to something like that?

He heard a sigh, like air slowly coming out of a tire. "Sorry, I shouldn't have blurted that out, or called you out of the blue like this. I just… I just don't know."

Crawford had no idea where this was going. "It's nice to hear your voice…are you still living in the city?"

"Yes, but we bought a house in Palm Beach, after Covid. The city, well, kind of lost some of its appeal."

"I understand. So, where's your house?"

"Jungle Road. 240. Bought it six months ago."

"One of my favorite streets."

"I'd say come over for a drink, but… that's probably not appropriate."

"Probably not."

Jill sighed again. "Well, I just wanted to say hi and let you know, so if you saw me walking down the street you wouldn't say, 'What the hell's she doing here?'"

"Well, welcome to Palm Beach. I think you'll like it. It's a great town."

"Except for those bad actors you go after, right?"

He laughed. "Yeah, don't worry about them. They're all in jail."

Jill gave a faint laugh.

Crawford, six-three with piercing blue eyes and a sturdy chin that had taken a few shots over the years, wore his dirty-blond hair a little longer than his boss, Police Chief Norm Rutledge, liked. Handsome without much fuss, he could have been a model if models wore clothes they bought on sale at Men's Wearhouse.

"Well, Charlie, it's good to hear your voice again. I…"

Whatever she was going to say, she seemed to think it better left unsaid.

"Good to hear yours, too."

"Hope to bump into you somewhere. Publix, maybe." The local supermarket.

"That would be nice." Even though he was a Winn-Dixie guy.

"Bye," she said and clicked off.

But *would* it be nice? Or would it be colossally awkward? It had taken Crawford a long time to get over his divorce. It marked a failure, one he had many regrets about. Things he hadn't done, things he'd done, things…so damn many things.

*****

What Crawford had never told his friend, Rose Clarke, the real estate agent on the purchase of his condo at the Trianon—1200 South Flagler Drive—was that he had a fear of heights. So here he was on the 14th floor, looking due east out over the Intracoastal and the Palm Beach Marina in the foreground and the skinny island of Palm Beach beyond. He could even see the ocean on the other side of Palm Beach, with the inevitable tanker steaming along, a mere speck in the distance.

Though he'd had his movers place two Adirondack style chairs out on his balcony, he never went out there. After a cocktail or two, he imagined a fierce cross wind sucking him out over the railing, or him clumsily tripping and plunging fourteen stories, a splat on the pavement next to the building's pool. He even imagined the building collapsing like the tragedy in Surfside. As a result of all the scenarios his fertile imagination conjured up, he was content to take in the view from well inside the condo. And a beautiful view it was: the *look-at-me* yachts moored at the marina straight ahead, Everglades Island off to the right, the majestic middle bridge over to Palm Beach to his left, and off in the distance, the elegant Breakers hotel.

Rose Clarke and Dominica McCarthy, his girlfriend—well, at the moment anyway— had both had a hand in decorating the condo. Rose had convinced him to chuck all his "old junk," as she called it, from his dumpy former condo and start from scratch at the Trianon. She took him to Restoration Hardware on Okeechobee, where he suffered acute sticker shock at the prices. Nevertheless, Rose twisted his arm and he bought beds, towels, sheets, wash cloths, and even something called a duvet, though he had no idea what it was for. Then he found two other places online—True Treasure and Circa Who— that sold, as one claimed, "gently used" furniture and furnishings. So he went to those places one Saturday morning with Dominica and bought a few things that didn't cost an arm and a leg, having already shot his wad at Restoration Hardware. A week later, his condo was ready for habitation. As for his walls, he found a few paintings at small shops on Dixie Highway and two vintage posters on line. He also bought an oil painting of a beach scene that was for sale at a restaurant he frequented in the Northwood section of West Palm Beach. Rose liked the painting until he told her where it came from, and Dominica said he could do better. He liked it, though, and kept it in a place of prominence in his living room. The hell with them—they didn't appreciate great restaurant art.

At the moment, 39-year-old homicide cop Crawford had more time on his hands than he would have liked. Nobody had gotten killed in Palm Beach in a while. He was sick of going into the office and staring at his partner Mort Ott all day long. He could tell Ott dittoed that.

He had more time than usual to ponder and replay the phone call from his ex-wife Jill. Something in her voice made him uneasy. So he had decided to call her sister Jessie. He'd remained friends with Jessie's husband, Jack Giordano, and went fishing with him whenever he and Jessie came down to their winter place in Port St. Lucie. He had emailed Jack for Jessie's cell number and just received it in response.

He dialed.

"Hi, Charlie," Jessie answered. "Jack said you might be calling. How are you?"

"I'm fine, how are you?"

"Oh, you know, older, fatter."

"Older, yes, fatter, I seriously doubt it," Crawford said. "So, I spoke to Jill. She told me about buying a house down here. How's she doing, anyway?"

"That sounds more like a detective question than an ex-husband's question."

"A little of both."

Jessie sighed deeply. "Well, I'll tell you, 'cause as you know, I'm not one to hold back. She's not doing too well. Giles started cheating on her like five minutes after they were married. Discreetly at first, then openly. I mean there are nights he doesn't even come home. He once… no, I'm not going to go there."

"Come on, tell me."

"You just want to hear a sordid story—"

"No, because she was my wife and I still care for her."

There was a long sigh at the other end. "Well, for one thing, Giles tried to talk Jill into a ménage à trois."

"You're kidding. What an asshole!" Crawford said with unrestrained vehemence. He had never liked Giles Simpson the few times he'd met him. "I mean, that's sick. I can't even imagine what Jill said when he asked her."

"Well, she sure as hell didn't say yes," Jessie said with a laugh. "But it was more what she thought. Like maybe it was time to seriously think about getting out of the marriage. But the next morning he told her he'd just had too much to drink and was kidding around."

"Guy's got a hell of a sense of humor."

"I know, right?" Jessie said. "Plus, he's just such an egotistical jerk. Wants to do what he wants to do, the hell with what she ever wants."

"And this is the way it's always been?"

"Yeah, pretty much, but it keeps getting worse. I wish she had never met the jerk."

"Well, maybe it'll be better now that they've got a place down here. At least she can get away from him when he's up in the city. Meet some new people, you know, change of scenery."

"I sure hope so."

"Does he come down on weekends? Or what?"

"Yeah, most weekends. Unless he's got a better offer up there."

Crawford groaned.

"Sometimes he'll come for a week," Jessie said, "if he's not operating."

"Sounds like he's *always* operating."

Jessie laughed. "I meant as a surgeon."

"She still playing tennis?"

"A little... but the problem is her cocktail hour seems to start earlier and earlier."

"Oh, God, really?" That had never been an issue before.

"Yeah, I've called her some mornings at around ten and I can tell she's halfway through her second Bloody Mary," Jessie said. "You know what it is: Giles berates her all the time. For dinner being overcooked, and—I don't need to tell you—she's a fabulous cook. For one lousy plate being in the sink, and the poor woman's a total neat freak. For a whole bunch of imagined stuff. I think she just reached the conclusion that she's better off dealing with him when she's drunk. She told me once she goes to bed at around eight o'clock most nights... or whenever, and wherever, she passes out."

Crawford felt a palpable pain in his chest. He felt like having a little talk with Giles Simpson... in a dark alley.

"I'm really sorry to hear that. I had no idea, but I could hear the pain in her voice." And maybe a Bloody Mary.

"Hey, it's not your problem, Charlie."

"Yeah, I know, but it still makes me sad. I mean, she deserves the best. She doesn't deserve that guy."

"I'm just glad they don't have kids," Jessie said. "That would be so much worse."

He couldn't imagine Jessie walking down the street with Giles's kids. Talk about painful.

"Well, thanks for filling me in. I just feel so bad for her."

"Yeah, me too."

"What do you think can be done about it?"

"For one thing, I'm going to step up my campaign."

"Your campaign?"

"For her to divorce the arrogant son-of-a-bitch and be done with the whole sorry mess."

*****

On his way home, Crawford took a little detour to a florist shop he had been to once before, the day of Dominica's birthday. He almost cheaped out and bought a thirty-dollar bouquet but then stepped up to a much larger one that cost a hundred and ten. He wrote on the card, "A belated welcome to our fair city. Well, town actually. Promise you'll love it here." He almost added three X's but thought he better not and instead just wrote, "All the best, Charlie."

CHAPTER THREE

Chet Egan had been manager of a successful restaurant on Clematis Street in West Palm Beach until Covid came along and put it out of business. Then he had collected unemployment for a while, trying to land a job at other restaurants in the area. But nothing had worked out except for one that paid about half of what he had been making. So, Chet had a lot of time to think. And a lot of his thinking was about how to get rich. Really rich. Palm Beach rich. His girlfriend Laurie was a pool cleaner and always told him about the fabulous houses in Palm Beach whose pools she cleaned, chlorinated, and repaired.

In particular, she told him about one old man who never left his house but was supposedly worth billions. How he'd watch her out of a big picture window as she performed her duties and always had a big grin on his leathery face when she showed up in cut-offs and a skimpy, red bikini top. Chet asked her a bunch of questions about him: like whether she ever saw cars in the driveway, how often people visited him, and if she ever saw him leave the house at all.

No, the guy's a total whatchamacallit, Laurie said.

A recluse? Chet asked.

Yeah, that's it. Dude never goes anywhere, and no one's ever come to visit him in the three years I been doin' his pool. Just looks out the window with that dumb grin on his face watchin' me skimmin' leaves and doin' my thang.

A week later, Chet had a plan. It was loosely based on an incident he had read about in the *Palm Beach Post* a couple of years before. He couldn't remember the exact details, but the gist of it was that two men had gone to an open house for a big Georgian home on Clarke Avenue and, as the real estate agent showed a couple around the downstairs, the two men had gone and hidden in the large walk-in closet in the master bedroom upstairs. After the open house was over and the realtor had locked up and left, they came out of the closet and waited for the owner to return.

An hour later they heard the clicking of a key in the front door. One of the men was apparently hiding behind the front door and the other one in a coat closet in the foyer. The owner, a middle-aged single woman, walked in and the man behind the door grabbed her from behind and covered her mouth with his hand. The other man came out of the coat closet and calmly explained that he had found her checkbook in her desk in the master bedroom and knew exactly how much she had in her account. In a relaxed tone accompanied by a friendly smile, he explained that she was going to write him a check for the entire balance. Then he pulled a pistol out of his waistband and said to make the check out to *Cash*... adding sinisterly, *Or else, pop, pop, pop.*

They gagged her—put duct tape over her mouth, Chet seemed to remember—then made her write out a check for just over $25,000. Then one of them drove her to her bank on Royal Poinciana Way. He went in and presented the check. The teller told him that because the amount was over $10,000 and was made out to Cash, she had to get her manager to approve it. The manager then called the woman, who had a gun to her head, and—without a second's hesitation—told him to go ahead and cash it.

Not a bad day's work, Chet thought, but so small-time. Penny ante. Plus, a check? That was so dated in a world of such innovative cybercrime. He seemed to remember that the two men had tried it again but had gotten caught that time. The manager had become suspicious, as he recalled, and had marked the money.

That incident became the germ of Chet's plan, but his grew to be much more complex and involved a lot more money.

*****

"So here's what you're gonna do," Chet said to Garrett Janney. "You're gonna call up your man at Bessemer Trust and tell him about your new lifestyle change."

Garrett Janney was so hunched over in the brown wing chair he looked almost U-shaped. "What are you talking about? What *lifestyle change?*"

"I told you. Buyin' a private island in the Exumas and a big-ass yacht. See, what happened was a guy came to you, told you about a major business reversal he had just gone through and offered to sell you the island and the boat for twenty-five cents on the dollar."

"Like I told you," Garrett said, "I get seasick on boats."

"Yeah, I heard you," Egan said. "Which is why they have shit like Dramamine…so as I was saying, this guy came to you with all these bona fide appraisals that said the island is worth sixty million and the boat another twenty."

"And in case your math's a little rusty, Mr. J.," said Laurie, "that adds up to eighty million."

Janney scowled. "I got it."

"Like I said, twenty-five cents on the dollar," Egan said. "So as a man who was known all your long successful business career as a shrewd negotiator with an eye for great investment opportunities, you jumped at it. Hell of a deal, wouldn't you say?"

"Hell of a racket is what I'd say," Janney said. "You don't really expect to pull this off, do you?"

"Matter of fact, we do. Because if we don't, my friend, you're a dead man," Egan said, studying Janney closely and seeing he was bent over so much that his chin practically touched his knees. "By the way, you really should do something about that posture of yours… just sayin'."

Laurie nodded fervently. "Yeah, come on, Mr. J., thrust out that chest, pull your shoulders back, look like that kickass captain of industry you once were."

Janney shook his head and scowled again. "Why don't you nudniks just take the money I offered you and go to Cancun or wherever? Get out of my house and give up on this hare-brained scheme."

Egan looked at Laurie and laughed, but then he glanced over at Janney, narrowed his eyes, and got dead serious. "So, I've been through the files in your office and read through all your accounts and investments. How long have you had that account at Bessemer Trust?"

Janney didn't answer.

"How long, Garrett?"

"What difference does it make?" Janney said, with a shrug. "A long time. Forty years or so."

"Wow, before I was born. And, according to what I read, they manage the bulk of your assets. Five billion plus."

"A lot of which is illiquid. Most of it, in fact."

"Hey, we're talkin' a mere twenty million here," Egan said. "You're never gonna miss it."

"Yeah, it's like a tip to you," Laurie said.

"So are you ready to call 'em up?" Egan asked.

"And say what?"

"You want twenty million wired into an account at Chase."

"They're going to want to know why."

"I told you why. You're getting this incredible opportunity. The island and the boat. And if your bankers have a problem with it, well, screw 'em. 'Cause you got five billion in their bank. What right do they have to question anything you want to do? Tell 'em if they don't hop to, you're gonna walk your money down the street to Citibank or some place."

Janney squinted up at Egan and tried again. "Why don't you just take the two million and walk away?"

Egan pulled closer to Janney. "You gotta get that out of your head, Garrett. We ain't goin' anywhere, my friend. The price is twenty million. Either that or you get your throat slit. *Comprende?*"

Garrett kept silent despite being threatened with murder two different ways: with a gun, and with a knife.

Egan pulled a knife out of a sheath on his right hip. "Maybe you oughta start rehearsing what you're gonna say, 'cause if this doesn't get done by tomorrow at five, you're gonna have a very difficult time breathing."

Janney started blinking rapidly.

"Got a little script here for you, Garrett," Egan said, pulling a yellow-lined sheet of paper out of his pocket. "You're gonna call up your friendly banker there and this is what you're gonna say. What's his name, by the way?"

"My banker?"

"Yeah."

"Lawrence," Janney said.

"Okay... *'Hey, Lawrence, it's Garrett Janney, I need you to wire twenty million dollars into an account at Chase.'*

"*'Sure, Garrett, anything you say. Mind telling me what it's for?'*

"*'A business opportunity,'* you tell him. And he goes, *'Do you mind being a little more specific?'*

"And you say, *'Do you ask me when you want to go buy a new Mercedes?'*"

Laurie nodded. "Yeah, let the dude know you're large and in charge."

Egan went on. "Then Lawrence says some crap like, *'I'm just trying to exercise my fiduciary responsibility on your behalf.'* So you sigh… kinda dramatically, and go, *'A former colleague of mine came to me with a deal I have to move fast on. He offered to sell me an island he owns in the Exumas—'*" Chet glanced over at Laurie and chuckled, "Wherever the hell they might be—*'along with a Feadship he's got docked down in Lauderdale. He's got bona fide appraisals saying they're worth eighty million between 'em, but he'll take twenty million if I move fast. I looked into his company and found out it's hemorrhaging cash. It's going to go under unless he can get some creditors off his back immediately.'* So then Lawrence starts in with more questions: *'What's the man's name? What's the name of his company? What do you need an island for? What do you need a Feadship for?'* Or whatever he comes up with. So you cut him off, say something like, *'Listen, don't start with that shit again. I promised the man anonymity.'* Then go, *'Look, time is of the essence here, I got plenty of money with you, so don't go screwing this up. If this deal doesn't get done in the next twenty-four hours, he's belly up and I miss a major opportunity. So I want you to get it done… fast!'*"

Egan looked up at Janney and smiled. "Now isn't that just how a big swingin' dick like you would talk?"

CHAPTER FOUR

Garrett Janney called Lawrence Duke of Bessemer Trust later that night. Egan and Laurie were sitting on either side of Janney on a large beige couch, Egan holding the knife menacingly close to Janney in case the old man was tempted to stray off-script.

To be absolutely sure Janney got the message, Egan told him, "You blab, you shout, you yell, you scream... you bleed to death all over your nice couch."

"I got it. Loud and clear," Janney said.

Egan dialed Lawrence Duke's number and handed Janney the phone when Duke answered.

"Hi, Lawrence, it's Garrett Janney."

"Oh, hey, Garrett, how are you? I saw you made the list as usual in the *Glossy*," Duke said, referring to *The Palm Beach Reporter*.

"What list?"

"The forty-three billionaires who own houses in Palm Beach."

"You know what I call the *Glossy*?"

"What's that?"

"*The Palm Beach Daily Bullshitter*." Janney tended to repeat himself.

"Yeah, I know," Duke said with a chuckle. "It's good to line your birdcage with."

"I don't have any birds," Janney said. "Okay, enough of the small talk. I need you to do something for me."

"Anything, my friend."

"Long story short, I'm going to need twenty million dollars wired into an account at Chase in the next twenty-four hours."

"Sure," Duke said. "That should be no problem. What's it for?"

"Let's just call it a business opportunity that won't be there unless I jump on it quick."

"Well, as one of the masters of capitalizing on opportunities when they pop up, I'm sure it's a home run. Can you just give me a little color?"

Janney's tone flipped from business-like to impatient. "You mean because it's your fiduciary duty to protect my interests?"

"Yeah, well, something like that," Duke said, "And as someone who's worked with you for a good portion of those forty years you've been with us, I want to pitch in where I can be helpful. Can you just tell me what the nature of it is?"

Janney sighed deeply, as if Duke were severely taxing his patience. "All right, here's the down and dirty. Someone I know professionally has what you boys call a 'liquidity crisis.' His company is about to default on a bond and unless he gets twenty million in a hurry, he's toast. So in order to raise cash I'm buying his private island in the Exumas and his 225-foot yacht for twenty-five cents on the dollar."

"Can you tell me his name?"

"No. That I can't do. It'll come out sooner or later, but I signed a confidentiality agreement and told him I wouldn't reveal his identity. And, as you know, I always keep my word."

"That you do," Duke said. "I'll get on it first thing in the morning."

"No, Lawrence, you'll get on it right after you hang up with me."

Duke laughed. "Yes, Garrett, that's what I meant to say."

CHAPTER FIVE

Crawford had just walked into his office when his cell phone rang. He looked down at the display: *Jessie*, it said.

"Hey, Jess, twice in a week. Lucky me."

"That bastard beat up Jill."

"Where'd it happen?"

"Their place in the city. She was up there for a friend's daughter's christening. It's not the first time."

Crawford's first reaction was to get one of his former New York cop friends to go rough up the lowlife son of a bitch.

"What did he do to her?"

"Started choking her then slapped her across her face with the back of his hand so hard it knocked her to the floor," Jessie said. "I just texted you a photo of her face."

"Hang on." He clicked her on hold and went to Messages. Jill had a puffy upper lip, a big bruise on her left cheek, and her neck was angry red.

"Jesus, you can see his finger impressions on her neck."

"I know," Jessie said. "She told me the whole thing was kind of a blur."

Crawford thought for a moment. "Is she on her way back down here?"

"Yes, right after the christening tomorrow."

"Good. She should tell him not to come down this weekend."

"Or maybe *any* weekend."

"I hear you," Crawford said. "Tell her if she wants to call me again, I'm happy to talk."

Jessie sighed. "I know you, Charlie. I know how you get."

"What do you mean?"

"What I mean is, you want to go beat the living hell out of Giles, don't you?"

"Well, yeah, matter of fact that *had* crossed my mind."

CHAPTER SIX

"I can see why you were such a kick-ass guy in business, Garrett," Egan said, sheathing the knife he had been menacing Janney with.

Janney didn't respond.

"Yeah," Laurie said, impressed, "you seem like a dude who gets it done."

Janney scratched his turkey neck. "Are those s'posed to be compliments?"

Egan laughed. "Well, yeah. Hey, we just like your style. Doesn't seem as though you've lost a step…you know, like a lot of guys your age have."

"Okay," Janney said, holding up his hands, "I did what you wanted. Now what?"

"Well, now Laurie's gonna go get us some dinner," Egan said. "I'm thinking an extra-large pizza. How's that sound?"

"I'd like lasagna, if you're getting take-out," Janney said.

"Lasagna it is my friend."

Janney nodded. "So, assuming my guy at Bessemer wires the money into your bank account tomorrow morning, then what?"

Egan stood up and took his wallet out. "Then, after I've gone to the bank, we go on our merry way and leave you in peace. I want to see how much the bank will give me in cash. The rest I'm going to want to get in certified checks."

"And that'll be the end of it?"

"Yup, we'll be set for life, and you, like I said before, won't even miss it," Egan said, taking two twenties out of his wallet and handing them to Laurie. "Get Garrett a lasagna and whatever he wants to drink and you and me can split a pizza. On my half, I want sausage and onions."

"I'm good with that. I'll make the whole thing sausage and onions," Laurie said, turning to Janney. "Mr. J., you want something to drink with that lasagna?"

"Seven-Up."

"*Please,* Laurie," Laurie instructed him.

Janney glanced at her, gave her an eyeroll, and said nothing more.

*****

Janney had concluded that it was unlikely he would be celebrating his eighty-fifth birthday.

It was obvious that they were going to kill him. They had no choice. Otherwise, when Egan left, Janney could simply call the cops and say there's a guy named Chet Egan who forced me at knifepoint to have my money guy wire twenty million bucks into my account at Chase. Egan hardly struck him as the type to accept Janney's promise to keep the whole thing under his hat.

Not a chance.

So Janney had to do something. But the possibilities were slim. Particularly since he was eighty-four and, for the most part, extremely frail. And because Egan had him handcuffed to himself or Laurie at all times, except when he had to take a piss or something.

It was 10:30 at night. Janney and Egan were watching season five of *Bosch,* a show Janney had never heard of. Normally, Janney would have been in bed by now. He usually knocked off between 9:30 and 9:45. They were sitting in the living room of Janney's guest house, which was above Janney's six-car garage.

Janney turned to Egan with a frown. "How does a Los Angeles detective get to have such a nice house?"

Harry Bosch, the hero of *Bosch,* had a glass box of a house overlooking Los Angeles.

"Just so happens, I know the answer," Egan said. "See, the story is that a movie was made of one of Harry's cases and he got a nice paycheck for it. Put that money into the house."

Janney nodded. "Hell of a view. I never was a big fan of Los Angeles, though."

"Oh yeah, why not?"

"All that smog and plastic people."

"Good-looking women and nice weather, though."

Janney shrugged and fell silent for a few moments.

"So, what are you going to do with me once the money's in your bank account?" Janney asked.

Egan didn't hesitate. "I told you. Not a damn thing. But, if you even think about callin' the cops, you're a dead man."

"I have no intention of doing that."

"That's good. So you'll just keep quiet about this whole thing?" Egan didn't wait for an answer. "Because if you're ever tempted to rat us out, I've got a man ready to take you down."

Janney didn't react.

"'Case you're unfamiliar with the term, that means kill you. Slowly and painfully."

"Yes, I knew what you meant."

"Just to lay it out nice and clear for you…I'm going to park twenty-five grand in a safe deposit box. And if you're foolish enough to call the cops, I'll call a very vicious friend of mine, tell him to go whack you, then how to open the box to pay for his services. *Capeesh?*"

"I got it," Janney said with a yawn. "I'm tired. I hope we're not sleeping in the same bed."

Egan laughed. "You got three bedrooms in the guesthouse here. Two with king-sized beds, one with two singles. We're both gonna be sleeping in one of the singles. Roommates, but not bedmates."

Janney rolled his rheumy eyes. "How cozy."

CHAPTER SEVEN

Chet had Laurie watching Garrett Janney the next morning as he left the guest house and drove down to the Chase bank at 411 South County Road. He parked, went into the bank, and walked toward the manager, whom he had briefly met when he opened up his account a few years before.

Wayne—Chet knew his name was Wayne because he had a gold name plate on his left breast pocket that said Wayne P.—was a man with thinning hair, large teeth, and a weak chin. He greeted Chet with a generic "How ya doin', sir. How can I be of service?"

"Name's Chet Egan, Wayne. I've been with the bank about three years now."

"And we appreciate your business, sir," Wayne said. "How can I help?"

"My question is, if a large sum of money is wired into my account, does that set off a lot of alarms? And, also, is any kind of freeze put on the money? I don't want to go through all that hassle, you know."

"When you say a large sum of money, how much are you talking?"

"Twenty million dollars."

Wayne's eyes got big. "Really?"

"Inheritance from my rich grandfather," Chet said, looking up in the air. "God bless his soul."

"Wish I had one," Wayne said with a chuckle. "In answer to your question, a deposit of that size is definitely going to attract attention from bank examiners and our compliance people. This is not something I've had a lot of experience with, but I remember once when a customer made a million-dollar deposit. It did attract a lot of attention."

"Why? What did they want to know?"

"Well, like where the money came from, for one thing. You know, was it a lawful source? Tell you the truth, I don't know that much about it. But I think the drug trade had quite a bit to do with tightening up a lot of bank regulations."

Chet, nodding, made a quick decision that this was *not* the way to go.

"Another problem is you're not allowed to withdraw more than ten thousand dollars at a time."

"Really? Why is that?"

"I honestly don't know. It's just the law."

It was clearly time for Plan B. And he had already come up with it.

*****

He was back in Garrett Janney's guesthouse. Janney was handcuffed to Laurie.

"Change of plan, Garrett," Egan said, sitting down opposite Janney.

Janney shrugged his scrawny shoulders. "Okay, so you don't want the money wired?"

"No. You're going to buy twenty million in gold instead from an outfit in Dallas called JM Bullion."

Janney was not about to throw up any roadblocks. He just wanted to give Egan what he was demanding and get him and Laurie the hell out of his life. "Okay, just tell me what you want me to do."

Egan turned to Laurie. "I love how cooperative he's being. Don't you?"

She nodded and said, "I always told you what a nice man he was."

"All right then," Egan said. "So I'm gonna call these bullion people, say I work for you, and work out the logistics. Then you're going to call that guy Duke at Bessemer and tell him you want to buy twenty million dollars' worth of bullion."

Janney just nodded.

"Then you can go back to watching girls skim leaves off your pool in their bikinis," Egan said to Janney. "'Course it won't be Laurie 'cause she'll be retired."

"Yeah," Laurie said with a smile. "Hung up my trusty skimmer."

*****

The other thing that Egan had looked into were bitcoins. Like the fact that a ten-thousand-dollar investment in bitcoins in 2012 would be worth three million dollars now. He read about how it all worked and found it tough to process, but finally was able to understand it. He read about how one bitcoin investor had obtained a $1.2 million mortgage to buy a house in Amsterdam from a Swiss company called Nexo and how the mortgage was collateralized by bitcoins. He read another article about a bitcoin billionaire, a former child actor, who had moved to Old San Juan, Puerto Rico, because there was no capital gains tax there and he felt the island was rife with opportunity. The article went on to say that many other American business men had moved their families to the island. A lot of rich hippies, too, the article continued.

Egan had given a lot of thought about his next stop. The West Coast, at first, but then he'd decided he'd better get out of the country. He considered moving to one of the tax havens like Panama, Belize, or the Caymans—after he changed his identity—but didn't know what the lifestyle would be like in those countries. The cultures were just so different. Puerto Rico, where he had once been on a gambling junket, seemed to have things that appealed to him and had the benefit of being an American territory. But, he was certain, he couldn't just show up with twenty million dollars and deposit it in a bank.

Enter the Cayman Islands. Or, as Egan joked to Laurie, "The No-Questions Asked Islands." There, it seemed, he *could* just walk into one of the many banks in Georgetown with a lot of gold bars and convert them into cash. From everything he'd read, they didn't seem to care much where it came from. Then he could buy bitcoins, a house, a big-ass boat, or any damn thing he pleased.

*****

Chester "Chet" Egan had grown up the son of aging hippies. He had been raised in a commune in Colorado, then spent time at another in New Mexico. His mother came from a rich family in San Francisco and his father from a poor one in Modesto, California. Chet wasn't entirely sure where his parents met but his mother thought it was Haight-Ashbury, though it seemed both his mother and father were almost always stoned back when they first crossed paths and couldn't remember much.

One of the benefits of commune living seemed to be that many of the leaders were extremely dedicated to home-schooling and had well-educated members who served as teachers. In fact, the leader of Egan's commune reputedly went to Harvard in the early sixties and became a disciple of Timothy Leary. In any case, Egan's SAT scores were off the charts, and he was accepted at both UC Berkeley and Duke.

Sight unseen, he chose Duke.

It was not a perfect match, and Egan dropped out halfway through his sophomore year after taking—much to the chagrin of his parents—as many gut courses as he could. He went back to the commune and was not welcomed warmly by his parents, who thought he had squandered his big chance. But one of the leaders, who had taken a liking to Egan, was a crafty man who created a fake transcript that portrayed Chet as a magna cum laude Duke econ major. A few months later, Egan was accepted in the training program at Morgan Guaranty in New York City. But once again, Egan crashed and burned. Part of the reason was that Egan drew a total blank when the man who hired him at Morgan mentioned the names of prominent economists John Maynard Keynes, Milton Friedman, and Paul Samuelson. The other part was his occasional use of somewhat indecipherable *hippie-speak* to express himself. So, after several months, he was told he wasn't exactly "Morgan Guaranty material" and was fired.

Egan once again returned to Colorado and a few weeks later got a job at a winery in a town called Palisade. Making wine, it turned out, was something he liked and was good at. And by age twenty-four, he was assistant manager of the winery. He was making good money and had a nice girlfriend, too. All was well with Egan until a year and a half into his relationship with the woman, when she cheated on him, and he beat her up and broke her neck.

Miraculously, she didn't die, but she would be on life support for the rest of her life. Egan was suddenly out of a job and in jail for the next seven years. After his release, he bummed around for a while before moving to Jupiter, Florida, first becoming a security cop, then working on a charter boat. He met Laurie in a singles bar in Jupiter and talked a lot about boats but kept his past to himself.

*****

Garrett Janney called Lawrence Duke of Bessemer Securities just after five.

"Lawrence, it's Garrett Janney. Listen, change of plan," Janney said. "I want to buy twenty million dollars' worth of gold from an outfit in Dallas called JM Bullion."

"What happened to wiring—"

"Long story, but I need you to get right on it."

"Well, Christ, Garrett, give me some details. I mean there are a lot of ways to buy gold. What exactly do you want me to do?"

"Okay, write this down. I want eighteen million dollars' worth of one-kilo Valcambi-cast gold bars. Works out to about three hundred twenty of 'em—" he read from what Egan had written on a yellow-lined pad—"and two million dollars' worth of ten-ounce Credit Suisse Palladium bars. A hundred of them."

"All right…what do you want to do with them?"

"I want to take delivery. Here."

A pause. "At your house?"

"Yes. At my house." Janney mustered his best tone of impatience.

Another pause. "But what are you going to do when you get the gold to your house?"

"That's none of your damn business," Janney said. "We're wasting time here. Just execute the damn order, will you?"

Duke sighed. "All right, Garrett, whatever you say. You're the boss."

"Yeah, and don't you forget it."

"Okay, okay… I'm just curious, how do you know so much about gold anyway?"

"When you been around eighty-four years, you either know a lot about everything…or else you've forgotten everything."

CHAPTER EIGHT

Charlie Crawford looked down and saw his ex-wife's phone number on his cell phone display.

"Hey, how you doin', Jill?" he said.

"Well, okay I guess. Jessie told me she told you what happened. So I'm back down here now."

Crawford was relieved. "Good. Alone, I hope."

"Yeah, Giles is up there…with his women and his squash buddies."

"Women…plural?"

"Oh, yeah. Last count was he had three of 'em."

"What a—" he cleaned up his language "—slimeball."

"I know," Jill said. "By the way, that was so sweet of you. Sending me those flowers.

I meant to call earlier, but—"

"—Don't worry about it. Picked 'em myself, you know."

Jill laughed. "I figured."

"So, how's the house? By now you've had plenty of time to work your decorating magic."

"It's great," Jill said. "Why don't you stop by and see—" she caught herself— "No, that's probably not such a good idea, right?"

"I don't think it is," Crawford said. "You got some friends you can play tennis with? Have over for a glass of wine?"

"Yeah, a few. But I'm just happy to veg out. Sit out at the pool with a trashy novel."

"I know what you mean," he said. "Well, I'm really glad you're down here. Have fun, It's good to be a thousand miles away from him."

Jill laughed. "I checked. Twelve hundred and eighteen miles, to be exact."

CHAPTER NINE

The man at JM Bullion promised he could get the gold to Garrett Janney's house in two days and acted like trucking in roughly 800 pounds worth of gold wasn't that big a deal. Egan told Janney to say he needed it the next day and he'd pay him an extra five thousand dollars to make it happen. The guy said he was a *can-do kinda guy*, and then, *consider it done*. He'd add it to the bill. Next, he asked where it should be unloaded. Egan was ready for the question and told Janney to tell the guy that he wanted it loaded into the back trunk of his Honda Accord. The man at JM Bullion hesitated a few seconds, as if he expected Janney to say the trunk of a Rolls or at the very least a Mercedes.

*****

The morning of the expected gold delivery Egan and Laurie had gone outside of Janney's guesthouse to talk. This time, Janney was handcuffed to the handle of the GE Profile refrigerator, duct tape over his mouth.

"So what are we going to do with him, once we get the gold?" Laurie asked.

They had discussed this a number of times but hadn't come up with a scenario Egan was satisfied with.

"I'm still thinking about it. Obviously, we've got to make it look accidental."

"Yeah, definitely," Lauric said.

"I've got an idea…ever hear of a tennis player named Vitas Gerulaitis?"

"Sounds like the name of a disease. Who's he?"

"Well, when I was a kid out west, I was a tennis fan. Vitas was one of my favorites; he had long hair, charismatic guy. Anyway, he was staying at a friend's house somewhere up north and died of carbon monoxide poisoning, I'm pretty sure it was."

Laurie took her iPhone out. "I'm gonna Google him—" she clicked its screen "—How do you spell his name?"

"V-i-t-a-s G-e-r-u-l-a-i-t-i-s."

"Okay, here we go, it says, 'An improperly installed pool heater caused carbon monoxide gas to seep into the guesthouse where Gerulaitis was sleeping, causing his death by carbon monoxide poisoning.'"

"Yeah, poor bastard," said Egan. "Never knew what hit him."

Laurie nodded. "What do you think? You're pretty mechanical. Think you could mess around with a heater a little, so it puts out carbon monoxide? Maybe check out a YouTube video or something, see how to do it."

He patted her shoulder. "Good thinkin'."

"Thanks." She puffed up her chest proudly. "And you thought I was just a chick who looked hot in a bikini."

*****

A day later, Garrett Janney's cell phone, in Egan's pocket, rang. Egan, seeing the display said "JM Bullion," handed it to Janney.

"Hello."

"Mr. Jenny?"

"Janney. Yes, who's this?"

"Name's Robert. I'm making the delivery from JM Bullion. Should be at your house in ten minutes."

"Okay, good. When you're on the street in front of the house, call again. I'll hit the button that opens the front gate."

"You got it. See you in a few."

Janney clicked off.

He turned to Egan and shrugged. "See, I'm doing my part. After you get the gold you'll release me, right?"

"Yeah, we're gonna put you back in the main house. Tie you up so you don't call the cops five minutes after we're out of here."

"Told you I wasn't going to do that."

"But you might change your mind," Laurie said. "We've got a friend who'll come untie you a few hours after we're gone."

Janney was more than a little suspicious, but what could he say?

A few minutes later, Janney got a call from the gold-delivery man.

Egan went over to the guesthouse buzzer and buzzed the truck in. Then he went outside and waited for it as it slowly made its way up Janney's chattahoochee pebble driveway. It was a Brinks-style white Volvo truck with big black letters on its side that said: *Fortress*.

Two men got out. Both had pistols at their hips.

"Mr. Janney?" said one with a wispy mustache.

"I work for him," said Egan.

"We've got instructions that only Mr. Janney can sign for the delivery," the other man said.

"He's eighty-four years old," Egan said. "Can't walk so good."

"Sorry, we gotta obey instructions," the man with the mustache said.

Egan sighed. "All right. He's up in his guesthouse. It's gonna take a few minutes to get him down here."

"We're in no hurry," Mustache said.

"Okay, I'll get him."

Egan went back to the guesthouse and up to the second floor. He took the key to Janney's handcuffs out of his pocket and unlocked them. Then he went over to a table where his silver Glock was sitting. He picked up the Glock and jammed it in the wide pocket of his cargo pants.

"Okay, Garrett, you gotta sign something says these guys delivered the gold."

Janney nodded.

"You blurt out anything or act funny in any way and you got three slugs in your back. Then the delivery guys get the rest of the clip. All clear?"

Janney nodded grimly.

"You just say hello, sign the papers, and come right back up here. Understand?"

Egan uncuffed the old man and, as gently as he could, peeled the tape from Janney's mouth so he could answer.

"I understand."

"Okay. Let's go."

They walked down the steps, then outside and over to the truck. The man with the mustache was sitting on the truck's bumper. He stood up and walked over to Janney.

"Hello, Mr. Janney," Mustache said. "Could we see some ID, please?"

Janney reached into his back pocket and pulled out his alligator wallet. He reached in, took out his Florida license, and handed it to mustache.

"Hey, your birthday's the day before mine," Mustache said, taking out his iPhone. "Just need to take a shot of this."

He clicked two pics of Janney's license with his iPhone, then handed it back to Janney. "Okay, so where's the car we're going to put the delivery in?"

Janney hesitated for a moment, then remembered. "My Honda over there," he said pointing at Egan's gray Honda Accord.

Mustache eyed the Honda disdainfully. "Not into cars, huh, Mr. Janney?"

"What do you mean?" Janney asked.

"Well, a guy like you could probably afford a fleet of Bentleys."

Janney paused for a moment. "Yeah, I'm not into cars."

CHAPTER TEN

It took the two men less than ten minutes to load the gold into Egan's Honda. Egan saw the rear bumper get closer to the ground and realized he wasn't going to be able to drive the car much over forty, fifty max.

Janney thanked them and gave each of them a twenty-dollar bill. They eyed him like they were expecting fifties or C-notes, then got into the truck without a word and drove down the driveway and out onto North Ocean Boulevard.

As Egan and Janney walked into the main house, Egan said: "That was the real reason they wanted to see you."

"What was?"

"They were looking for a tip," Egan said, with a chuckle. "A little more than a couple twenties for a twenty-million-dollar drop."

Laurie opened the door of the guesthouse and walked outside. "No problem, huh?"

"Nope. Garrett played it like a champ."

"I'm not surprised," Laurie said with a smile. "Well, guess we just tie him up and hit the road."

Egan nodded and all three went inside the main house.

Garrett Janney had a worried look on his face.

CHAPTER ELEVEN

Miami is a town full of sketchy characters. And nobody seemed much sketchier than Dieter Roentsch (pronounced *Wrench*), yacht salesman at Luxury Yacht Sales on South Bayshore Drive in Miami.

After having looked at ten or fifteen sport-fishing boats, Chet Egan and Laurie had decided on a Viking 53 convertible to make the trip to Georgetown in the Cayman Islands. Roentsch, a rotund, oleaginous man, had just spent five minutes complimenting Laurie, first on her tan, then her sunglasses, and finally her "bew-ti-ful" smile. Egan wanted to get on with the purchase of the boat, so he fished a 2.2-lb. gold bar out of the pocket of his cargo pants.

"So, I'll give you four of these for the boat," Egan said.

Roentsch studied the shiny bar for a full fifteen seconds. "Oh my God, what is it?" he finally asked.

"It's a one-kilo Valcambi cast gold bar," Egan said. "As of this morning, it's worth fifty-six thousand two hundred fourteen dollars and ninety-five cents. So, in case you're slow on the math, I'm offering you two hundred twenty-five thousand dollars for a boat that's over twenty years old and that you're asking only two hundred thou for."

Roentsch didn't hesitate. "How do I know that thing's worth what you say? Or that it isn't counterfeit?"

Laurie burst out laughing. "Counterfeit? Are you kidding? Look at it."

Roentsch did. "Can I hold it?"

"Sure," Egan said. "Just don't run away with it. I'll have to shoot you in the ass."

He still had the Glock in the front pocket of his cargo pants. He handed the bar to Roentsch.

"Wow, it's heavy."

"No shit, it's heavy. It's pure gold."

Roentsch cocked his head, still not sold. "Why don't you pay like everyone else does?" he said. "A certified check or wired money?"

"Look, man, *everyone else* is going to hondle you on the price. Offer one-seventy-five or one-eighty. I'm giving you ten percent *over* the asking price."

"Have you ever been offered $225,000 for a $200,000 boat before, Dieter?" Laurie asked.

"But it's in gold."

"Damn right it is," Egan said.

"Ever hear the expression, *good as gold?*" Laurie asked.

"How 'bout you give me five bars?"

Egan started to say, *How 'bout you go fuck yourself?* but caught himself.

"Oh, you mean, $280,000 for your $200,000 boat that's over twenty years old?" Egan asked in disgust. Then to Laurie. "Come on, let's get out of here."

"All right, all right," Roentsch said. "If what you said it's worth is true, I'll take the four bars. Where are the other three?"

"Don't worry, we'll get 'em," Egan said. "How 'bout you just go take care of the paperwork."

CHAPTER TWELVE

Three days later, the Nicaraguan cleaning ladies found the body of Garrett Janney. The smell was overpowering as they walked into the house. Anna Sofia, the one who could speak English a little, called 911 right away. Two Palm Beach PD uniforms, Wes Horton and Jose Pena, arrived five minutes later and walked into Janney's living room. The four cleaning ladies were huddled in the far corner like frightened rabbits.

"What the hell's that smell?" Pena asked Horton.

"Whaddaya think," Horton said, holding his nose and pointing at Janney's body, lying on the carpeted floor.

"No, I don't mean him," Pena said. "Smells like gas or something."

"Oh, yeah, now I smell it."

Pena pointed toward the kitchen. "Maybe the stove," then he glanced over at the cleaning ladies and said in Spanish, "Okay, all of you, get out of here. Go outside and wait."

The women scurried toward the front door.

"Come on, man," Pena said to his partner, pointing to Janney's body, "let's move him out of here."

"What's the point? Dude's dead."

"So we can look him over outside," Pena said. "Come on, let's go."

The two cops each grabbed one of Janney's arms and dragged him toward the front door. He only weighed about a hundred-fifty pounds, so it wasn't hard work. They dragged him out the front door onto the wide brick front porch. Then Pena went back inside, ran up the steps to the second floor, and pulled a blanket off a bed. He ran back downstairs, out to the porch, and covered the body of Garrett Janney.

Then he dialed his cell phone.

"Who you callin'?" Horton asked.

"The ME," said Pena, referring to the medical examiner. "Crime-scene techs, too."

"Why?" his partner asked. "It was an accident."

"You don't know for sure."

*****

Dominica McCarthy was one of the two Palm Beach Police Department techs to arrive twenty minutes later. She was standing one step down from the front porch at Garrett Janney's house. She had just snapped off ten shots of Janney's body on her iPhone. She turned to the other tech, Sheila Stallings. "Check out his wrists."

Stallings, on the porch, got down in a crouch and examined Janney's wrists.

"Yeah, I see what you mean. What do you think?"

"I don't know. Like something really tight. A ligature."

There were indented red marks on both of Janney's wrists.

Dominica, wearing vinyl gloves, raised one of Janney's hands. "The marks go all the way around."

"Some kind of restraints," said Officer Pena.

Dominica nodded.

"What kind?" Wes Horton asked, observing from the lawn.

"I'm guessing plastic ties, but maybe handcuffs," Pena said. Then to Dominica, "Right?"

Dominica nodded again. "Sure looks like it."

She stood up and dialed her cell phone. "Hey, Charlie, it's Dominica. I got a dead body you're gonna want to have a look at."

CHAPTER THIRTEEN

Charlie Crawford and Mort Ott got there in ten minutes and parked behind the two squad cars, the crime scene techs' vehicle, and an old Chevy van, which was the cleaning ladies' ride. The ME had not arrived yet.

They got out of their car and walked toward the cluster of four at the front porch.

"Your favorite tech," Ott said, spotting Dominica.

"Stallings?" joked Crawford.

Ott chuckled. "No, not Stallings."

They walked up to the porch. Nods all around.

"So, what do we have here?" Crawford asked.

Ott lowered his voice. "And who are those Spanish babes?" He flicked his head at the cleaners, now huddled on the front lawn.

"Cleaning ladies," Pena said. "They found the body."

"Well, you can tell them to call it a day," Crawford said. "Unless they know something that might be useful."

"I interviewed 'em," Pena said, pointing at Janney's covered body. "All they know is that when they walked in, there was the body."

"What's his name?" Ott asked. "The deceased."

"Garrett Janney. Eight-four years old. Lives here alone, it seems."

Crawford caught Dominica's eye and lowered his voice. "I can see something's got you suspicious."

Dominica pointed. "Check out his wrists."

Dominica and Sheila Stallings stepped aside so Crawford and Ott could get closer looks. The two men got down in squats and examined the vic's wrists.

Ott turned to Crawford, smiled, and said under his breath. "Dude's a little old for BDSM, wouldn't you say?"

Dominica overheard him. "Oh, nice, Mort."

"Sorry," Ott said, then to Crawford. "Let's look around. See what we find."

Crawford nodded, then he glanced at Dominica. "Can you guys give us a hand? This is a pretty big house."

"Not to mention a big guesthouse," Dominica said, pointing.

"Which is probably five times the size of my apartment," Ott said.

*****

The first thing Crawford, Ott, Dominica, Sheila Stallings, and the two uniform cops did was go into the main house and open every window on the first and second floors. Then Crawford went into the kitchen and turned the knob on the stove that was wide open and which they could hear gas pouring from.

Then the six of them divided up in twos and went room by room through the main house. It took over an hour, as there were thirty-seven rooms. They found nothing to indicate that anything violent or in violation of the law had taken place. Then the six moved on to the guesthouse, where there were eight more rooms.

Crawford and Ott were in a bedroom where it was clear that at least two people had recently spent the night because the two beds there were both unmade. Dominica and Sheila Stallings were scanning the bathroom for the two single-bed bedrooms.

"Charlie," Crawford heard Dominica shout, "come in here quick."

He and Ott quickly walked into the bathroom where Dominica and Sheila were hovering over an open drawer of an ancient, three-drawer, wooden medicine cabinet. The women stepped aside to let Crawford and Ott see. On the bottom of the lowest drawer, written in toothpaste, it said: *Chet Egan did it. G. J.*

Dominica opened the drawer above it, revealing a half-used tube of Colgate toothpaste.

"Holy shit," Ott said, as Crawford took a few shots with his iPhone camera. "So the old guy knew it was coming."

Dominica was already on her iPhone having typed in Chet Egan on Google.

"So, now we got a homicide, huh, Charlie?" Sheila Stallings said to Crawford.

Crawford nodded, then said to Dominica, who was scanning her iPhone, "Got our suspect there?"

"I got a Chet Allen who was a child actor and committed suicide in 1984. A Chet Egan who's a project superintendent at Cook Brothers in Tallahassee, another one who's a saxophonist." Dominica clicked her screen. "I'm going to try Chester now."

"I'm already there," Crawford said, scrolling down his iPhone. "I got a Chester Arthur Egan from Alachua, Florida who's... forget it."

"What?" asked Ott.

"A hundred and one years old."

"Never know, could be the world's oldest living murderer," Ott said.

Crawford ignored his partner. He had surfed to a site he used frequently when looking up a suspect.

"I'm checking out *Arrest Records—Florida*," Crawford said.

"Anything there?" Ott asked.

Crawford punched the keyboard and shook his head. "Nah, nothing."

"What next?" Ott asked Crawford.

"Well," Crawford put his hand on his chin. "First, we gotta contact the old man's family. Do a next of kin. Try to track down a friend or two. Also, take a closer look at that home office of his. Might be some answers there." He turned to Dominica. "You're going to dust the bedroom and bath here for prints?"

She nodded.

"That toothpaste tube, too," Crawford said. "Might come up with prints other than the old man's."

Dominica nodded. "Yeah, we're gonna need to spend a lot of time here."

Ott looked in the drawer again and read Garrett Janney's note. "Something tells me this has to do with money. Probably lots of money."

"Usually does," Crawford said. "I saw a bank statement that said Bessemer Trust on his desk."

"What's that?" Dominica said.

"A company that invests very rich people's money. Got an office on Royal Palm Way," Crawford said. "Main office is up in New York, I think."

"Maybe we should go there now?" Ott asked. "To Bessemer."

"Yeah, good a place as any."

*****

Crawford and Ott were sitting in the glass-paneled office of Lawrence Duke at Bessemer Trust. It was a lot fancier than any office at Crawford's bank, PNC. Upon arriving, they had asked who handled Garrett Janney's account and been introduced to Duke.

It fell to Crawford and Ott to tell the banker the news about Garrett Janney.

Duke was shaking his head slowly. "I'm going to miss that man. He could be difficult, but he was a real decent guy. Damn...I knew something was funny."

"What do you mean?" Crawford asked.

"Well, Garrett and I had a series of conversations over the last few days. It was a little strange. First, he wanted me to wire some money into a local account. At Chase. I was all set to do it when he called up and said he changed his mind. Then he instructed me to buy twenty million dollars' worth of gold from a company in Dallas."

"Twenty *million*?"

"Which isn't that much for a man worth six billion."

"Did he say why? Give you any idea why he wanted to buy gold?"

"Here's the thing about Garrett. He was a very shrewd investor. That's how he got to be a multi-billionaire. He gave me a quick explanation what he wanted the money for. Said someone he knew needed a bunch of money in forty-eight hours or his company was going under. Default on a big bond payment, he said. I started to ask some questions and he got pissed off. The way only Garrett could. Told me I was wasting time and he needed to move fast. He did say that the twenty million was collateralized by the man's Feadship worth twenty million and some island he owned in the Exumas worth another sixty million."

"Did he say the man's name?"

"No, I asked him, and he told me it was none of my business."

"But it was your business, wasn't it?" Crawford said.

"Yeah, but that was typical of Garrett. He played his cards close to the vest. That was just the way he operated."

"And was he still doing deals like this...at his age?"

"That's a good point. As far as I know, and I *would* know, it's been a few years since he made any kind of a significant deal. I was kind of surprised to hear that, you know, he was back in the game."

"What did he do besides invest and make deals?"

"What do you mean?"

"Well, I mean, did he play golf? Invest in art or anything like that—" Crawford was racking his brain to come up with old rich guys' pastimes. "Have any women friends?"

"None that I know of," Duke said. "I think he just read history books. Knew everything there was to know about every American president and their entire cabinets. Read every book ever written about Winston Churchill and Catherine the Great, he told me once."

"Catherine the Great, huh?"

"Yes, I don't know what that was about."

"So, the gold? He just bought that as an investment? As a hedge?"

"That was the weird thing."

"What was?"

"He took delivery of it. At his house."

Crawford nodded. "What was it? Bars, coins, what?" He was not very knowledgeable about gold. It had never been much of a factor in his life.

"Bars. One-kilo Valcambi bars, they were called," said Duke.

"Valcambi?"

"Yes, he told me, and I looked it up. It's a refinery in Switzerland."

"Do you know what a kilo is in pounds?" Crawford asked Ott, who was generally more knowledgeable about obscure things like that.

"A kilo is 2.2 pounds," Ott said

He nodded then he looked back at Duke. "So why in God's name—"

"I asked him why. He just said that was the terms of his deal."

"To give this person twenty million dollars in gold?"

Duke shrugged. "Well, I assumed he had some kind of contract. A bill of sale or something."

"You've worked with Mr. Janney a long time, I take it?" Crawford asked.

"Close to thirty-five years. I used to be up in the New York office when he first became a client."

"So, tell us about his family," said Ott.

"Not much to tell. He has one son, who he has kind of been estranged from. His name is Roland, lives up in New Canaan, Connecticut."

"Married?"

"No. As far as I know, he never was. He's a doctor. A shrink, actually."

"Do you have a number for him?" Ott asked.

"Yes, I do," Duke said, reaching for his phone. "It's in here somewhere. I haven't spoken to him for a long time. He doesn't have an account with us."

He scrolled through his phone and gave Ott Janney's son's number.

"So any brothers or sisters still living?" Ott asked.

"No, I don't think so."

"Well, thank you, Mr. Duke," Crawford said, getting out of his chair and standing. "We'll let you know when we know something."

"Thanks," Duke said with a sigh. "I'm really going to miss that crusty old bastard."

CHAPTER FOURTEEN

Crawford and Ott were in the elevator, descending from the Bessemer offices.

"I hope they say that about me," Ott said.

"What's that?"

"I'm really gonna miss that crusty old bastard."

Crawford laughed. "Even with all your bad habits, you're gonna outlive everybody."

On their way to Chase Bank, which was just one block away from Bessemer, Crawford called Garrett Janney's son, Roland. He went straight to voicemail and asked Roland Janney to call him back.

"What's your take on this?" Ott asked as they walked through the front door of Chase.

Crawford shrugged. "That a guy named Chet Egan is out there somewhere with a shitload of gold. Unless he sold it or traded it already. That's about all we got."

"I Googled what a bar goes for, then did the math," Ott said. "Twenty million bucks works out to about seven-fifty, eight hundred pounds of the stuff."

Crawford nodded as he approached an interior glass-enclosed office.

The man at a desk inside saw them, stood up, and walked toward them.

"Hello, gentlemen," he said. "I'm Wayne Pearson, the manager. How can I help you?"

"I'm Charlie Crawford and this is my partner, Mort Ott. We're detectives with the Palm Beach Police."

"Well, welcome, fellas. Come on in to my office," Pearson said. "What can I do for you?"

Crawford and Ott followed him in and sat down facing him.

"Does the name Chet Egan, or Chester Egan mean anything to you?"

Pearson cocked his head. "Yes, it does. Not sure from where exactly."

"Did a man ever call you," Crawford asked, "or maybe come in and inquire about wiring a large sum of money into his account?"

Pearson nodded. "Oh, yeah, now I remember. The man who inherited twenty million dollars?"

Crawford and Ott both leaned forward in their chairs.

"That's what he told you?" Ott asked.

"Yes, it was that man you mentioned, Chet Egan," Pearson said. "After he left, I looked him up and he typically had a balance of around three or four hundred dollars and had been overdrawn a number of times."

"Can you describe Egan, please?" Ott asked.

Pearson did.

"So, when he came in, what exactly did he say?" Ott asked.

"That he was expecting a large amount of money to be wired into his account. From his rich grandfather who had just died."

"Did he say his name?" Ott asked. "The grandfather?"

"No, never mentioned it," Pearson said. "He just asked me questions about whether a deposit like that would set off a bunch of bells and whistles."

"What did you say?"

"I said it most certainly would. With examiners and my superiors at Chase. Not so much when it was wired in, but if he planned to take out a lot of it at once. Plus I told him that, theoretically, he could only withdraw ten thousand dollars at a time. But then I checked myself on that and said the law is, a customer can make bigger withdrawals than that, we just need to report those transactions to the feds."

"So then, what did he say?" Crawford asked.

"That was pretty much the end of the conversation. He thanked me, got up, and left. That was when I checked him out."

"Not one of the bank's larger depositors, huh?" Ott said.

"Matter of fact, one of the smallest."

Ott turned to Crawford and said under his breath, "And a cold-blooded killer to boot."

CHAPTER FIFTEEN

The main reason Chet Egan bought the boat in Miami instead of Palm Beach was that he could kill two birds with one stone in Miami. A guy he knew in Jupiter was a low-level drug dealer who bought coke and weed from a supplier in Miami, then brought it up and sold it in the West Palm and Jupiter areas.

A few weeks back, Egan had met him for a drink at a bar on Clematis Street. A few drinks had turned into lots of drinks and in the course of it, Mel—he called himself Mel Jastrow—told him about growing up poor in Puerto Rico.

"I'm thinking about moving back there," Jastrow said.

"Why? So you can get your house wiped out by a hurricane?"

"Hey, that was like the storm of the century. It won't happen again any time soon."

"You never know."

"I'd buy a place in Old San Juan. Beautiful city…if you've got a little money, you can live like a king."

"And, I'm guessing, you've got more than a little money."

Jastrow smiled. "I've saved up. Plus there's no capital gains taxes there. No income taxes, no nothin'. You can live pretty reasonably there. City's been around five hundred years. No hurricane's ever done much damage to San Juan itself. Plus, they got great restaurants, great bars…great women."

"Sounds pretty nice," Egan said, making a mental note to Google it later.

"Might even take my old name back."

"What do you mean?"

"I grew up in the barrio. My name then was Lupe Fernandez."

"Why'd you change it?" Egan asked.

"'Cause I had a record when I moved to Miami. You know, needed a fresh start. Changing it was a piece of cake."

"So, wait a minute, with all the names you could have chosen, you went with Mel Jastrow?"

"Yeah, why? What's wrong with it?"

"I mean, shit, man, you could have been...Jake Remington...or, or Slade Kincaid, or some badass name like that."

"Sound like gunfighters in the wild west."

"Yeah, well, Mel Jastrow sounds like a fuckin' accountant," Egan said. "So how'd you change your name?"

"Somebody told me about this lawyer who created new identities for Colombian dealers who came here. So I looked this guy up and a thousand bucks later, bye-bye Lupe Fernandez."

"And hello, Mel Jastrow."

"Exactly."

"So what did he do, the lawyer?"

"Well, he started the process out by claiming I was the victim of identity theft."

"Smart."

"Yeah, then there were a bunch of other steps, like filing a petition in Dade County to move the process along. Then getting my Social Security card changed, along with my driver's license, passport, the whole nine. It really wasn't that big a deal."

"How long did it take?"

"I had him rush it...less than two weeks."

"So what's the name of the guy?"

"The lawyer?"

"Yeah."

"Rufus Badger."

Egan took a long sip of his Mojito. "While he was at it, why didn't he change his own name?"

*****

So, two weeks before holing up in Garrett Janney's house on 1231 North Ocean Boulevard, Egan had called Rufus Badger, said he was a friend of Mel Jastrow, and started the process of changing his name. He told Badger he'd pay him two thousand dollars if he could get it done in two weeks. Badger said he'd do his best.

And sure enough, when Egan and Laurie rolled into Miami, laden with eight hundred pounds of gold in the Honda's trunk, Badger presented Chet with all the paperwork. He was about to start a new life as Jake Kincade.

*****

Jake Kincade, formerly killer Chet Egan, had been around boats. First, as a mate on a charter fishing boat in Jupiter. Then, a few years later, when the captain had a heart attack and retired, Kincade became the new captain. The job's pay was decent, but he didn't love bouncing around on the sea and getting verbally abused by drunken fisherman.

Kincade's big question in getting to the Caymans from Miami by boat was which side of Cuba to go around—the east or the west end. The east side meant going through the Bahamas, then hanging a right through the Windward Passage between Cuba and Haiti, then past Jamaica to the south and on to the Caymans.

Instead Kincade decided to go down Hawk Channel to Key West, then around Cuba on the westerly side.

They fueled up in Key West, then again in Los Morros, just before Cape San Antonio, at the western tip of Cuba. Then another fuel stop at a place called Nuevo Gerona on the Isla de la Juventud, an island south of Cuba. From there, their last stop was Caya Largo del Sur, another Cuban island, before making the final run to Georgetown, the capital of the Caymans.

Miraculously, their four days at sea were pretty uneventful despite hitting some rollers that looked as tall as Mount Everest between Havana and Cape San Antonio. *Destiny*, as the Viking 53 convertible sports fisherman was named, despite being over twenty years old, held up well. It had three staterooms and two heads. Its only problem was the washer/dryer conking out just before they reached the Caymans.

Kincade knew his way around boats and—though Laurie didn't—she was an eager and willing first mate and, maybe most importantly, didn't get seasick.

Unlike the late Garrett Janney.

CHAPTER SIXTEEN

Crawford had called JM Bullion in Dallas and worked his way up the ranks and was talking to a man named Jay Montell, a Vice President of Sales at the firm.

"Yes, I got the paperwork here, Detective. Five days ago, delivered to Mr. Garrett Janney, 1231 North Ocean Boulevard, Palm Beach, Florida. Delivery made at 12:41 p.m., signed by Mr. Janney, and there's a photo of his license here."

"Any more details in that file?"

Montell was silent for a moment. "No, not really. I've got the names and numbers of the men who made the delivery, if that's any help."

"Yeah, thanks, give me those, please."

Montell gave him their names and numbers.

Crawford thanked him and hung up.

He called one of the men, a Robert Moultrie, and got an answer on the first ring.

"Mr. Moultrie?"

"Yeah, who's this?"

"My name is Charlie Crawford, I'm a detective in Palm Beach. I want to ask you about a delivery you made here five days ago."

"The old guy? House on the ocean?"

"Yeah, that's it. When you were there, did you see anyone besides Mr. Janney, the owner."

"Sure did. A guy who said he worked for him."

"Did you get his name?"

"No, sorry."

"What did he look like?"

"Umm, I'd say mid- to late-thirties. Kinda curly dark hair, average height, I guess you'd say. Five-ten or so. A bit stocky."

"Anybody else?"

"No, just the old guy and him."

"Anything else that you remember about the delivery?"

"Just the car that we were loading the gold into."

"What about it?"

"Well, it was a Honda. I would have expected something a little more, you know, upscale, for a guy who lived in a mansion like that. Like a Rolls or a Bentley. Guy's house had to be worth millions."

Crawford's guess was thirty to forty million. "It was definitely a Honda?"

"Yeah, kind of a beater, at that. I even said something to the old guy, 'Guess you're not into cars?'"

"What did he say?"

"Said, yeah, he wasn't."

"What model Honda was it? And the color?"

"It was a gray Accord. Coulda used a wash."

"Anything else?"

"That's about it. Pretty routine delivery."

"Well, thanks, I appreciate your help."

"No problem," Moultrie said and clicked off.

Crawford walked down to Ott's cubicle and told him what Moultrie had just said.

"Now we're getting somewhere," Ott said. "Should be enough to get an ID on the guy, don't ya think?"

"Yeah, unless he's a Chet Egan from out of state."

"I got a hunch he lives somewhere around here. A local boy. You don't just come down here out of the blue from St. Louis or Boise and pull off something like this."

"I agree," Crawford said with a nod. "It's almost like he had some kind of inside knowledge."

"You mean like those cleaning ladies, or a contractor or someone who did work at the house?"

"Yeah. Apparently, the old man was practically a hermit. Never went anywhere, never had anyone come visit him."

"I hear ya. So no golf, no hobbies, no fun, no nothin', huh?" Ott said.

Crawford nodded.

"So why don't I put a list together of people who worked there. Landscapers, garbage pick-up—"

"Probably had people come wash the windows, too…you know how it is on the ocean."

Ott nodded. "Pest control…."

"Yup."

"Hookers?" Ott said with a waggle of his eyebrows.

"Jesus, Mort, why does your mind always have to go to places like that?"

CHAPTER SEVENTEEN

It took a while and included forty-five minutes spent at the Motor Vehicle Department, which could have been accomplished in five, but Crawford eventually tracked down Chester J. Egan and was convinced beyond any doubt that he was the man they were looking for. His address was 541 Alley Milne Drive, in a little development off of Military Trail.

As he pulled into the driveway, Crawford saw what he knew was a bad sign: There were four *Palm Beach Post* newspapers covered in red plastic near the garage door. Moments after he pulled in, a blue Lexus turned in right behind him. He reached for the Sig Sauer pistol on his hip while, in his rearview mirror, he watched a man climb out of the Lexus. The man, who looked to be in his seventies and about a hundred pounds overweight, was clearly no threat.

Crawford re-holstered his Sig, opened his door, and climbed out.

The older man approached Crawford. "You a friend of the deadbeat?"

"I'm a Palm Beach Police Department detective. Name's Crawford."

"I'm Jerry Stovall. I own this place. Guy's three weeks late on his rent… as usual."

"Can't help you with that," Crawford said. "Can you let me inside, Jerry?"

"Yeah, why? This guy do something?"

"I don't know for sure. I'll probably know more after I look around a little."

"Let's go," Stovall said, taking a key ring out of his pocket that had about ten keys on it.

"Guess you own a bunch of places?"

"Yeah...don't ever become a landlord. Complete pain in the ass."

They walked around to the side of the one-story house and Stovall unlocked the door.

Crawford followed him in and felt a distinct chill in the home's interior.

"Goddamn igloo," Stovall said, going over to the thermostat and turning it up. "Gonna be a big goddamn electric bill."

It was neat inside, which surprised Crawford. He figured guys who were habitually late on their rent and killed people were likely to be slobs. He walked into the larger bedroom of the two, then its bathroom. No toothbrush, toothpaste, razor or shaving clean. A sure sign Egan was in the wind. Then he walked over to a closet. It had five wooden hangers on the floor and was only half full. Another sign Egan was long gone.

Jerry Stovall wandered in. "You think he skipped?"

Crawford turned to him. "Yeah, I do. What do you know about him?"

"Not a hell of a lot. He was a charter boat captain, I'm pretty sure. Or first mate, maybe. Then he worked in a restaurant, I think. I can't remember exactly."

"You mind providing me with his lease? Or any file you have on him?" Crawford was thinking there might be some financial information or even the name of a person he used as a reference.

"Yeah, sure. I think all I have is a basic lease."

Crawford nodded as he walked over to a desk and chair. There was a printer on it and a small calculator. "He own the charter boat, by any chance?"

"I don't think so."

Crawford looked in a waste basket. There were crumpled-up pieces of paper in it. He reached down, uncrumpled them, and started reading. It was a five-page Wikipedia article entitled *Tax Havens*. Crawford folded the pages up and put them in his jacket pocket.

More proof that Chester J. Egan was history. The question, of course, was where to?

*****

Meanwhile, Mort Ott had been hard at work tracking down the tradespeople who had worked for Garrett Janney. The cleaning ladies from Nicaragua were the only ones who had access to the house, it seemed. He spoke to someone at the window-cleaning company, the trash-hauling company, and Janney's landscaper to see if their employees ever went inside Janney's house. With the exception of the window cleaner, who was let in by the old man, none of the others ever went inside. He also had interviews with the actual employees to see if any of them had ever seen any suspicious activity at the house. They all gave similar answers: They never saw any suspicious activity, or much of any activity at all, nor did they even know what the owner looked like.

Having questioned the obvious candidates, Ott called local pest-control companies until he found one that serviced Janney's house. The person who answered at Cole Pest Control gave Ott the cell phone number of the attendant who worked onsite at Janney's residence.

Ott called him. "Hi, Jason, my name's Ott, I'm a detective with the Palm Beach Police. I'm calling about one of your customers. His name's Garrett Janney at… 1231 North Ocean Boulevard."

"O-kay." Jason sounded apprehensive.

"I just have a few questions: Did you ever meet Mr. Janney?"

"Yes, I met him once a couple years ago. I've been servicing the place since then. When it was time for me to go there, I'd call him, and he'd leave a side door open."

"When you were there—in the last six months, say—did you ever see any other people in the house? Or anything that you thought was…unusual?"

Jason didn't say anything at first. Then finally. "Ah, I don't wanna get anyone in trouble. Did something happen there?"

"What were you about to say?"

Another long pause. "Well, one time I called to say I was on my way…."

"Yeah?"

"It just went to voicemail…and so…I got there…but the door was locked. I heard splashing coming from the pool…."

"Yeah, keep going."

"So I went around to the pool. You know, to ask Mr. Janney if I could get in the house, spray for pests…."

"Go on."

"And, and, I saw him in the pool… buck naked. You know, like skinny-dipping."

"Okay? Was he alone or what?"

"No, he was with the girl…the girl who cleans the pool. Laura, I think her name was. Or maybe Laurie. She was, ah—" he coughed to clear his throat— "bare-ass, too."

CHAPTER EIGHTEEN

Garrett Janney had one of those big binder-like checkbooks with three checks per page and Ott had photographed ten pages' worth, which was how he confirmed all the companies that did work at Janney's house. Janney's pool company was called Cool Chicks Pools. Ott figured if he was choosing between National Pool Service, Preferred Pool, Total Pools, or Cool Chicks Pools, he might just give Cool Chicks Pools a whirl. Apparently, he and Garrett Janney thought alike.

He had called the number for Cool Chicks Pools three times and left messages but hadn't heard back. He decided to go the address on their website. It was just across the south bridge in West Palm. A hand-lettered sign on a one-story cinderblock ranch house announced, *COOL CHICKS POOLS, cleanest pools in the Sunshine State.* Ott walked in the front door. It was not the cleanest office in the Sunshine State. Not by a long shot. In fact, it looked like it needed three hours' worth of work from those Nicaraguan cleaning ladies who had formerly dusted, scrubbed, and mopped Garrett Janney's house.

A bleached-blonde woman in her thirties was standing behind a counter, writing something on a pad.

"Yes, sir, welcome to Cool Chicks. Can I help you?"

"I hope so. I'm looking for Laurie."

The woman groaned. "Laurie doesn't work here anymore."

"You know how I can reach her?" Ott asked, showing her ID. "I'm a detective… Palm Beach Police."

"Hi, I'm Cheryl. She quit five days ago. I can give you her cell number."

"That would be great. Also, do you know where she lives?"

"Over in one of those college streets."

"College Streets?"

"Yeah, you know, College Park in Lake Worth, I think it's called. Streets are named after colleges. Harvard, Yale, umm…Georgia Tech."

"What is Laurie's last name?"

"Reback. Laurie Reback."

Ott wrote it down.

"Does the name Chet Egan mean anything to you?"

"Sure, her boyfriend. He probably knows how to get in touch with her."

"Did she say why she was quitting?"

"No, just that she was going away somewhere."

"Like on vacation?"

Cheryl shook her head. "Kinda seemed more permanent than that."

"What gave you that idea?"

"Well, she said Chet had a really good business opportunity."

"But she didn't say what or where?"

Cheryl shook her head. "But I heard her talking to some guy on the phone about buying her car."

Ott nodded. "Did she have a desk here or anything?"

Cheryl pointed to a cluttered desk.

"You mind if I have a look?"

Cheryl shook her head. "Go ahead. It's kind of a mess."

Ott walked over to it. You could hardly call it a desk. More like a slab of white Formica on four rickety legs, with nothing useful on top of it.

"I'd appreciate it if you'd give me that cell number. And if you could dig up Laurie's exact address."

She did.

Ott thanked her and walked out.

He decided to take a run down to Laurie's address at 131 Cornell Drive. First, though, he dialed her cell phone number. "This number is no longer in service," said the recording. He'd kind of expected that might be the case.

It was only a ten-minute drive to a small, neat ranch made of that orange brick that nobody wanted anymore, if ever they did.

Ott parked, walked up to the front door, and hit the buzzer. Unsurprisingly, nobody answered. He walked around to the side of the house and looked through a picture window. The living room was sparsely furnished. He walked around to the back and saw what appeared to be the master bedroom. There were several wire hangers on the carpeted floor along with discarded cellophane of the sort that protects dry-cleaned clothing. It all had the look of someone who had packed up in a hurry.

Then he walked over to the mailbox. It was half full. He went through the mail, hoping to find a personal letter, his intent being to call the letter writer and ask whether they knew where Laurie was intending to go.

There was nothing but bills that would never be paid.

CHAPTER NINETEEN

Crawford was on his cell phone when Ott walked into his office. He was wearing an uncharacteristic frown when he motioned Ott to have a seat.

"But is she okay?" Crawford asked the person on the other end of his call.

He listened and appeared to wince.

"Jesus, that doesn't sound okay at *all*."

He kept listening.

"All right, if anything happens again, I'm gonna go there personally, handcuff him, and drag him away. See if he likes our jail cell as much as the house on Jungle."

He looked at Ott and shook his head.

"All right, well, thanks for letting me know, Jess. Keep me in the loop." He nodded. "Talk to you soon."

"What's that all about?" Ott asked. "Who you gonna cuff and put in a cell?"

"My ex-wife got beaten up by her husband."

"Up in New York?"

"No, down here. Didn't I tell you? They bought a house here a while back."

"First I heard of it."

"Yeah, I guess he's got a bunch of friends and clients who have houses here. She's got a few friends, too. You know how it is, a lot of rich people from up north spend winters here. Go back and forth a little."

Ott nodded. "So what was it about? Why'd he beat her up?"

Crawford leaned back in his chair. "You ever notice how guys who cheat on their wives suspect everyone else cheats?"

"Yeah, know what you mean."

"Well, seems like her husband Giles has screwed around from day one and somehow got it in his head that Jill was, too. Even suspected she was cheating with *me*. Which would have been pretty tough, considering I haven't seen her in five years."

"Not to mention, you got your hands full."

"What?"

"Well, there's Dominica and Rose and probably a few others I don't know about."

Crawford shook his head. "Okay, cut the shit. Anyway, the poor woman had a busted lip, bruises all over, and cuts on her cheeks."

Ott's eyes got hard. "What an asshole."

"No kidding."

"Sorry to hear that, Charlie."

Crawford nodded. "Yeah, thanks. So what did you come up with?"

"No, you go first."

Crawford nodded and tapped his desk top. "Okay, so I found out where Chet Egan lived and went there. Up in Jupiter. I got there and right after I pulled in this old guy showed up. Told me he was Egan's landlord, and he was there 'cause Egan was three weeks late on his rent. We were both out of luck 'cause Egan had clearly split recently. But a couple interesting things came out of it. One, the landlord told me Egan used to be a charter boat captain."

"That's what he did before he went into the murder business?"

"Yeah, and while I was looking around the house, I found these crumpled pages in a wastebasket. Turns out to be a five-page Wikipedia article on tax havens."

"So the guy's headed to Switzerland or something?"

"Switzerland used to be rich guy's favorite tax haven, but because they got so much pressure from the U.S. government, it's apparently not so popular anymore."

"Gotcha. So where do people go now?"

"I looked into the whole thing when I got back here and there're a bunch of them in our part of the world. The Bahamas, Panama, Costa Rica, Belize, the Cayman Islands, Andorra, Nevis—"

"Andorra, Nevis…where the hell are they?"

"Islands to the south of us somewhere."

"Hell, man, I coulda guessed that."

"There're also other ones around the world. Hong Kong, Mauritius, Lichtenstein, Monaco—"

"That's where I'd go. Monaco. Party with that crazy dude Prince Albert."

Crawford ignored that. "So that's what I found out. What about you?"

"So, for one thing, a woman named Laurie Reback worked for a company called Cool Chicks Pools."

"Catchy."

"Yeah, and I found out from the pest-control guy that he spotted her splashing around naked in Garrett's pool one day. *With* the old man...also buck naked."

"So that's maybe how she got inside the house? Got cozy with the old man."

"Coulda been."

Crawford started tapping his desk. "So it's starting to come together," he said. "Laurie told Chet about the old man and his billions. And that nobody ever came to visit Janney and he never went anywhere. And Chet gets the lightbulb over his head and comes up with a plan."

"Yeah, or else Chet came up with the plan first. Then just had to locate a rich old guy, of which there are many in Palm Beach. Then Laurie shows up in a skimpy outfit and pitches Cool Chicks Pools."

"Either way, it was easy to get in the house."

Ott nodded. "Oh, I also found out that Laurie sold all her possessions and her car."

"So they definitely got the hell out of Dodge. You know who she sold the car to?"

"Yeah, Shifty Al's Used Junkers or something. I've got it written down. Somewhere on Dixie Highway. So what do we do now? You go to Hong Kong. I go to Monaco?"

"How 'bout you go to Shifty Al's, see what you can find out. I'll go to Motor Vehicle, see if Egan sold his car, too. Maybe that'll lead somewhere."

"Okay. Sounds like a plan."

"This is gonna be a tough one, Mort."

"I know."

"Those two could be anywhere by now."

CHAPTER TWENTY

Shifty Al's Used Junkers was actually called Honest Al's Auto Sales. It was on Dixie Highway and had lots of colorful balloons and banners so you couldn't miss it. There were three salesman sitting around and watching a NASCAR race on TV when Ott walked in.

"Yessir," one said enthusiastically, getting out of his chair. "What are you looking for today, my friend?"

Ott flashed the man his ID. "Just a little information. Ott's my name. I'm a detective, Palm Beach PD."

"O-kay," the man said. "What kinda information?"

"Did one of you buy a car from a woman by the name of Laurie Reback in the last few days?"

"That would be me," said a skinny, red-faced man wearing a Tampa Bay Buccaneers T-shirt.

"Go Tom Brady," Ott said with a fist pump. "What can you tell me about her?"

"I just know she worked for a pool company…was hot…and not a half-bad negotiator."

"Anything else?"

"Not that I can think of."

"Did she say why she was selling the car?"

"Yeah, actually she did. Said she was getting a boat."

"Really? She have a boat all picked out?"

"She didn't say."

"So when she dropped the car off, someone must've picked her up, right?"

"Yeah, a guy in a Honda."

Ott looked around at the lot where the cars for sale were parked. "Those security cameras work?"

The skinny guy shrugged. "I guess so."

"Yeah, they work," the man next to him said.

"You must be Honest Al?" Ott said.

"In the flesh."

"You mind if I check out your cameras? I want to get the tag number on the Honda that picked the woman up."

"Sure," said Honest Al. "I'll give you a hand with it. Always happy to cooperate with law enforcement."

"That's what we like to hear."

*****

Ott called Crawford on his cell. "So, I got Chet Egan's tag number."

"Good work. How'd you get it?"

"It was on a security cam of my new best friend, Honest Al, smiley used-car dude," Ott said. "Plus, a salesman there told me Chet and Laurie were in the market for a boat."

"Mm-hmm."

"So, I'm thinking they pack the gold in a boat and head for one of those tax havens you were telling me about," Ott said.

"Yeah, can't exactly lug that much gold onto a plane."

"Unless they rent private metal."

"Never thought of that," Crawford said. "Can you look into Signature, Galaxy, and—what's that other private plane company?"

"Jet Aviation."

"Yeah, see if Egan chartered a plane between the time of Garrett Janney's death and now, though my bet's still on a boat. Meanwhile, I'm gonna head over to Motor Vehicle, see if there's any record of Chet selling his Honda."

"Sounds good. Let me know."

*****

An hour later, Crawford called Ott. "So, I got good news and I got a head-scratcher."

"Gimme the good news first."

"I'll give you both. A man named Jake Kincade sold a gray Honda Accord with Chet Egan's tag number."

"How can that be?"

"That's the head-scratcher. Only thing I could come up with is that Chet Egan changed his name."

"How do you even do that?" Ott asked.

"It can be done. It's not that easy, though."

"So…you thinking he might have changed his identity so he could start a new life in some place like Panama or the Bahamas?"

"That's what I was thinking."

"Makes sense."

"I also found out the name of the place in Miami that bought Egan's car. We should take a little run down there," Crawford told Ott.

"And do what?"

"Lift some prints from the Honda. Confirm that Jake Kincade used to be Chet Egan. And if so, find out if he bought a boat down there."

"Only problem is there's got to be a million places to buy a boat in Miami."

"Tell you what, I'm gonna round up a bunch of staff at the station to make calls all over Miami."

"Yeah, good idea," Ott said. "We'll get 'em, Charlie, but we'll probably have to do some traveling. I just hope it's to somewhere with good food and nice beaches."

CHAPTER TWENTY-ONE

Jake Kincade and Laurie Reback were sitting at an outdoor bar on Seven Mile Beach outside of George Town in the Cayman Islands. Earlier that day, they had taken a submarine tour of George Town harbor, followed by two hours' worth of snorkeling, then a tour of a local rum distillery. The night before, they had stayed in a suite in the Ritz-Carlton, where they planned to stay for the remainder of their time in the Caymans.

Jake was drinking something called a Nitro Stout from a local brewery and Laurie a Mojito.

"So, this guy at the bank told me forty of the fifty biggest banks in the world have branches here and the Caymans are the second largest captive domicile in the world," Jake said.

Laurie cocked her head. "What's that mean?"

"Beats the hell out of me," Jake said. "I think the gist of it is that lots of rich people park a lot of money in the banks here."

"Rich people…like us, you mean," Laurie said with a wide smile.

Jake raised his beer bottle and clinked Laurie's glass. "Exactly."

"Hey, by the way, speaking of money stuff, I thought you didn't want to use a credit card?"

Kincade thought for a second, then nodded. "Oh, you mean for the hotel. Well, see, I had to 'cause I ran out of cash. All the gas and shit on the way down. I won't use it again."

"'Cause all the cash you got for the gold?"

Kincade patted her shoulder and smiled. "You catch on quick."

Laurie leaned back in her cushioned rattan chair. "So tell me again how those bitcoins work? Maybe I'll understand it better with a little booze in me."

"Okay, now listen carefully," Jake said and explained how he had bought five million dollars' worth of bitcoins and how his hope was they'd have a nice appreciation.

At the end of Jake's explanation, Laurie still looked lost. "Well, as long as you understand how they work, that's all that counts."

"What didn't you get?"

Laurie shrugged. "Hey, I could never balance my checkbook, so bitcoins are like understanding Einstein's theory of whatchamacallit."

"Relativity's what you're going for," Jake said, then patted Laurie's tanned arm. "Hey, I'm impressed you've even heard of Einstein."

"The dude with the funny hair," Laurie said. "And tell me again why you want to live in Puerto Rico? You were a little fuzzy about that."

"Well, that's another pretty long story, but I'll sum it up. I've been reading these articles about a group of American expats living in Old San Juan. Sounds like a bunch of hippies who made a pile of money—"

"Selling weed probably."

Kincade laughed. "Could be. Anyway, you can live there pretty reasonably; Puerto Rican tax laws are lenient, and the States are just a quick plane ride away," Kincade said, taking a pull on his Nitro Stout. "You did such a good job as first mate on the *Destiny*, are you up for another boat ride?"

"To Puerto Rico, you mean?"

Jake nodded.

"How far is it?"

"Umm, a little over nine hundred miles."

"That's a long haul."

"Yeah, but here's the thing. I'm thinking about us spending a couple of days on the beaches in the Dominican Republic, which is a little over halfway there."

"That sounds nice. A good way to break up the trip, huh?"

"Exactly. It's a place called Casa de Campo. Where all the rich people go."

"Like us," Laurie said again.

Jake clinked his bottle on her glass again.

"Would you ever go back to the States?"

"As Chet Egan? Never. As Jake Kincade? I think it might be safe after a year or two."

"So, if we ever run out of money, we could go find another old, rich guy in Palm Beach, huh?"

Jake leaned across the table and gave Laurie a fist bump. "We could, but don't worry, we're never gonna run out of money. Because I got most of it in bitcoins, which are gonna go up, up, and away."

"You sure they're safe?" Laurie was still not absolutely sold.

"Yeah, I am. Plus, I told you about that guy who financed the purchase of a million-dollar house with bitcoins as collateral."

Laurie put her hand on Jake's. "Are we gonna get a million-dollar house, Chet?"

He shook his head. "It's Jake, remember. And I'm thinking, no, we're gonna get a *two*-million-dollar house. With a gym, a hot tub, and a pool. And, since you're retired, we're gonna hire somebody to clean the pool."

"That's good, because I can't tell you how sick I got skimming bugs and leaves and shit out of people's pools."

"Yeah but look where it got us. Meeting a nice old man worth six billion dollars…may he rest in peace."

CHAPTER TWENTY-TWO

Crawford was looking out the window of his office, wondering how he and Ott could find out whether Chet Egan, who, it seemed likely, was now calling himself Jack Kincade, had bought a boat in Miami and, more importantly, where the boat was heading.

His cell phone rang. It was Jessie Giordano.

"Hey, Jess, how's it goin'? How's Jill?"

"Well, the good news is her face has healed nicely and the even better news is she's divorcing that asshole Giles."

Crawford slapped his desk. "All right! That is *really* good news. I was wondering if it was going to come to that."

"It's come to that," Jessie said. "I mean, once he accused Jill of having an affair with you…. Forget about it."

Crawford shook his head. "Maybe someone should point out to him that's it's impossible to have an affair with me unless she sees me, which she hasn't."

Jessie laughed. "The guy's delusional. What can I tell ya?"

"Is she going to be all right for money?"

"More than all right. She has a good pre-nup."

Crawford laughed. "Something she never got from me."

"You mean she never got her hands on that vast Crawford fortune?" Jessie said. "Must have married you for love."

That put a smile on Crawford's face. "Well, listen, keep me up to speed. Seems like she's doing the right thing."

"Oh, she's definitely doing the right thing."

"Where do you think she's going to live?"

"I don't know yet. Maybe get a smaller place here, but she's definitely a city girl. Loves it there. Even after the whole Covid thing."

"Yeah, but she might bump into Giles."

"It's a big city, Charlie."

CHAPTER TWENTY-THREE

Ott had been down to Miami only once before, for a Miami Dolphins-Cleveland Browns football game, which he told Crawford was a colossal "penalty-strewn muddle-fuck of a game between the two worst teams in the league." Crawford had been to the city a couple of times. Once, with the actress Gwen Hyde, whom he met on a movie shoot in New York and had a brief but passionate three-month fling with eight months after his divorce. The other time was after his final New York City burnout, when he desperately needed a beach and a dozen margaritas to help him leave his woes behind.

Crawford had recruited at least half of the Palm Beach Police Department personnel who weren't flat-out busy to help him track where, or if, Jake Kincade and Laurie Reback had bought a boat in Miami. He had actually made a game of it, saying that whoever found out where the boat was bought would win lunch for two at an "exclusive Palm Beach bistro," but didn't tell them that the exclusive Palm Beach bistro was, in fact, Crawford's own beloved lunch spot, Green's Pharmacy. At the end of the day—and after probably several hundred calls—Bettina at the front desk struck gold. She found out that a salesman named Dieter Roentsch at a place called Luxury Yacht Sales had made the sale.

When told that she had just won lunch for two at the not-so-exclusive Green's, Bettina was justifiably disappointed and walked into Crawford's office with a big frown on her face.

"Green's?" she asked. "Why not just make it Burger King, Charlie?"

"Sorry, I run kind of a low-budget operation here," he told her.

"Okay, but the deal is, at least you have to take me there. Me and you," Bettina said.

Crawford reached across his desk and offered his hand. "You got a deal. Just gotta wait 'til things slow down a little again."

"Okay," Bettina said, shaking his hand, "but not too far down the road."

Crawford nodded. "Not too far. I promise."

*****

With Ott behind the wheel, they pulled into the parking lot of Luxury Yacht Sales on South Bayshore Drive in Miami and walked into the showroom

"Hi, is Dieter Roentsch here?" Crawford asked the receptionist.

She gave him a warm smile. "And who should I say is here to see him?"

"Detectives Crawford and Ott, Palm Beach Police Department."

"Cool," she said. "Never met a detective before."

"Let alone two," Ott said.

"I know," she said. "Just a sec, I'll get the D-Man."

"That's what he calls himself?" Ott asked.

"Yeah, that or Deets."

"Well, great," Ott said. "Just tell him the C-Man and the M-Man are here to see him."

The woman laughed and went over to a desk next to a circular front window where a man wearing sunglasses and reading a magazine was leaning back on a chair. The receptionist went up to him and pointed back at Crawford and Ott. The man got to his feet and walked over.

"Welcome to Luxury, gentleman," Dieter said.

Crawford and Ott introduced themselves and Dieter asked them to come over to his desk.

So, you want to know about my sale to Goldfinger?" Dieter said, chuckling as he sat. "My little joke...Mr. Kincade, I'm talking about."

"So I'm guessing, based on what you said on the phone, he paid for the boat in gold?" Crawford asked, hoping Dieter would lose the sunglasses but guessing it was part of his hip-salesman brand.

"Sure did. I actually had a local gold dealer come here and check out the bars. Man said they were the highest quality. I did a little negotiating with the buyer and got him to pay more than the asking price. I think he wanted to do a quick deal."

"The buyer?" Ott asked. "Can you describe him, please."

"Sure. Dark curly hair, average height, a little heavy, late-thirties, I'd say. Had these long, skinny sideburns, a little scar to the right of his nose…no, left of his nose."

"And he was with a woman, right?" Crawford asked.

"Yeah, a knock-out. Beautiful tan, tall, nice curves to her…." He made that little click-click sound of approval. "I always remember women like her."

"So the boat was a Viking 53 convertible sports fisherman, correct?" Ott asked.

"Yup, exactly."

"Did they ever mention where they were going? On the boat. I mean, deep-sea fishing? The Bahamas? You remember anything about that?"

"The guy was very interested in how far they could get on a full tank. So my guess is… far."

"But they never said where?" Ott asked.

"No, sorry."

"Did you get the sense they were going to leave right away?"

Dieter thought for a few moments. "Yes, I'd say so. They drove their car as close as they could get it to the dock and started loading right after he signed the papers and gave me the gold bars. Took 'em a while to load up. They had a ton of suitcases. Almost like they were going on an around-the-world-trip or something."

Or all those suitcases were stuffed with gold bars, thought Crawford.

He got to his feet and offered his hand.

Dieter shook it. "Well, if you boys ever want a boat, I'll give you a really good deal."

Ott nodded as he shook his hand. "Thanks, D-Man, we'll keep that in mind."

They walked out of the Luxury Yacht sales office.

"So, what do you think?" Ott asked, turning to Crawford.

"I think we gotta get Norm to authorize getting us a fast boat to go after 'em."

*****

On his way back to Palm Beach, Crawford called his friend, David Balfour. Balfour had once been a partner at Goldman Sachs in New York and knew his way around all things financial. Crawford told him he needed to pick his brain and Balfour invited him to come on over, he'd leave the front door open. He'd be out at his pool, working his first rum drink of the day.

Balfour didn't mention that he had a poolside companion. When Crawford and Ott walked through the house and out to the pool, they saw a topless woman lying in a chaise next to Balfour, wearing only a banana-peel-sized bikini bottom. When she looked up and saw the two men in jackets, she quickly covered herself, smiled, said hello, then went back to her *Vanity Fair*.

Balfour introduced them all, suggested Crawford and Ott take off their jackets, loosen their ties, and pull up a pool chair.

"So, you boys have a question about stocks and bonds?" Balfour asked.

"Not exactly that," Crawford said. "But here's a hypothetical question for you: Say you bought a boat in Miami and loaded it up with twenty million dollars in gold—"

"Wait a minute," Balfour interrupted. "This has to do with Garrett Janney's murder, doesn't it?"

"Yup," Crawford said. "You read about him in the *Glossy*?"

"*The Glossy. The New York Times, The Wall Street Journal....* So, you guys think the people who killed him took a bunch of gold down to Miami—"

"And bought a boat. And the question is, if it was you, where would you go with the gold?"

"Presumably to liquidate it into cash and do a Robert Vesco?" Balfour asked.

"Who's that?" Crawford asked.

"Before your time. This fugitive financier and all-around scammer from like forty years ago. Absconded with $200 million in investor money—back when $200 million was real money—and ended up in some place like Panama or Costa Rica."

"So what would you do... *today*?"

Balfour glanced over at his female companion, smiled, then returned Crawford's gaze. "If I had twenty million in ill-gotten gains, i.e., gold bars, I'd take my friend Brooke here to the Bahamas or the Caymans and sell it—" Balfour reached for his iPhone on the pool deck— "Hang on a sec, I want to check something. I think I'd rule out the Bahamas 'cause I'm pretty sure they gouge you with a big VAT tax—" he scrolled down on his iPhone— "Yeah, here it is, a 7.5% VAT tax."

"Which means they take that right off the top?" Crawford asked.

"Exactly, so that's like a million five to two million… poof, gone. Let me check the Caymans," Balfour said, scrolling down. "Okay. So here's a place called Strategic Wealth Preservation that buys gold. Here's another one called Cashwiz…. I don't know, with a flashy name like that, you might want to steer clear of that one."

"This is great," Crawford encouraged him. "Let me ask you this, if I were to go into one of those places, you think I could get them to tell me if they just bought a big pile of gold from someone?"

"No."

"That's what I thought. Because it's basically a country that's all about discretion and keeping everything financial a secret, right?"

Balfour nodded. "Absolutely. Anyway, since there's no VAT tax in the Caymans, I think that might be my destination. Or maybe Panama, but, I forget, do they still have a dictator there?"

Crawford shrugged. "Nah, pretty sure he's long gone."

"Like the guys with the gold, huh?" Balfour said.

Crawford nodded grimly. "A guy and his girlfriend."

"What about Andorra?" Ott asked.

"How'd you come up with that one, Mort?" Balfour asked.

"It's a tax haven, right?" Ott shrugged. "Sounds like it might be a nice place to go."

"You know where it is?" Balfour asked, furrowing his brow.

"Yeah, a little island somewhere down around Cuba, I think," Ott said. "Or maybe Puerto Rico."

Brooke put down her *Vanity Fair*. "Are you crazy? Andorra's in Europe. Between France and Spain."

"Oh," Ott said with a shrug. "I'm a little geography-challenged."

"Clearly," said Brooke, going back to her *Vanity Fair*.

"So," Crawford asked Balfour, "is the Caymans a place you'd go to if you were planning to start a new life?"

Balfour thought for a moment. "Um, I wouldn't say so," he said. "I don't know what there is do there. I mean, they have beaches and, I guess, a couple of golf courses, but I've never heard anyone say,

When I was in the Caymans I had the time of my life. You know what I mean? It's just a place where you go for business, particularly to hide money."

"Well, thank you, that's really helpful. We appreciate it," Crawford said, pushing himself up from the pool chair. Then he turned to the woman. "And thank you, Brooke, for straightening us out on where Andorra is."

CHAPTER TWENTY-FOUR

By Crawford's count, Chief Norm Rutledge had between seven and nine brown suits. There was the one with the white chalk stripe, the one with the black chalk stripe, and the one with the orange chalk stripe. And God was that one ever hideous. Brown and orange, despite being the colors of Ott's football team, the Cleveland Browns, was about as ugly a combination as you could get. Then there were lighter shades of brown and darker shades of brown, and the special suit that Ott referred to in classically blunt Ott-ese as "shit brown." And…well, the list went on.

Today's was plain brown with silver buttons. Rutledge had just ushered Crawford and Ott into his office as he finished up a call.

He clicked off and looked over at the two. "I was beginning to forget what you boys looked like." His way of saying, *Why the hell haven't you checked in on the Garrett Janney case? A high-profile murder and I don't know jack shit about what's happening…*

"What can we tell ya," Crawford said with a shrug. "We've been flat-out since we found the body."

"I figured, but hey, maybe a postcard or something." Rutledge's sense of humor was best ignored, and Crawford and Ott did exactly that.

Crawford spent the better part of the next twenty minutes, with occasional Ott interjections, telling Rutledge everything they knew about Janney's murder and the flight of Chet Egan (now Jake Kincade) and his girlfriend, Laurie Reback, formerly a pool skimmer with Cool Chicks Pools.

"We're thinking it's time we took a trip down to the Caymans," Ott said. "What do you think?"

"Are you serious?" Rutledge asked.

Crawford nodded. "Yeah, he's serious. How else are we going to get these two?"

Rutledge leaned back in his chair and knotted his hands together. "First thing I'm going to say is, if you knew with absolute certainty that they went to the Caymans, I'd entertain it. Second thing is, what kind of reciprocity do we have with them? I mean, imagine you go there and can't arrest them and bring 'em back."

"Okay," Crawford said. "Second one first: We checked with the city attorney, who said his initial sense was that we do have reciprocity with them but he's going to confirm it and get back to me. Number one, we think it's an 80% chance they went there, but we've got someone checking hotels and dock registrations. Don't worry, we wouldn't go there unless we're 100% sure."

"Okay, and what are you going to charge 'em with if you do catch 'em?"

"Premeditated murder."

"You think you can prove that? I mean, as opposed to a gas leak. Accidental death."

"I'd say that note in toothpaste goes a long way to proving it."

Rutledge nodded. "I hope you're right," he said. "Okay, assuming the attorney says we're good on the reciprocity thing and assuming you can track 'em down to the Caymans, I'm good with it. I'll authorize you going down there—" he turned to Ott—"but no late nights in bars quaffing rum drinks and chasing skirts. I know how you like your cocktails and cocktail waitresses, Ott."

"Good one," Ott said, dialing up his insulted look. "Why are you directing that at me? What about Chuck here?"

"He's a little more…discreet than you."

"You mean 'cause he's got skirts chasing him. 'Stead of the other way around."

*****

Crawford spoke to the city attorney, who told him he had two conversations with people in the Caymans government who assured him that if a fugitive from the United States had fled to their country, they would most assuredly allow the U.S. to extradite him back.

One down, one to go.

Then Ott heard back from one of the police department clerks that she had found out a Mr. Jake Kincade was registered at the Ritz-

Carlton in George Town. The hotel would only reveal to the clerk that Kincade had used a credit card in his own name – not the type or card number.

Ott went into Crawford's office and reported what he'd discovered.

"I'm kinda surprised," Crawford said.

"Oh, you mean using his own credit card?"

"Yeah, I would have figured a guy changing his identity, and the dude's whole MO in general, would be too smart for that."

"Yeah, I hear ya."

"Okay, so no Motel 6 for Jake and Laurie," Crawford said. "How long they been there?"

"Three nights. Checked in on Wednesday."

"Okay, I'll get Bettina to book us on the next flight."

"Cool. Let me know when take-off is. I'm gonna go home. Get some tropical duds and my toothbrush."

*****

Turned out they got a flight out the next morning on Jet Blue. It was a two-and-a-half-hour flight and featured a lot of breathtaking ocean views all the way down. One flight attendant was a tad grouchy, and the captain prattled on as if he were narrating a travelogue, but, all in all, it was a good ride.

Ott had made the reservation at the Westin Grand Cayman on Seven Mile Beach after unsuccessfully trying to talk Chief Rutledge into letting them stay at the Ritz-Carlton, "in order to be a stone's throw from our perps."

On the way in from the airport, Ott made a call to the Ritz-Carlton and put it on speaker.

"Hi, I'm just calling to confirm that my friend, Jake Kincade, is staying at the hotel."

He waited a few moments.

"I'm sorry, sir, but Mr. Kincade checked out this morning."

Crawford whispered to Ott. "See if he left any forwarding info."

Ott nodded. "Did he happen to mention where he was going next?"

"I'll ask the clerk who checked him out."

He came back on a few moments later. "Just that wherever he was going, he was going by boat. Left from the Barcadere Marina."

Ott jotted that down on his hand. Crawford and Ott went straight to the Royal Caymans Island Police office in George Town and asked for Inspector Palmer Bentz, whom Crawford had spoken with the day before.

A bald man with a trim mustache and a crisp uniform came out to the front desk.

"Gentlemen," Bentz said, eyeing Crawford and Ott. "Welcome to headquarters."

"Thanks," Crawford said, shaking Bentz's hand. "I'm Charlie Crawford, who you spoke to, and my partner, Mort Ott."

Ott shook Bentz's hand. "Thanks for seeing us."

"Happy to help in any way I can," Bentz said. "What do you want to do first?"

"Go to the Barcadere Marina. That's where they docked their boat when they first got here. They left earlier this morning."

"Sure," Bentz said. "That's not far from here."

The three drove to the marina and spoke to a man working there. He confirmed that the American couple had left first thing in the morning after paying more than six hundred dollars in cash. They did not mention what their next stop was or say what direction they were headed. The three thanked him and went back to Bentz's car.

"I'm thinking we split up," Crawford said. "Mort, you go back to the Ritz-Carlton and find out what you can." He turned to Bentz. "Meantime, you and me hit some places that buy gold. Our theory is that our suspects had about eight hundred pounds of it. Probably wanted to lighten their load."

"Eight hundred pounds. Good God, how much is that worth?" Bentz asked

"Um, somewhere in the neighborhood of twenty million dollars."

"Minus the $225,000 for the boat they bought with four gold bars," Ott added.

Crawford nodded.

"So you're thinking they'd want to convert as much as they could into dollars?"

"Dollars, euros, marks, pesos… any stable currency."

"And then do what with it?"

"That we don't know," Crawford said. "Go buy a place somewhere and live happily ever after, would be my guess."

"Which we need to make sure never happens," Ott said.

CHAPTER TWENTY-FIVE

Ott, good schmoozer that he was, wasn't able to get much out of the desk clerk who had checked out Jake Kincade and Laurie Reback. He didn't sense she was withholding anything, she simply didn't know anything more than the fact that the couple had checked out. He started to ask her what kind of credit card Kincade had used and, even more significantly, what the number, expiration date, and security code was. But then he realized the chances were slim to none he could get her to give him that information. But an inspector from the Royal Cayman Island's police force in a nice, crisp uniform with a nice, crisp English accent asking her those same questions had a much better chance of being successful.

Ott had just asked her if she had any idea what the couple might have done during the day while they were staying at the hotel.

"Well, I really don't know except the lady went to the shop in the hotel. I think she went there a couple of times. I saw her walk past here with a big shopping bag."

"Where's the shop?" Ott asked.

She pointed. "That way. Not far."

"Great. Thanks," Ott said, knowing she had probably not seen the last of him.

He walked in the direction she had pointed and saw the shop. It was called Calypso.

He walked in, scanned it, and saw that it had everything from jewelry to watches to bathing suits. All of it looked very expensive.

A flashy-looking blonde with a face full of freckles was on her cell phone behind a counter. She gave him one of those finger flutters and hung up. "Hello, sir, how can I help you?" she asked.

Ott slid the photo of Kincade and Laurie out of his jacket pocket. "Just wondered if you've seen a couple of friends of mine staying in the hotel. She loves to shop so I'm pretty sure she'd find her way here."

The woman looked at the photo Ott handed her. "Oh, sure, Laurie. Yes, she's one of my best customers."

"Well, here's the thing. She and Jake, that's her boyfriend, left without me having a chance to give Jake back a fishing rod I borrowed from him. A very expensive fishing rod, I might add, and I want to FedEx it to him. You don't have any idea where they went, do you?"

Ott hoped the woman wasn't the suspicious type, as the story he had just rattled off contained a few holes in it.

The woman's expression was blank at first, but she soon lit up. "I do remember her mentioning something about maybe going to the 'Old City.' Like I was supposed to know where that was. But I had no clue where the 'Old City' was. I mean, there're lots of old cities, right?"

Ott nodded. "Yeah, I suppose there are. Is there anything else you can remember? I'd really like to get that rod back to Jake."

The woman shook her head. "I'm sorry, but that's all I remember. Did you talk to the girls at the reception desk? Maybe they can help."

"Yes, I did. Unfortunately, they don't remember hearing much," Ott said. "Well, thanks, I appreciate it."

"You're very welcome," she said, walking over to a rack of Hawaiian shirts and pointing at one. "You know, I was just thinking how great you'd look in that."

The shirt had every color of the rainbow in it. It was too loud even for Ott.

Ott walked over for a closer look and turned the price tag over: $199.

"I like it," he said, "but the last time I spent $199 on clothes, I got two suits, a shirt, and a nice white belt at Overstock.com."

*****

Crawford and Palmer Bentz had been to three places, including Strategic Wealth Preservation, which paid cash for gold, and none of the three had recently bought one-kilo Valcambi gold bars. Or else they lied convincingly. But why would they? That was their job—buying and selling—and besides, wouldn't they want to get on the right side of a prominent Caymans law-enforcement officer?

At the fourth place—as Bentz said to Crawford—"We struck gold. Sorry, couldn't resist."

It was a place called Global Investments and it looked like someone had spent a small fortune on the décor. It clearly was designed to look like a prosperous, well-heeled establishment that catered to the international fat-cat set which didn't want their respective countries knowing how much they were worth or how much they had squirreled away. A tall, rail-thin man in a natty gray suit greeted them. Bentz started the conversation.

"I'm Inspector Palmer Bentz from GCIPS and this is my colleague from America, Detective Charles Crawford." The last time Crawford was referred to as Charles was when he made a rare public appearance at church in West Palm and the minister struggled to remember his first name. "We have a few questions for you, if you don't mind."

"Yes, of course. I'm Basil Humphrey. I don't mind at all."

"Thank you, Basil," said Crawford. "I'm here in pursuit of two fugitives—a man and a woman—looking to sell a large quantity of gold. Specifically, in one-kilo Valcambi bars from a Swiss refinery."

Basil nodded. "You came to the right place. I bought three million dollars' worth from a Mr. Kincade."

"That's all he sold?" Crawford asked.

"He wanted to sell ten million dollars' worth, but three million in U.S. currency was all I had. In fact, I had to go to my bank and get it," the man said and smiled. "It's not like I have three million dollars sitting in my cash register."

"Understand," Crawford said. "When was this?"

"Well, he first came in here to inquire if we could effect the transaction yesterday morning. I made some calls and said I could. Then, yesterday afternoon he came back with the bars. Fifty kilos, to be exact, So, let's see, that was just before five o'clock."

"Were you the only one he dealt with?" Crawford asked.

"Yes, both times. My associate," he said and flicked his head at an older woman with wire-rim glasses across the room, "originally met them when they came in, but then turned them over to me."

"Gotcha. So in the course of the time the couple was here, did they ever happen to mention where they were going from here?" Crawford asked.

"Well, let me think...I know they came here from the States by boat, but you probably know that already." Crawford nodded. "I also got the impression they were not going back to the States."

"What did they say to lead you to that conclusion?"

"Well, the man focused on the transaction and the woman did a lot of the talking. She was kind of...well, a chatterbox. She said something about 'island hopping.' One of the places she mentioned was the Dominican Republic."

"You mean, that was their destination?"

"I'm not sure whether that was their final destination or just one of their stops along the way. I was only half-listening while I was on hold with my bank. Then, the bank official came on and I didn't hear what they were saying anymore."

"I understand. Was there anything else that you think might possibly be helpful to us?"

"Not really. Just that she said they were about to go on that submarine ride."

"What's that?" Crawford asked.

"It's a tourist ride in the harbor. Quite popular with visitors."

Crawford nodded and thought for a second. "Anything else you can think of?"

"Well, let's see, the man asked me for a card and said, 'If I gave you a week, how much cash do you think you could raise?'"

"For more gold bars?" Crawford asked.

"Yes. I told him I didn't know for sure, but maybe five million."

"What did he say?"

"He seemed pleased and said, 'Well, maybe I'll come back then.' I said, 'Great, just let me know.'"

Crawford nodded at Bentz. "I can't think of anything else," then he turned to Humphrey. "Thanks very much. I really appreciate your help."

"Yes, thanks," said Bentz.

"You're very welcome," Basil said, then broke into a wide smile. "On the one hand, I hope you catch them...on the other, for my sake, I kind of hope you don't."

Crawford nodded. "I get it," he said. "You'd like to do another deal or two with 'em, huh?"

The man only smiled.

*****

Ott called Crawford shortly after he and Bentz left the Global Investments office.

"How you coming along?" he asked.

"Good. We found the place that converted some of the gold into three million in cash."

"That's all?"

"That's all the dealer had access to in dollars. How about you?"

"I got a couple possible leads. Tell you when I see you," Ott said. "Hey, could you and Bentz meet me at the Ritz-Carlton desk? I'm thinking he might be able to get the manager there to give us the information on the credit card Kincade used to pay with."

"Yeah, that could come in very handy. Following the trail of where it's used in the future."

"You got it."

"I'm thinking one of the places might be the Dominican Republic," Crawford said.

"Why there?"

"'Cause the guy at the place where they sold the gold overheard something Laurie said about them going to the Dominican Republic. Are you near the Ritz-Carlton desk now?"

"Pretty close."

"How about we meet you there in ten minutes?"

"See you then."

*****

Ott's theory was right. Bentz met little resistance with the clerk at the desk of the Ritz-Carlton as far as getting her to divulge Jake Kincade's credit-card information. She did balk slightly at first, but Bentz acted a little huffy and told her that she would be impeding an "international homicide investigation" unless she immediately did her civic duty and turned over the vital information. She didn't need to be asked twice and told him it was an Amex card and gave him all the pertinent numbers. After that Bentz, Crawford, and Ott went and had a late lunch—it was two in the afternoon—at a place Bentz recommended.

They were seated at a booth that reminded Crawford of his beloved Green's back in Palm Beach.

"What's this place remind you of?" Crawford asked Ott, who had just picked up a menu.

Ott nodded. "The one and only Green's," he said. "Wonder if they've got your favorite—the sardine platter with tater tots."

Bentz grimaced. "No offense, but that sounds disgusting. You'd actually eat that?"

Crawford nodded. "Yeah, probably at least twice a week."

"And usually has seconds," Ott added.

The waitress came over and they ordered.

Crawford took a long sip of water. "Okay, Mort, solve a mystery: Where are these two going?"

"Well, I'll tell you where they're not."

"Where?"

"Andorra."

"Funny," said Crawford. "See, I've been thinking about the Dominican Republic, but I see that as more a place you go on vacation, not a place where American expatriates actually end up. They go to places like Costa Rica or Portugal or Spain maybe."

Ott pulled out his iPhone and typed in "Dominican Republic maps."

"What are you looking up?" Crawford asked.

"Just want to get a quick geography lesson," Ott said. "So, the Dominican Republic is between here and Puerto Rico. Actually, pretty close to Puerto Rico."

"Maybe that's where they're going. Puerto Rico."

"Could be. But farther north are all those Bahamas islands. Hmm…Turks and Caicos is supposed to be really nice."

"Yeah, but remember what David Balfour said about that VAT tax taking 7.5% right off the top."

"Yeah, that was the Bahamas. We don't know about Turks and Caicos. And also, that's only if the authorities find out about the gold." Ott put his phone down on the table. "Sorry, Charlie, wish I could solve the mystery but there're a lot of islands, big and small, out there."

Crawford sighed. "Yeah, I hear you. So I guess it comes down to trying to follow the money. Or in this case, the Amex card."

Bentz was going from Crawford's face to Ott's like he was watching a ping pong game.

"So, Palmer," Crawford said, "do you know how long it takes to get from here to the Dominican Republic by boat?"

"Depends on the boat, but, ballpark, I'd say between a day and a half to three days," Bentz said. "Their boat, being a Viking 53 sports fisherman, I'd figure closer to the short side— a day and a half."

Crawford turned back to Ott. "So, if they left this morning, earliest they'd get there would be, say, tomorrow at noon."

"Or maybe late afternoon, then call it a day," Ott said. "We could get someone at the station to try to track purchases on that card. As soon as they use it, we'll know exactly where they are."

Crawford thrummed the table. "Problem is now that they got a hell of a lot of cash, they might never use the Amex card."

"True. We could just call around, all the resorts and hotels in the D.R. See if they got a Jake Kincade and Laurie Reback staying there."

"How many resorts and hotels you suppose there are in the D.R.?"

"I don't know. Lots, I'm sure. But it's safe to assume they're not going to be staying at some 2-star dump. We can get a bunch of staff at the station calling the good places, might just track 'em down. Hey, it worked for finding out where they bought the boat."

"True," Crawford said, thinking about having to shell out for another lunch at the "exclusive bistro," Green's Pharmacy.

Ott shrugged. "Or we could rent a plane, head for the Dominican Republic, and when we see the boat, parachute down on 'em."

Bentz laughed. Crawford didn't. "Come on, Mort."

"Sorry, that was lame."

"We got the same problem if they go somewhere else."

"What do you mean?" Ott asked.

"I mean, they could just use cash."

"Yeah, true. But it's not as though they have any clue we're hot on their heels. Plus, I'm guessing the game plan is to conserve cash. That was the whole purpose in coming here in the first place."

"You're right. So we're back to where we were. Questions are, are they going to the Dominican Republic, number one? And if so, are they going to stay there? And if not, where are they going next?"

"That's a lot to find out," Ott said, then a moment later he slapped the table so hard that the salt and pepper shakers jumped. "*Holy shit!* I know where they're going!"

"Where?"

"Isn't there a part of San Juan, Puerto Rico, called Old San Juan?"

"Yeah, I think so. Why?"

"I bet they also call it the 'Old City.'"

"They do," Benz chimed in.

"This shopkeeper in the Ritz-Carlton remembered Laurie saying something about going to the 'Old City' to live."

Crawford raised his fist and gave Ott a knuckle bump. "That's good info. Narrows things down a lot. So the next question is, if that's where they're going, then when the hell are they going to get there?" Crawford looked out a window at the George Town harbor.

Bentz spoke again: "My guess is, even they don't know."

"Yeah," Ott said, "'cause they're probably in no rush at all."

CHAPTER TWENTY-SIX

Crawford and Ott decided that the prudent thing at this point was to go back to Palm Beach. It could take a week to as long as two weeks, or even longer, for Jake Kincade and Laurie Reback to make it to their final destination. Maybe that *was* going to be the "Old City" of San Juan, but then again, maybe it wasn't. They could always change their minds. Maybe decide they loved the Dominican Republic and decide to stay or go somewhere else altogether. They could even sell the boat, hop on a plane, and go to…God-knows-where. Crawford and Ott talked about flying to Puerto Rico and waiting. Be the welcoming committee for the two peripatetic fugitives. But where? And wait for how long? No, that didn't make any sense, so they both agreed, it was time to head home.

So, they thanked Palmer Bentz for all his help and went back to their hotel. The first flight back to Miami left the next morning. Before the three parted ways, Crawford had an afterthought.

"One last thing, Palmer," he said.

"What's that?"

"I want to tie up a loose end. I'm thinking because Global probably made a fair amount of money on the gold trade with Jake Kincade, Basil Humphrey might want to keep open the possibility of doing another deal with him. I mean, he all but said that. See where I'm going…?"

"Yes, I'm with you," Bentz said. "You're suggesting that I have a conversation with Basil, tell him that if he ever contacts Jake Kincade and warns him that you're in pursuit, that he'll be charged as…as what?"

"Well, let's see, how 'bout 'aiding and abetting a murder suspect,' punishable up to five years in prison?"

Ott looked eager to throw in his two cents' worth. "Or accessory to commit an international monetary conspiracy across foreign waters."

"Oh, I like that," said Bentz.

Crawford chuckled. "Whatever the hell it even means."

"Whatever it means," Bentz said, "consider it done."

*****

Crawford and Ott were having dinner at a place called The Funky Chicken, which was more upscale than its name suggested. It was a beautiful, humidity-free night in the Caymans and Crawford had ordered swordfish, and Red-Meat Mort ordered a well-done steak.

"I saw that old movie, *The Firm,* on Netflix a while back. You ever see it?"

Crawford put down his glass of red wine. "Yeah, part of it took place here, right?"

"Sure did. Tom Cruise, I think his name was Mitch somebody in the movie, is an ambitious lawyer who cheats on his wife with a hot local number when he and Gene Hackman are down here on some kind of dubious business trip."

"They're both lawyers in the same firm, right?"

"Yeah, hence the title. Hackman turns out to be a bad guy who's mentoring Mitch while at the same time up to all kinds of skullduggery."

"Like murder, as I recall."

"Like multiple murders. And the mafia's involved, and the FBI, and Mitch's wife finds out he cheated and threatens to cut him loose. So then...oh, yeah, Mitch makes a deal with the FBI, then the mafia, and Hackman gets whacked, and Mitch reconciles with his wife and...everyone lives happily ever after."

"Except Hackman."

"Yeah, well, 'cause he was dead."

"Right."

"So, what do you want to do tonight, Charlie?"

Crawford polished off his glass of red wine. "Um, watch a movie, I'm thinking."

"What? We're on an exotic island in the Caribbean and you're gonna go back to the hotel and go to bed?"

"I said I'm going to watch a movie."

"Same thing."

"No, it's not."

"My big chance to hit the town with the playboy of the Western World and scare up some Grand Cayman poon."

Crawford threw up a hand. "Stop," he said. "Will you quit draggin' out your lame junior-high-school lingo?"

"Okay, okay, I just thought we'd hit a couple of bars and—"

"Not happening."

"Is it 'cause of Dominica or Rose? I never can keep 'em straight."

Crawford laughed. "It's 'cause I want to watch a movie."

"Okay, I can see that's your story and you're sticking to it."

"Yup."

Their swordfish and steak arrived, and they dug in. They went conversation-free for a few minutes, until two young, attractive women walked in and sat a few tables away.

"You see what I see, Charlie?" Ott whispered, flicking his head in the direction of the women.

"Mort, you gotta give it a rest."

Ott sighed dramatically. "What a total killjoy you turned out to be."

CHAPTER TWENTY-SEVEN

The next morning, Crawford and Ott had a smooth flight from the Caymans back to Miami. They got their police vehicle from the airport parking garage where they'd left it and drove up to Palm Beach. Then they parked at the station and went in to Norm Rutledge's office to catch him up on the trip.

After Crawford explained how they suspected their fugitives might, ultimately, be fleeing to Puerto Rico, Rutledge weighed in. "So, you want to go on *another* junket in a week to ten days, to Puerto Rico."

Crawford gave Ott a quick eyeroll. "Or we could leave it up to Puerto Rico's finest to bring the two back here."

"Nah, we ain't doin' that," Rutledge said, leaning closer to them. "I noticed you both got a little color."

"Yeah, we met a couple hot babes," Ott said, "went to this really amazing nude beach."

Rutledge leaned in toward Ott, his eyes large, like he was envious. "Seriously?"

Crawford shook his head. "Not much he says is serious. You oughta know that by now."

"All right, so basically you're gonna wait 'til you get a hit on that credit card number, is that it?" Rutledge asked.

Crawford shook his head. "There's no guarantee they'll use it again," he said. "I mean this Kincade's a smart guy and he's loaded with cash now."

"But how convinced are you they're headed to Puerto Rico?" Rutledge asked.

Crawford shrugged. "We're basing it on a remark one of the suspects made to a hotel shopkeeper."

"So, more than a hunch then?"

"Oh, yeah, definitely," Crawford said.

"Good. 'Cause a hunch and three bucks'll just get you a cup of coffee," Rutledge said.

"Not at Green's," said Crawford. "They'll throw in toast, too."

*****

Crawford got a call on his cell as he headed back to his office.

It was Dominica.

"Hey, how's it going?" he said.

"Charlie," she said, sounding more somber than he'd ever heard her before, "I'm at a crime scene. A homicide."

"Okay...where are you?"

"240 Jungle Road."

The address registered instantly. "That's...that's my ex-wife's house."

"I know."

His whole body tensed. "Oh my God, is she...."

"I'm so sorry," Dominica said with feeling.

"Oh, Jesus. I'm on my way."

He ran out of the back of the station, got into his car, and gunned it. He got it up to seventy on South County Road where the speed limit was thirty. He hung a hard, squealing left onto Jungle, hit the brake pedal, and skidded into the 240 Jungle driveway. He jumped out of the car and ran inside through the open front door.

"Dominica?" he shouted.

"In here!" she shouted back.

He walked to where her voice had come from. She and another tech, Robin Gold, were hunched down over a body, two uniforms behind them with their arms over their chests.

Dominica looked up and caught Crawford's eye. "Oh, Charlie, I am so sorry."

Crawford took three steps closer and looked down. Jill's eyes were open, and her face was covered with bruises. Blood matted her hair and had coagulated below her nose. Her once-perfect, heart-shaped mouth had not escaped the brutal battering—her lips were puffy and dark-colored. Dried blood had gathered at the corners of her mouth.

If he were alone, Crawford wouldn't have been able to hold back the tears. He would have fallen into a crouch, cradling Jill's broken, lifeless body.

Instead, he wanted only to go find Giles Simpson and beat him senseless with his fists, the butt of his gun, whatever was handy.

But, as shocking, heartbreaking, and infuriating as this unthinkable scene was, he had a job to do.

He looked over at Dominica. "Fill me in. Who found her?"

One of the uniforms, Larry Bowles, stepped forward. "I did."

"Did someone call in or what?"

"Yes, a friend. Stephanie Meyers her name is," Bowles said. "Said the vic was supposed to come to her house for dinner last night, then play tennis with her this morning. Never did either one. Said she got worried."

Crawford's eyes narrowed. "Do me a favor, Bowles, don't ever call her 'the vic' again. She's got a name. Jill Simpson."

"Sorry, I just—"

"That's okay," Crawford said, turning to Dominica. "What's your best guess when it happened?"

"Um, late afternoon, early evening yesterday. That's my best guess."

Crawford looked around at the others. "Anybody found a murder weapon?"

"No, nothing yet," said Les Rackoff, the uniform next to Bowles.

Crawford nodded. "Hawes coming?" he asked, referring to the medical examiner.

"On his way," Dominica said.

"So what else?" Crawford said to no one in particular.

Dominica understood what he was asking. "The place was burglarized, Charlie. Turned upside down. Her jewelry box empty, a gun case broken into, looks like either rifles or shotguns taken, plus two smaller TVs and a painting."

"We're guessing the good silverware, too," the other tech, Robin Gold added. "Two drawers were cleaned out."

"Anything else?" Crawford asked.

"We just did a quick check," Dominica said. "Don't know what else."

Crawford nodded.

"Looks like he…or they…used a crowbar or something to get in the back door," Bowles said.

Crawford looked up quickly. "A break-in?"

"Yeah, looks like all the doors and windows were locked," Bowles said. "Don't know if you remember, Charlie, but there was a burglary a few streets down three weeks ago. Another one a little before that. We're thinking that whoever it was broke in, thinking no one was here, and they attacked Ms. Simpson when they realized she could ID them."

Crawford looked back down at Jill's viciously smashed face and thought for a few moments. "This was no burglary gone bad," he said. "This was premeditated murder."

Dominica cocked her head. From having been to a number of crime scenes with Crawford, she knew he was not a detective who made conclusive statements without definitive proof. She no doubt wondered if this were merely a hunch of his.

He looked to Robin Gold, who was dusting for prints. "Go over the house, top to bottom, will ya, Goldie?"

She nodded. "Don't worry, I will."

He turned to Bowles. "Show me the back door, please?"

Bowles nodded and walked out of the living room, Crawford and Les Rackoff right behind him.

Bowles led Crawford, who was putting on vinyl gloves, to the back door. It was pushed in and splintered. Crawford got down in a crouch and looked it over, not saying anything for a few moments. "Yeah, looks like somebody took a crowbar to it. Not the usual way a burglar enters. Makes too much noise. Neighbors could hear it."

Both Bowles and Rackoff nodded. "I agree," said Bowles. "But what are you thinking?"

"I don't know yet," Crawford said, going outside and looking at the door from a different angle. "Hey, come out here a sec."

Bowles and Rackoff walked outside.

"So, if you're a guy thinking of the best way to burglarize this house, what would your first thought be?" Crawford asked.

Rackoff pointed. "I'd knock out that pane of glass and open the window. Maybe use one of those gizmos that can cut a hole in the glass."

Crawford nodded. "What about you, Larry?"

"I'd pick the damn lock," Bowles said. "Isn't that what burglars do?"

Crawford nodded. "Yeah, there are a least a few other ways that would be easier and less noisy than taking a crowbar to the door."

"Plus," Rackoff said, "for the most part, burglars aren't killers."

"Yeah, unless they're trapped. Gotta kill or be caught," Bowles added.

"Except I doubt whoever did it would be thinking she was going to catch him. I mean, what could she do?" Crawford asked.

"Good point," said Rackoff.

The three walked back into the house.

Crawford heard familiar footsteps coming toward them.

Ott appeared, his shirttail out, looking like he'd been running. Their eyes met—Ott's were red-rimmed and shiny. "Shit, Charlie. I'm so damn sorry."

It looked like Ott wanted to hug him. Probably would have if Bowles and Rackoff weren't there.

"Thanks, man." Crawford had nothing more to say.

"We'll get the bastard," Ott said, his eyes focused and his nostrils flaring. "I promise you that."

Crawford nodded. "Damn right we will."

"What we got so far?" Ott asked.

"Used a crowbar to bust through the back door off of the family room. Took a bunch of stuff...."

"You think it might be the same guy who hit the other houses around here?"

Crawford put his hand on his chin and looked down at the floor. "I doubt it." He spoke more quietly. "I got my suspicions, Mort. Fill you in later."

"Okay, man, understood," Ott murmured, then turned to Bowles and Rackoff. "You guys talk to the neighbors yet?"

Bowles shook his head. "Not yet,"

"Well, come on, what the hell you waiting for?" Ott said. "After that go string up some yellow tape, then stay out there and keep people away."

Bowles and Rackoff nodded.

"Yeah, four police cars are gonna attract a lot of attention," Crawford said.

"Already have," Ott said.

"On it," said Rackoff, and Bowles and he walked out.

Ott gave Crawford a sad look. Then he came over and threw a bearhug around him. "I am just so goddamn sorry, man. You all right? No, course not. How could you be?"

Crawford hugged Mort back, then pulled from their embrace. "I spent eight...mostly happy...years with that woman, Mort. I loved her very much."

"I know, I know. I don't know what to tell you except.... Christ, my heart goes out to you, brother."

Crawford took a step toward Ott. "You know who did this, right?"

Ott didn't hesitate. "I know who you think did it. Her husband."

Crawford nodded. "Or had someone do it for him. Look at the facts. She was divorcing him, maybe for half of what they were worth. He thinks she's cheating with every man in New York and Palm Beach, myself included. He's beaten her up in the past, the last time really bad. I mean, isn't that enough? The guy's violent, delusional, and afraid of losing his money."

"Yeah, I hear you. Where's the husband now?" Ott asked.

"I have no idea. I'm going to call my sister-in-law and get his number... after I tell her what happened."

"Who called it in, Charlie?"

"A woman named Stephanie Meyers. She's apparently a friend of Jill's who got concerned because Jill was supposed to go to dinner at her house last night and play tennis with her this morning but didn't. She called the station and asked us to check on her."

"But she doesn't know what happened?"

"No, but the neighbors have all got to be wondering, seeing our cars and everything. You know how fast rumors spread in this town."

Ott nodded. "Sure do. Well, I'll let you call her sister. I know you gotta get on that."

"Yeah, I'm going to do that right now. Tell her and get Giles's number at the same time. Then call Jill's mother."

"That's gonna be a tricky call. The Giles call, I mean," Ott said. "Because you don't know for absolute certain he did it. So, on one hand it's a condolence call, on the other, you want to find out where he is and whether he's our guy or not."

"Put it this way, Mort, I'm ninety per cent certain he's our guy." Crawford shook his head. "A burglary gone bad? I'm just not buying it."

"I hear you, but this wouldn't be the first burglary that turned deadly."

Crawford sighed deeply. "True."

He heard light footsteps as Dominica walked in. "Just wanted to see how you're doing."

He could tell she wanted to throw her arms around him and comfort him. He could have used it.

"Like I told Mort, I spent a lot of good years with that woman. She's only thirty-six years old—" he couldn't use the past tense— "way too young to die."

"I know, I know. Again, I'm so sorry," she said. "For what it's worth I can guarantee you everyone will work overtime and do whatever it takes to catch whoever did it."

"Thanks, I appreciate it. You find anything yet?"

"Not much. I mean, the guy comes in, obviously wearing gloves, so likely no DNA to speak of. Maybe something under her nails, but I'm not seeing much chance of that. We'll keep looking, cover every square inch of this house."

Crawford nodded. "Thanks. Well, I'm gonna make a call I really don't want to make. Jill and her sister were really close."

"We'll give you some privacy," Ott said, walking toward the door.

Dominica nodded and followed him out.

Crawford took out his cell and thought about what he was going to say. Then he dialed.

Jessie answered after the third ring. "Hey, Charlie, how are you?"

"Jessie," he said, taking the simple but direct approach, "I've got terrible news."

CHAPTER TWENTY-EIGHT

Jessie Giordano was not the hysterical type, but she broke down and cried for a full two minutes before she could pull herself together enough to speak. "So, he did it. That bastard did it," she said at last.

"Well, put it this way," Crawford said. "It was made to look like a burglary, but, like you, I've got serious doubts."

"Serious doubts? Charlie, you *know* it was him! He either hired someone or did it himself."

"I'm sorry, Jess. I can't tell you how sorry I am. I keep thinking how young she was, how much life she should have had left."

Jessie started sobbing again. "Oh God, oh God...I can't believe he'd go this far."

"Do you know where he is? Giles?"

"No idea."

"Do you have his cell phone number?"

Jessie gave it to him

"So, you'll come down here?"

"Yes, of course. I'll book a flight right after I hang up."

"Will the funeral be up there?"

"Jesus, Charlie, I don't know! I haven't had a chance to process any of this yet."

"I know, I know. I'm sorry. Again, my condolences."

Jessie sniffled and blew her nose. "I guess Giles makes the call on all the funeral arrangements. Unless you put the bastard in jail first."

"If he did it, you can be sure I'll try."

"He did it and you damn well know it."

"All right, Jess, I'm in her house now. I've got more to do here."

"Find whatever evidence you need, Charlie."

"Trust me—I will."

*****

He dialed Giles Simpson's number.

"Hello?"

"Giles, it's Charlie Crawford in Palm Beach."

"Charlie Crawford… And to what do I owe the pleasure of this call?"

"Giles, I'm sorry to have to tell you but Jill…well, she's been murdered. Happened yesterday some time."

"Oh…Jesus. I can't believe it—" he sounded truly shocked. Not like he was faking it— "What…what in God's name happened?"

"We don't know much more than she was found in the living room of your house here beaten to death. It appears that a burglar, maybe two, might have ransacked your house. I am very sorry."

"When did it happen?"

"Sometime yesterday. I'll know more after I speak to the Medical Examiner," Crawford said. "Where are you now?"

"In New York."

"How long have you been there?"

A pause. "What do you mean how long have I been here? I've been here for weeks. I live here, I work here. I was down at my Palm Beach house with Jill about a month ago."

"So, you haven't been back here since then?"

"What are you getting at? Are you thinking *I* had something to do with this?"

"Giles, I'm a detective doing my job. Asking a lot of questions is part of it. I'm sorry if you're offended, but this is what I have to do. I want to find Jill's killer, just as much as you want me to."

"Okay, I'm gonna book a flight. Get down there as fast as I can."

"All right. I'll get back to you with any new information we come up with."

"Thank you," Simpson said and clicked off.

Crawford looked out his window and thought for a few minutes. If he were in Simpson's shoes, he figured, he might have asked a lot more questions. Not to mention how business-like Giles sounded—not really shaken up except for his initial reaction…not much emotion there at all.

But maybe that's just the way the man was.

CHAPTER TWENTY-NINE

Crawford had another call to make. To Jill's mother, Lucy. He dialed her straightaway because he still had her number in his contacts. He almost didn't want her to answer it. Next-of-kin notifications were the worst part of the job. But ones where you knew the people were even more horrible.

Lucy Dellasandro did answer, in the end. He told her what happened. Said how sorry he was. She cried profusely. He said how sorry he was again. She asked him who did it. He said he didn't know yet, but he'd keep her informed since it was his case. She cried again. He said he was sure he'd be back to her shortly. He repeated how sorry he was. Lucy thanked him, said she loved him, and that was the end of the conversation.

*****

Crawford walked out of the kitchen and into the living room of the house on Jungle Road. The Medical Examiner, Bob Hawes, was down on his knees taking close-ups of Jill. He looked up as he heard Crawford approach.

"Oh, hey, Charlie, I'm so sorry about your loss," he said, a grim look on his face. "Terrible thing."

"Thank you, Bob. Found anything yet?"

"She's got a broken hyoid. Strangulation is the COD."

"Really," Crawford said, glancing down at Jill's body. "So not the result of a beating."

"No, that was what I originally speculated. I mean, she was beaten badly, but it was the hyoid."

Crawford put his hand to his chin. "Let me ask you this:, if you were a burglar and got caught in the act, what would you do?"

"Run. Get the hell out of there," Hawes said.

"Okay, but what if you thought this person could recognize you, testify against you, and put you in jail."

Hawes didn't hesitate. "Shoot her or strangle her, like he did."

"But would you choose to actually approach her and strangle her?"

Hawes thought for a few moments. "On second thought, I guess I wouldn't. I wouldn't want to get close to her 'cause who knows what could happen? I mean, shit, she could be a karate expert for all I know."

A karate expert was about the last thing Jill was, Crawford thought. "But if whoever did it came up to her, planning to strangle her, that would have given her plenty of time to scream. Loud enough so the neighbors might hear."

"Yeah, true," Hawes said, nodding. "Obviously, the neighbors never heard anything, or they would have called in yesterday."

"I have a couple guys interviewing 'em right now, but yeah, if anybody ever heard a scream, we would have definitely gotten a call yesterday."

He spent the rest of the afternoon going through the house with Ott, Dominica, Robin Gold, and Hawes. One of the best clues, he felt, was an open hardcover book lying on the living room floor and a reading lamp with the light still on. He pictured Jill reading and suddenly dropping it to the floor when one of two things happened: either she heard a burglar jimmy open her back door with a crowbar; or it was her husband, or someone hired by her husband. They came at her and beat and strangled her. It could have been Giles Simpson, Crawford thought. He could have killed Jill and beelined straight back to New York. Crawford calculated that with the pedal down, a minimum of stops, and a fast car, which he no doubt had, he could make it from Palm Beach to New York in sixteen or seventeen hours. Flying commercial would make no sense, as it would leave an electronic trail. Flying private…?

Crawford reminded himself that Giles could have hired somebody. But how would a seemingly reputable surgeon ever find a killer for hire? That was one of the few areas Google couldn't help much with. But someone who could administer the terrible beating that Jill's sister had described a month before could probably ratchet it up a level or two. Yes, he felt reasonably certain, Giles Simpson could have done it.

It made even more sense that he, in fact, *did* do it because of the point Crawford had discussed with Bob Hawes. No neighbor had called in the killing. No screams heard, apparently. So, if Giles did it, he'd simply come up to his wife, put his hands around her neck, and strangled her to death before she had a chance to scream.

As he was working through the scenario, Larry Bowles and Les Rackoff came back into the house and approached Crawford in the living room.

"We didn't really come up with much, Charlie," Bowles said. "We spoke to the neighbors on either side and across the street, and nothing. We'll go back out and speak to the ones further down the street but just wanted to update you, nothing so far."

"Okay. So definitely none of them heard a scream?" Crawford asked.

"Nah, none of 'em."

"Did any of 'em report hearing any unusual noises? Like the sound of the guy using the crowbar on the back door."

"Sorry, man. Again nothing."

Crawford wasn't surprised. "Okay, what about something one of 'em may have seen? Someone on foot? A car coming or leaving?"

"Well, yeah, matter of fact," Bowles said.

"Matter of fact what, Larry?" Crawford asked, taking a step closer to Bowles

"The neighbor across the street said she saw a black car pull out of the driveway."

Crawford's eyes narrowed. "When the hell were you gonna tell me this? A black car? Did she say what kind?"

"I asked her, but she didn't know," Bowles said. "Just that it looked like a nice one."

Crawford shook his head. "*A nice one.* That's not real helpful."

"Yeah, I know."

"Go back and ask her again. A *nice* big one? A *nice* small one? A *nice* convertible? Or what?"

The two nodded.

"Did she say when she saw it?"

"Just said yesterday afternoon. She wasn't sure exactly when."

"Wow. You got a real star witness there, Larry."

Bowles shrugged. "Wish we got more. We'll go ask about the car, then check the other houses."

Crawford nodded. "Okay. Probably the farther away, the less you'll get."

"Let's hope not," Bowles said.

Crawford nodded, knowing he should personally follow up with the people Bowles and Rackoff had interviewed.

The two went toward the front door and Crawford walked back over to Hawes. "What's your best guess on time of death, Bob?"

"Sorry, man, I can't really pin it down yet. But I'd say somewhere between one and four in the afternoon. Could have been a little earlier or a little later."

"Understand," Crawford said, looking at his watch. It was six-fifteen. "All right," he said to Hawes, "I'm gonna leave. If you find anything I should know about, call me. Otherwise, I'll just read your report when you get it done. I plan on coming back here later."

"Okay, but one last thing."

He didn't like the look on Hawes' face or his tone.

"What?"

Hawes lowered his voice. "She mighta been raped," he said. "I'm really sorry, man. I…"

Crawford put his hand up. He was all out of words.

He didn't want to be in the same room with Jill's lifeless body anymore. He was having flashbacks now, scenes involving the vibrant, vivacious, passionate, beautiful, fiery—the Italian in her—Jill. A woman of enormous vigor and spirit and enthusiasm and oftentimes feistiness. God, she was a fantastic woman and what a fool he had been to let her go.

What a complete and total fool.

He needed a drink.

In some dark joint where he didn't know a soul.

CHAPTER THIRTY

He knew of such a place.

Yeah, it was a bit of a dump.

But when he went there, he realized it was not worthy of drinks in memory of Jill. She deserved a high-class bar to be remembered in. A place that had pickled eggs and a box of Slim Jims behind the bar wasn't gonna cut it. Just plain not appropriate and not in keeping with the thoroughly classy woman Jill was.

So he went to the bar at The Breakers in Palm Beach and shot his wad. Drinks there were around fifteen to twenty bucks a pop, but so what? It was for a really good cause.

Jill Dellasandro Crawford Simpson.

*****

He had had two drinks at HMF, the bar named after the noted robber baron and railroad magnate Henry Morrison Flagler. He was having one of what they referred to as their "bespoke" cocktails. His drink selection at the moment was one called a Floozy, which was made of tequila, ginger, cucumbers, jalapeno, and lime. Traffic was light, so the bartender and he had a little back and forth going.

"So *bespoke*...isn't that what they call custom-made suits? Usually from London?" Crawford asked.

"I guess. I like to think I custom-make my drinks."

"I'd say you do. They're damn tasty."

"Well, thank you."

He had heard somebody a few stools down order something called a Blueberry Bootlegger. Some of these names were a little too cutesy for the serious drinker Crawford considered himself to be.

He waited until the bartender passed by him.

"So, what exactly's a Blueberry Bootlegger, Jack?"

Jack leaned toward him. "That would be Pisco, freshly picked blueberries, lemon, and ginger. Also bespoke."

"Of course. But what the hell's Pisco?"

Jack chuckled. "Hell, man, you haven't lived if you've never had Pisco. It's a brandy. A very tasty, high-proof brandy."

"Gotcha. I notice you seem to like ginger in your drinks?"

"Sure do. Gives 'em that little zing."

"I'm a big fan of zing."

Crawford leaned back in his barstool, his intention being a little Jack-free contemplation of the all-too-short life of Jill Dellasandro Crawford Simpson. He remembered when they first met. She was someone else's date at a frat party at his alma mater, Dartmouth. They had been opponents in a game of Beirut, the ping-pong ball-tossing drinking game that had allegedly been conceived at Dartmouth in the sixties. That was one of Dartmouth's claims to fame, along with—again allegedly—the place that the *Animal House* fraternity, Delta Tau Chi, had been patterned after: a notorious Dartmouth frat house.

In any case, Crawford called her up a few days later, and they had a skiing date, followed by dinner the next weekend. Calling it dinner was a stretch since it consisted of pizza and beer, which was in line with the limited budget of juniors in college. Their next date was when Crawford and Jill and six others piled into a Rent-a-Wreck and went to a Rolling Stones concert in Boston. They limped back to Hanover, New Hampshire, in the pitiful Plymouth Breeze, singing Stones songs the whole way back.

Crawford knew Jill was the one after those two dates. Not only did she have a sneaky-funny sense of humor and a big-hearted personality, but she was also drop-dead gorgeous. Plus a few dozen other qualities you couldn't quite put your finger on.

For example, there was an Asian girl in their class who looked to be sixteen years old max who didn't fit in at all. She was the stereotypical grind and didn't try to hide it the way other grinds did, and never seemed to smile or get much joy out of anything. Even A-pluses on papers. Despite her inscrutability, though, she apparently suffered silently from the ostracism. Crawford knew because Jill befriended her and told Crawford what she'd told her.

"Can you imagine," Jill said, when they were at a table in a Dartmouth coffee shop, "what it would be like, you going to…I don't know, Kowloon or somewhere…and having nothing in common with anyone? No one to play lacrosse or football with. No one to guzzle grain alcohol with."

Crawford chuckled. "I do occasionally go to classes, you know."

"I know. I was just making a point," Jill said. "Point is, it's pure hell for the girl. I mean, she's just absolutely miserable here."

Jill, one of the "popular" girls, made an even bigger effort to befriend the Chinese student, even though they had very little in common. Then, one night, the Chinese girl slit her wrists. She didn't die and Jill interpreted the act as a message to her parents: she hated it at Dartmouth and wanted to come home.

Apparently, her parents got the message. Four days after the attempt, Jill helped the girl pack up her few belongings and rented a car to take her to Bradley Airport in Hartford. The two hugged and had a tearful parting.

"Hi, this seat taken?" asked a woman standing next to Crawford. He had been a million miles away.

He looked up at her and smiled. "No," he said, opening his hand. "All yours."

She sat down. She was a short, attractive woman, in her early thirties, he guessed. She had about the shiniest hair he'd ever seen and freckles that you couldn't place much better on a human face.

She glanced over at him. "I hear this place is known for its creative drinks."

"Yeah, creative names, too."

"Like what?"

"Well, like one called Chanel # 6, another called The Redhead and one I can personally recommend one called The Floozy."

The woman laughed. "The Floozy, huh. I'm Charlotte, by the way. *Not* a floozy."

Crawford laughed. "I'm Charlie. *Not* a redhead."

She laughed back. "I can see. Are you from here?"

"Yes. Well, I work here but I can't afford to live here. How 'bout you?"

"I'm from D.C. Here on business."

Jack the barkeep came over. "Get you a drink, ma'am?"

"Well, my friend here told me about The Redhead and The Floozy. What's Chanel # 6 like?"

"It's a member of the bubbly family," Jack said with gusto. "Ketel One, Chambord, pineapple juice, and champagne."

"That sounds good," Charlotte said, nodding. "I'll give it a try."

"You got it."

She turned back to Crawford. "So what do you *do*, Charlie?"

"I'm a cop."

She drew her head back. "A cop? Really?"

"Well, a detective."

"No kidding. I thought all cops and detectives were fat and had buzz cuts."

He laughed. "I used to have a buzz cut. Used to be a little chubby, too. What do you do, Charlotte?"

"I'm a fashion consultant to boutiques. Staying here at the hotel."

"And I thought all fashion consultants to boutiques were anorexic and had pixie cuts."

"Touché," she said. "And, by the way, I'm impressed you know what a pixie cut is."

"Thank you, but I don't really."

"So what are you doing here anyway? Isn't there a nice cop bar in Palm Beach?"

"Nearest one's in a dubious part of West Palm."

"Seriously, why are you here?"

And he told her. He left out the part about Jill having been murdered but told her his ex-wife had died and he was very sad about it. She said she was sorry and mentioned she was single. He said that was surprising, and she asked why. He said because she obviously had a good career or she wouldn't be staying at the Breakers, plus she seemed nice and was nice-looking.

"Is that all men care about? Nice-looking?"

"No," Crawford said. "It's also important that they like to watch football."

She looked at him, her head cocked to one side. "You're kidding, right?"

He looked at her and just smiled.

"So are you in a relationship, Charlie?"

He hated that expression. "Kinda," he said. "You?"

"Nah. Too busy."

"Well, if you're going to be around for a while, I got a buddy looking for female companionship."

"Translation: he's horny. Right?"

"Why would you say that?"

She didn't answer. "Is he a cop?"

Crawford nodded.

"A cute cop?"

"Well, yeah, kinda." Though he was pretty certain Ott had never been called cute before.

One drink more, and twenty minutes later, he was on his way home.

The bar tab, Crawford was pretty sure, was the largest of his entire life as a drinking man.

Even bigger than the one from a hazy Mardi Gras fifteen years back when the elbow-bending began at eleven in the morning followed by an all-nighter celebrating something long since forgotten.

He left HMF at twelve-thirty in an Uber, losing count of how many Floozies he'd had before shifting to an 18-year-old Macallan single malt at fifty-two bucks a pop.

Charlotte had turned out to be a good listener and he'd waxed on with Jill stories, then listened as she talked about the various airheads in the fashion business she had to endure and how there was such a paucity of good men out there who weren't "totally self-absorbed." That's when Crawford jumped in and made another Mort Ott pitch, but when Charlotte asked him to describe Ott physically, she didn't seem all that interested.

He kissed Charlotte on the cheek outside of the Breakers, knowing it could go further but he was not interested. Then he slid awkwardly into the Uber driver's Toyota Corolla and was driven to his condo building in West Palm Beach. He faked a sober hello to the man at the reception desk in the lobby and concentrated hard on walking a straight line to the elevator without any stumbles.

It wasn't easy.

He started stripping down immediately upon stepping into his apartment, got to his bed, and wrestled with his socks, then gave up after being unable to peel one off.

CHAPTER THIRTY-ONE

He woke up in massive, head-splitting pain at eight o'clock and, with huge difficulty, got vertical and lurched toward the bathroom, where he shook out four Bayers and downed them without benefit of water.

He was at his desk at the station at 8:40 with a large Dunkin' Donuts coffee in front of him and a 16-ounce Coke off to one side, when Ott walked in.

Seeing Crawford's face and the quart of Coke, Ott, good detective that he was, put it all together.

"Little bender last night?"

"Big bender last night. I'll be lucky to get through the day."

Ott said down opposite him. "Jill, huh?"

Crawford nodded in pain. "Of course. A pretty pathetic way to mourn her death, I know."

"Maybe, but I sure understand," Ott said. "So, you ready to get this guy?"

"Damn right. I'm going to go back and question the neighbors again. I was going to last night, but…."

"I get it," Ott said.

Then Crawford gave Ott his theory why Jill had never screamed: her husband had approached her, maybe even with a smile on his face, then had put his hands around her neck and strangled her before she could ever get a sound out.

"Makes sense," Ott said. "You talk to him yet?"

Crawford nodded. "Yeah, he's coming down here. May be here already."

"How'd he sound?"

Crawford thought for a second. "Like a doctor, is the best way I can describe it."

"What do you mean?"

"Cool, calm...like it was just something he had to deal with."

Ott shook his head slowly and said, "Doctors and lawyers, my favorite lowlifes."

Crawford nodded. "Okay, so let's change the subject. Anything new on our boat friends?"

A big smile rolled across Ott's potato-shaped face. "That's what I came in here to tell you. Know how I had everyone calling all over the D.R? Well, Shaw found a Mr. and Mrs. J. Kincade staying at a place called Casa de Campo. I checked it out and it looks like a place where the high rollers hang. So I called there, described Kincade, and he's definitely *our* Kincade."

"Good work. When did they check in?"

"Three nights ago. They checked out this morning."

"Typical of our luck. Check out right after we find out they're there."

"I know. But the good news is Kincade asked the guy at the desk whether there were any places to get gas between there and Puerto Rico."

"Bingo. So that *is* where they're going."

"Gotta be. Hotel guy told him there's nothing but water between the D.R. and Puerto Rico."

Crawford raised his fist. "How do you feel about going there solo?"

Ott frowned. "Without my wingman?"

"Yeah, I'm gonna need to stick around here."

"I figured. Well, Charlie, I'll miss you, bro," Ott said, putting an arm around Crawford, "but to be honest, you didn't show me much in the Caymans. I mean, watching a movie on a Saturday night?"

Crawford smiled. "Yeah, well, I guess maybe I have lost a step or two."

CHAPTER THIRTY-TWO

"So now that you're a geography expert of the Caribbean," Crawford asked Ott, "how far is it from the Dominican Republic to Puerto Rico?"

"Two hundred and thirty-seven miles, to be exact," Ott said. "For all I know, they could be pulling into Old San Juan any minute now."

"So I guess you just do what you did in the D. R. Get everyone you can round up to get dialing every hotel in Puerto Rico."

"Yeah, we got two things going for us," Ott said. "One, we know those two have expensive tastes and like to stay at high-end places and, two, they can't use fake IDs 'cause high-end—well, most places, I guess—make you show 'em your license."

"Yeah, exactly. Maybe you should book a few flights. Like one for tomorrow, one the day after."

"I was thinking the same thing."

Crawford nodded. "You go take down those two, then hurry back and help me on Jill."

"I'd like nothing more. How you doing, anyway? I mean, how's your head?"

"You know, I was thinking, she's only the second person really close to me to die. The first was my dad."

"I hear you. When did you see her last?"

"Oh, Christ... right before I came down here. Five years, give or take. Long time."

"Then she and Simpson bought that house on Jungle."

"Yeah. I didn't think it was a good idea to see her. Figured sooner or later I'd bump into her...somewhere."

Neither one said anything for a few moments.

"So, you want to take someone with you to Puerto Rico?" Crawford asked.

"Yeah, a hot babe."

"Seriously. Driscoll maybe?"

"I don't know. I'm not really sure I need someone."

"All right. I think you're probably good going solo, but it's totally your call," Crawford said. "Hey, speaking of babes, I was talking you up in a bar last night."

"You were? To who?"

"Name was Charlotte."

"And?"

"I don't know, man, I wouldn't stop paying your Match.com dues quite yet."

"Did you tell her I was ruggedly handsome in a Jason Alexander kind of way?"

"I would have, if I knew who Jason Alexander was."

"You know, George Costanza… *Seinfeld?*"

Crawford shook his head. "Come on, Mort, you're selling yourself way short."

"Well, I wouldn't want her expectations to be too high."

Crawford's office line rang. He punched the button. "Hello?"

"Charlie," said Natalie at the front desk, "there's a guy here named Giles Simpson wants to see you."

Crawford paused, not at all sure he was ready for Simpson. "Okay, I'll be right out." He clicked off and turned to Ott. "Jill's husband."

"Want me to leave?"

Crawford stood up. "No, I want you here. Need your read on the guy."

"As our killer?"

Crawford shrugged. "You tell me."

He walked out to the reception desk and saw Simpson dressed in khakis and a blue, button-down shirt.

"Hello, Giles," Crawford said. "Once again, I'm sorry about Jill. My condolences."

"Thank you," Simpson said. "Can we sit down somewhere?"

Crawford waved his hand. "Come on back to my office. My partner's back there."

Simpson was around six feet tall, with brilliant blue eyes, a cleft chin, light brown hair parted on the side, and a small button nose. He looked like a guy who'd wear green pants with a sweater draped around his neck and be right at home in David Balfour's golf foursome at the Poinciana Club.

As the two walked into Crawford's office, Ott stood. "I'm Mort Ott," he said. "Sorry about your loss, Mr. Simpson."

"Thank you," Simpson said stiffly.

"Have a seat, Giles," Crawford said.

Simpson and Ott sat facing Crawford.

"So, catch me up on what you've found out," Simpson began.

"Not as much as we would have liked," Crawford said. "A dark car was seen leaving your house day before yesterday in the afternoon. And, pursuing the burglary angle, there was a break-in down the street on Banyan a few weeks back and another one a week before that."

Simpson held up his hands. "That's it? That's all you got? A black car that could have been anybody and a couple break-ins down the street. I'm guessing you haven't caught the burglar yet?"

Crawford nodded. "That's someone else's case, but the answer is no, we haven't."

"What do you mean, 'someone else's case'?"

"We're approaching this as both a homicide and a burglary. Mort and I cover the homicide angle; a man name Netzker covers the burglary angle."

Simpson shook his head. "Swell. Just fucking swell."

"Mind if we ask you a few questions?" Crawford asked.

"Yeah, so let me guess, because you got nothing, you're going to try to pin it on the husband? The husband who was twelve hundred miles away."

Crawford ignored his hostile tone. "Look, this is just a necessary part of any homicide investigation. Questioning the husband. So where were you the day before yesterday? You have a surgery, meeting with patients, or what?"

"I took a few days off," Simpson said. "Went to my brother's summer house up at a place called Lake Waramaug in Connecticut."

"In the winter?"

"Yeah, it's nice up there now."

"Where in Connecticut?" Crawford asked.

"Near Danbury."

"And besides your brother, who else saw you there?"

"My brother wasn't there." Simpson shot Crawford a little smile. "Just me and... a friend."

Crawford had an urge to cold cock the son-of-a-bitch right on the spot. He fought the impulse. "Okay, and your *friend*—I'm assuming it's a she—what's her name?"

"Can't tell you."

"She's your alibi, Giles."

"I don't need an alibi. I was twelve hundred miles away."

Crawford glanced over at Ott, who was trying to hide his disgust. "Got anything, Mort?"

Ott always had something. "Mr. Simpson, have you ever driven from Palm Beach to New York? Or the other way around?"

"The hell kind of a question is that?"

"Have you?"

"Yeah, once."

"And how long did it take you?"

"How the hell would I know? I wasn't timing it."

"Funny. 'Cause most people do. Or at least have a rough idea how long it took."

"Look…is your name really Mort Ott?"

"Yeah, it is."

"Okay, Mort Ott," Simpson said, his tone heating up, "you clowns obviously got nothing, so you're asking me a bunch of stupid questions. Why don't you go do your fuckin' job and find the guy who did it instead of wasting your time on me?"

"You came here, Giles. We didn't ask you to come," Crawford said.

"Yeah, assuming you'd have something, at least."

Crawford tapped his desktop. "I understand that Jill was filing for divorce," he said. "Is that the case?"

Simpson's undersized nostrils flared. "What's that got to do with anything?"

"Everything," Crawford said. "It opens up a lot of possibilities."

"Like losing half your money, maybe," Ott said. "Now, she doesn't get any."

"Or like hurting your professional reputation as a stable, happily married man."

"What's that supposed to mean?"

"Meaning not a guy taking a bimbo up to Lake Wormhog," Ott blurted.

Crawford almost laughed, but he kept his eyes on Simpson's reaction. It was predictable.

"I don't know who the fuck you are," Simpson said, glaring at Ott, "but with you working on my wife's murder, I have zero confidence it will ever get solved."

"We've been through this. My name is Mort Ott, and Charlie and I have a pretty good record for solving homicides. We'll solve this one, too."

Simpson stood up to leave, shaking his head. "Maybe, if you call in the FBI… or *someone* who actually knows what the hell they're doing."

CHAPTER THIRTY-THREE

"Well, that went well," Ott said with a straight face after Giles Simpson walked out of their office in a huff.

Crawford laughed. "So what's your take?"

Ott thought a few moments. "A condescending asshole, yes. A killer...um, not so sure?"

"Yeah, I hear you," Crawford said.

"Tell you this, it's hard to see what Jill saw in the guy."

"I get it," Crawford said. "Guys like him can be charming when they want to be. When it pays to be. I can imagine him talking people into doing twenty-thousand-dollar surgeries, can't you?"

"Yeah, I guess I could."

"I have a cousin like him. All the women used to think he was the cat's meow; guys like me who played sports with him and knew him on an everyday basis thought he was a total dickwad."

Ott shook his head. "Still can't see him with Jill."

Crawford laughed. "Just sayin', I get it."

"Just sayin', I don't."

Neither one said anything for a while.

"I'm gonna be taking a trip, too," Crawford said, finally.

Ott nodded. "New York, huh?"

Crawford nodded. "Yeah, no way I'd miss the funeral."

"When is it?"

"Don't know yet. I guess Giles is going to have a say in it," Crawford said, looking at his watch. "Wasn't Netzker supposed to be coming by?"

"Yeah, he'll be here."

Crawford started tapping his desk again. "I still think Simpson could have loaded up on Dexedrine, knocked back a six-pack of Coke, and made the run to New York straight through. Maybe take an hour-long nap along the way."

"And, for all we know, he could have answered your call when he was on the road. You know, in Virginia or Maryland or somewhere along the way. On his way back up."

"True."

"What about the Lake Whatever-it-was story?"

"I'm gonna check that out. Problem is, I can't force him to tell me who the woman was."

"I know. Assuming there was one."

"I'm buying that he has a girlfriend… hell, maybe two or three… but it's also a pretty convenient alibi that I can't disprove."

"Unless you can prove he was somewhere else."

"You mean like cell-tower triangulation or something."

"Yeah, we'd probably need a judge's order, though."

A man wearing a narrow black tie and black sports jacket poked his head into Crawford's office. "Knock, knock."

Crawford turned to him. "Oh, hey, Netz, come on in."

Paul Netzker was a lifer on the Palm Beach Police Department and headed burglary investigations. He nodded at Ott and sat next to him.

"So, first question is," Crawford said, "does this job on Jungle look like it was done by the same guy who did the ones on Banyan and El Brillo?"

Netzker shook his head. "Nah, on El Brillo the guy found an unlocked window. Thing was a piece of cake. The one on Banyan, the guy picked a lock. On both of them, they were after cash and jewelry. He managed to get into a wall safe in the one on Banyan. But didn't bother with shit like breaking into a gun cabinet or stealing silverware. These guys' MOs were *quick-in/quick-out/bye-bye*. My impression about the one on Jungle was the guy was a rookie if it was a burglary at all. You know, like his first job, maybe. I mean, no pro ever takes a crowbar to a door. Just too goddamn noisy. Neighbors would hear something like that, know what I mean?"

"Yeah, I do."

"Also, the ones on El Brillo and Banyan might have been boat jobs."

"Why do you say that?" Ott asked.

"Well, because both houses were pretty close to the ocean. Almost on South Ocean Boulevard. Plus, on the second one—Banyan—

we found a footprint behind the house that matched up to one on the beach, close to the water."

"Sound like pretty thorough investigations," Crawford said.

"Hey, just trying to keep up with homicide," Netzker said. "Hey, what's with that guy Giles Simpson anyway?"

"What do you mean?"

"I mean he had that reporter from WPEC—the cute one— in the house when I was there, and it was like he was trying to put the moves on her."

"How? What was he doing?"

Netzker scratched the back of his neck. "Like trying to impress her. Like here's my Matisse and here's my so-and-so—the burglar didn't get either one. And over there's my Remington sculpture or whatever."

"I'm not surprised," Crawford said.

"Guy's a douche," said Ott.

"Clearly," Netzker said. "Well, look, if it's a burglar and he keeps hitting houses, eventually he'll slip up."

Crawford and Ott both nodded.

"Anything else you want to know?" Netzker asked.

"No, man," Crawford said. "That was helpful."

Netzker stood. "Just doin' my bit for the team."

"Thanks," said Ott.

Netzker walked out.

"A rookie, huh?" Ott said.

Crawford nodded. "I'm thinking Giles Simpson might be rookie of the year. But all we gotta do is find a hole in his alibi."

"All *you* gotta do. Me, I'm headed down to the Commonwealth of Puerto Rico, Island of Enchantment."

CHAPTER THIRTY-FOUR

The next afternoon Ott heard from the same police officer who'd told him where Kincade and Laurie were staying in the Dominican Republic.

"I found 'em again, Mort," he said simply.

"No shit, Shaw, where are they now?"

"It's called the Condado Vanderbilt Hotel. 1055 Ashford Avenue, San Juan."

"You're amazing. I'm gonna nominate you for the Cop-of-the-Year Award... if there is such a thing."

"How 'bout just a couple beers at Mookies?"

Ott stopped by Crawford's office and told him about Shaw having located their fugitives and that he had booked a four o'clock flight to Puerto Rico that afternoon.

"Well, that's convenient," Crawford said, "I got a Jet Blue reservation at 4:20 to New York. We can both go in my car, save the department some parking money."

"Rutledge will love that."

Crawford nodded. "Hey, we aim to please. By the way, I'm meeting my sister-in-law at Jill's house in half an hour."

"Want me to come?"

"No need. I think part of it is going to be handholding. Although she'll probably need to comfort me as much as I'll need to comfort her."

Ott nodded. "So, what time do you want to meet?"

"Ah, let's say 2:45, here. That'll give us plenty of time."

*****

Jessie Giordano told Crawford on the phone that she was meeting her brother-in-law, Giles Simpson, at the house on Jungle at around noon, after which he had a tee time at the Poinciana Club at 1 o'clock.

"Are you kidding?" Crawford said. "Two days after his wife's murder he's out on the links with his golf buddies?"

"You believe that?" Jessie exclaimed.

Crawford thought for a second. "Yeah, actually I do."

He got to the house on Jungle at just past one and pushed the door buzzer.

A few moments later, Jessie came to the door. Her eyes were red-rimmed, and she clutched a handkerchief. She was wearing light mascara that had already run in one spot.

She hugged Crawford before saying anything. Then: "Oh, Charlie. I just can't get over it."

He patted her back. "I know, honey. She was an amazing woman. The world's not going to be same without her."

He thought clichés were just fine at times like these.

"Come on in," Jessie said, wiping her eyes.

She led him into a den—he knew she would be avoiding the living room—and they sat facing each other.

"Do I dare ask you about your meeting with Giles?"

She sighed deeply. "He was actually all right. Except at the end, when he kept looking at his watch."

"Well, he probably wanted to hit some balls on the range before his game."

Jessie nodded. "Thanks for coming over."

"I've been thinking about her a lot in the last few days. Can't think of anything *but* her, in fact."

"Well, you're allowed a mourning period...then I want you to go nail the guy."

"Don't worry, I'm all over it," he said. "So, back to Giles...what do you think?"

"I don't know. Thinking of your brother-in-law as a murderer... it's kind of tough to wrap my head around. What do *you* think?"

Crawford wanted to be absolutely sure before he said anything with certainty. "We're looking into a few burglaries that took place around here. And, of course, Giles. That's really all we have so far."

She looked at him and smiled. "It's clear to me what you really think."

Crawford nodded. "Maybe, but I've got a lot more work to do."

"I know."

"Don't worry, I'll keep you up to speed. Promise. I'm heading up to New York later this afternoon, but don't tell Giles."

"I won't. I doubt I'll be talking to him again until the funeral."

Crawford scratched his forehead nervously. "I almost hate to ask this question 'cause it makes it so real, but when is the funeral? Made any plans yet?"

"Not yet. Jack is flying down later today. I'll talk to my mother, and we'll figure out when it's going to be."

"Just let me know."

"Of course," Jessie said, then put her arms around Crawford and kissed his cheek, "You're the best brother-in-law a girl could ever have."

CHAPTER THIRTY-FIVE

Jake Kincade was having a Mojito with his friend, Martin Gulden, at an outdoor café in a square in Old San Juan. The square was surrounded by Spanish-style buildings and the nearby streets composed of uneven cobblestones. It reminded Jake of when he went to St. Augustine, Florida, a few years back. Especially the two old forts that Gulden told him had been there for four or five hundred years, each.

The backstory on Gulden was that he and Jake had briefly gone to college together and Gulden now ran some kind of a tech business that employed fifty people. He'd been a zealous bitcoin investor for five years. He had moved to the "Old City" three years before because of the tax advantages. Also because he had just gone through a bloody divorce that soured him on American lawyers, judges, and the American legal system in general.

"So the good things are obvious," Kincade said, meaning the weather, the appealing architecture, the city's long and fabled history, and the fact that there were no federal taxes or capital gains. "What are the negatives?"

"Well, let's see. As you'll find out, it's actually cheaper to live in a place like Florida than here...plus Spanish is the primary language. Oh, and it's got a pretty high crime rate in certain parts of the island."

Jake chuckled to himself: *Just what I want to get away from, criminals.*

"But you're glad you did it, right? Made the move?"

"Yeah, I also like the fact that it's becoming the world headquarters for the crypto bros," Gulden said.

"The 'crypto bros,' as in guys into cryptocurrency and bitcoins?"

"You got it. They're buyin' up half the old city. Started with the Children's Museum and an old hotel called the Monastery. One of 'em calls this place *Puertotopia*. I hear all kinds of things they're up to. Like they're gonna buy this old nine-thousand-acre naval station that has two deep water ports and an old airport. And build a new city on 250,000 acres somewhere."

"Wow, sounds like it could be good for the island."

"Yeah, we'll see, could just be talk," Gulden said. "What about you? What are your plans?"

"I don't really know. Just veg out for a while. See what comes along. I sold my businesses, so I don't really need to work."

"What were your businesses? I don't think you ever told me."

Jake'd had a lot of time to dream up fictitious companies while he and Laurie bobbed across on the Caribbean.

"I had two, actually. A Porsche dealership in Jupiter and a Viking dealership up in Stuart. Thank God for rich people," Jake said, raising his fist.

They bumped fists.

"And now you're one of 'em," said Gulden.

*****

It was only a two hour and forty-minute flight from Miami to Puerto Rico. Ott checked into the Sheraton Old San Juan on Brumbaugh Street—which didn't strike him as a particularly Spanish-sounding street name— at 7:45 p.m. He'd had dinner on the plane, so he'd only gone down to the bar to have a drink. There were three other couples present when he climbed up onto a barstool.

The bartender came up to him. "Yes, sir, what can I get you?"

"You guys are pretty famous for your rums. What would you recommend in the rum department?"

"That's a hard choice. Of course, there's Bacardi, but my favorite is Barrilto."

A man a few stools away raised his glass. "No, man. Ron Llave."

The woman next to him raised hers even higher. "There's only one: Mount Gay."

"Yeah, but that's from Barbados," said the bartender.

Ott smiled and eyed the bartender. "Wow, pretty controversial subject. Maybe I'll have vodka, so I don't insult anybody."

"Or just have three different rums."

Ott pointed at him and nodded. "That's a way better idea."

CHAPTER THIRTY-SIX

Ott had decided not to rent a car at the airport because he didn't plan to do much driving. When he needed to get somewhere he'd just take a cab, which he was doing at the moment.

On his way to the Sheraton Old San Juan the night before, Ott told the cab driver to take him past the Condado Vanderbilt Hotel. It looked like an expensive place. Ott didn't know what Condado meant but he was certainly familiar with the name Vanderbilt. He guessed the robber baron may have detoured down to Puerto Rico for a little entrepreneurial pilferage at some point in his long and prosperous life.

Now Ott was on his way to the Policia de Puerto Rico, Santurce precinct, where he had a meeting scheduled with a homicide detective named Fabrice Del Toro.

Ott had contacted the local cop more or less out of the blue while waiting at the Miami airport for his flight. He had been bounced around from one person to another until he ended up with a man with a commanding voice who said, "Fabrice del Toro, how can I help you, sir?" Ott identified himself and told him he had a warrant for two fugitives who were murder suspects in a Palm Beach, Florida, homicide and they were registered at the Condado Vanderbilt Hotel. Then he gave Del Toro their names and told him they had arrived in Old San Juan in a boat called *Destiny*.

"Well, I'll be happy to assist in this matter," Del Toro had said in a heavy Spanish accent.

Ott had thanked him for his help, said he'd be landing that night, and scheduled a meeting for mid-morning the next day.

Ott had arrived at 10:15 and they were seated in a remarkably neat and well-decorated office which seemed to have the air conditioning set right where Ott liked it: high 60s.

Ott had just filled in Del Toro on the murder and the flight of Jake Kincade and Laurie Reback, having given him only sketchy details during their brief conversation the night before.

"So, they absconded with twenty million dollars?" Del Toro asked.

Ott nodded.

"Jesus, man, that's a lot of money."

Ott just nodded.

"Okay, here's what I know. Your couple was seen at the pool at the Condado a short time ago, after doing some early sightseeing," Del Toro said. "They're getting around on a motor scooter. I've also located their boat."

Ott was surprised. Pleasantly. "How do you know all this?"

"What do you think? I've been sitting on my hands? After you gave me their names and said they were staying at the Condado, that was all I needed. I've got two men keeping an eye on them at the moment."

Ott nodded and smiled. "I'm impressed."

"I know what you Americans think. That we just sit around all day, take three-hour siestas in the afternoon."

"I didn't think anything. I just—"

"Would you like to go see their boat?" Del Toro asked.

"Sure," Ott said, thinking there was an outside chance the couple might go there next.

Ott and Del Toro arrived at the marina and five minutes later were face to face with the *Destiny*. It looked like a vessel that had been ridden hard for the last week or ten days on the high seas. Ott did a quick calculation and guessed the boat had done 1800 miles since the death of Garrett Janney. It showed in places, too—halyards had signs of fraying, a sheen of rust was noticeable on certain metal surfaces, dried salt was everywhere…. Even the tattered American flag on the flagpole looked like it had been in a marine battle. Like maybe how the *Monitor* and the *Merrimac* had looked after trading cannonballs.

Ott observed the *Destiny* at a distance before he got close to it. It was clearly a seaworthy boat that needed a nice, long rest. He was sure its sailors—Kincade and Laurie— were happy to be sleeping in beds with plump pillows for a change. Not being buffeted by winds and tossed around by waves.

"This baby's logged some miles," Ott said. "Miami to Grand Cayman to the Dominican Republic to here."

Del Toro did some calculating. "That's about two thousand miles."

"Pretty close," Ott said as Del Toro's cell phone rang.

He clicked it and listened for a few moments.

"Thanks, Alvaro," Del Toro said, hitting speakerphone. "I'm going to speak English, so my American friend can hear. But I'll take it from here."

"What do you want us to do?" Alvaro asked in Spanish.

"Nothing, man, I don't need you guys. Too many of us and they might spot us, get suspicious. Yeah, *adíos*."

Del Toro looked up at Ott. "The man and his girlfriend are having lunch at an outdoor café near the Condado."

Ott stood up. "How far from here?"

"Fifteen minutes."

"*Vamanos*," Ott said, flashing the detective a big smile.

*****

Del Toro parked his unmarked Chevrolet Impala a few doors down from the imposing Condado Vanderbilt Hotel on Ashford Avenue.

"What's with these street names?" Ott asked, "Brumbaugh and Ashford, I mean...?"

"What? You think they should be Sanchez and Garcia or something?"

"Well, yeah."

"You got any Spanish street names in Miami?"

"I don't know. I'm not from Miami." But Ott saw his point since there were plenty of Spanish street names in Palm Beach.

Del Toro flipped his head in the direction of an outdoor restaurant. "I think I see them."

Ott looked where Del Toro had signaled. And sure enough, there they were, the man and the woman in the photos. Jake Kincade and Laurie Reback, larger than life. Kincade had a scraggly beard and Laurie had a full-blown Coppertone tan. They were sitting at a table that had a spectacular view of the water, a bottle of white wine between them. Off to one side there were bikes in a rack and a few motor scooters.

"All right, let's talk about how we're gonna play this," Ott said, hand shading his eyes like he was admiring the view of the water.

"Simple," Del Toro said, observing the couple, "We just walk up to 'em and I say, *Jake Kincade and Laurie Reback, we have a warrant for your arrest for murder.* Then we give them the Miranda. Same way you'd do it in the States."

Del Toro was probably seeing a headline or two and maybe a promotion in his future. That was okay with Ott, who was studying what Jake Kincade was wearing. A tight, red bathing suit, a black T-shirt, and white Nikes.

"No way the guy's packing in that Speedo," Ott observed.

"No kidding," Del Toro said. "All right, let's do this."

Before Ott could react, Del Toro was walking quickly in the direction of the table.

"Slow down, man," Ott said under his breath, worried that the two might get spooked by the man coming at them full-tilt and with a purposeful stride.

But Del Toro ignored Ott and walked even faster to their table, Ott a few steps behind. "Jake Kincade"— Del Toro skipped Laurie Reback—"I have a warrant for your—"

And that was as far as Del Toro got because Kincade put his hands on the table edge and rammed it into Del Toro. It caught the cop at waist level, and he groaned and fell backward into Ott, knocking him off balance. Del Toro went down hard on the cobblestone pavement as Jake Kincade sprinted away.

Ott, despite his ample girth, was a speedy runner, but by the time he regained his footing, Kincade already had a fifty-yard head start. Ott caught a glimpse of Laurie, still sitting at the table, one hand over her mouth, shocked by the quick turn of events. And, no doubt, by the fact that Kincade was making his getaway without her.

As Ott's short, bandy legs churned, he flashed on what Del Toro had said about Kincade and Laurie sightseeing on a motor scooter. Kincade was clearly headed toward that scooter. Sure enough, he ran up to a pea-green Vespa, mounted it, turned the key, and took off. Ott, looking around, saw nothing but bikes in the bike rack.

Then he saw a young woman paused on a scooter twenty yards away. He ran toward her, pulling out his wallet and badge. "Police emergency, I need your scooter." The woman looked dumbfounded. Ott was pretty sure she didn't speak English. She didn't move.

"Get off, please," he said, pushing her off the scooter with his forearm as gently as he could.

He threw a leg over the scooter as she rattled off something in Spanish and cranked the throttle full-bore. He saw Jake Kincade disappear over the top of a hill.

The last two-wheel mode of transportation Ott had ridden was a Harley.

This was no Harley.

At full speed, it made a whining sound like a swarm of angry bees, but soon he was able to get it up to forty miles an hour. As he crested the hill Kincade had just disappeared over, Ott saw his quarry about a football field ahead, head down, trying to cut the wind resistance. Ott could see that the road became extremely narrow ahead, where it followed the shoreline. Kincade was headed up another hill now. Ott had closed the distance to seventy yards. It was now a matter of who had the faster scooter and Ott thought he might. He only wished he were thirty pounds lighter.

Soon he realized that he had been closing the distance because Kincade was going uphill. Kincade disappeared over the top and Ott felt his scooter lose speed as it climbed. Then it got to the top and suddenly gained a surge of power as he went downhill.

Ott saw a pack of six brightly clad bike riders ahead of Kincade, doing what packs of cyclists always seem to do: hog the road. The full lane's worth, in fact.

Ott sensed he was catching up but guessed it would take a mile or so before he'd be on Kincade's tail pipe. Once again, the road went uphill along the water. There was a thin, ten-foot sliver of beach between the cliffside road and the ocean. The bikers were climbing the hill—slowly, then even more slowly—Kincade fast approaching them and Ott now fifty yards behind.

To get by the bikers, Kincade had to either pick his way through them or go wide to the left. He chose to go wide to the left. That was when Ott heard the blast of a horn and saw the top of a truck cresting the hill. Ott, immediately behind the bikers now, cut back on his throttle as he saw Kincade steer the motor scooter hard to his right and just miss crashing into the lead biker's front wheel. Kincade turned to straighten but found himself on the pebble-strewn shoulder of the road. The scooter wobbled right, then left, clearly out of control, then disappeared from Ott's sight.

Ott decelerated, letting the cyclists surge ahead.

It didn't look good for Jake Kincade.

*****

Ott guessed that Kincade had plunged close to fifty feet into the shallow water of the ocean below.

Ott U-turned his scooter, raced back down the road, ditched the scooter on the shoulder and ran along the beach to where he saw Kincade's body. Kincade was floating, not swimming or even dogpaddling, about twenty yards from the shore. Ott swam out to him, grabbed him around the shoulder, and paddled with one arm back to shore.

When he got to dry land, he was exhausted from the running and swimming. Clearly not in the best shape of his life....

He dropped Kincade's body on the beach out of reach of the waves and lay on his back, panting and trying to catch his breath. After a few moments, he heard a groan, turned, and saw Kincade slowly get to his feet.

"Oh, shit," Ott said with a deep wheeze, "don't make me chase your ass again."

Kincade slogged forward a few steps, unsteadily, as Ott got to his feet. His old-football-injury knee creaked but he gamely started after Kincade. It was like a race between a three-legged rhino and a morbidly obese hippo, but Ott was gaining, just as he had on the scooter. Finally, he dived at the back of Kincade's legs, pulled him into the sand, and reached back to his handcuffs. In one swift and practiced movement, he had the man's wrists cuffed together.

It was then he remembered his Glock, which had been in his hip holster the whole time. "Christ," he said to Kincade. "I shoulda just plugged you in the ass."

CHAPTER THIRTY-SEVEN

Fabrice Del Toro ran down to the beach a few minutes later. He looked recovered from getting slammed in the gut by the table. The five cyclists had stopped, along with the truck's driver, watching the action from the road above. The truck driver had snapped off a bunch of photos, starting with Ott's rescue of Kincade at sea and culminating in the ultra-slow-mo foot chase.

Ott was walking behind the handcuffed Kincade when Del Toro reached them.

"As I was saying before," Del Toro said, authoritatively, "Jake Kincade, we have a warrant for your arrest for a murder committed in Palm Beach, Florida." Then he read Kincade the Miranda. "Oh, by the way, your wife's really pissed off at you. Running off and leaving her like that."

Still breathing heavily, Kincade mumbled. "She ain't my wife, dude."

*****

It was only 1:30 and Ott had booked a 3:45 flight back to Miami.

He caught the 3:45 and got into Miami at around 6:30. He called Crawford on his cell phone during the drive up to Palm Beach. He knew his partner would be impressed that he'd wrapped the whole thing up in a day.

"Jesus, Mort," Crawford said. "Sounds like a chase scene in a James Bond movie."

Ott chuckled. "Yeah, I get compared to James Bond all the time."

"Not very grateful, that Kincade."

"What do you mean?"

"Well, I mean, you save his ass when he's floating out to sea, then he takes off on you. That's not right."

"I know. You believe that shit?"

"So, I'm assuming those two need to be extradited from Puerto Rico."

"Yeah, process will take about a week or so, they tell me."

"Why so long?"

"Between you and me, I think the honchos there saw it as an opportunity to take credit for being in on the capture of two dangerous mainland murderers."

"Okay, but they'll be in a cell on South County Road soon enough?"

"Unless they pull an El Chapo with some kinda escape tunnel," Ott said. "But enough about my heroics…what have you been up to in the Apple?"

"Compared to you, not much," Crawford said. "Spent last night at a friend's house in Brooklyn."

"A cop friend?"

"Yeah, we had a few cocktails…then a few more. He and his wife and me and Jill were pretty tight. I got an early start this morning."

"Where'd you go?"

"To Simpson's office. Had a nice chat with his receptionist and his assistant."

"So what did they have to say?"

"That he took two days off before Jill was killed. Didn't say he was going anywhere or doing anything, just that he was going to take a little break."

"Did you get the sense they knew anything about a girl or Lake Wobegon or whatever?"

Crawford laughed. "Waramaug."

"Yeah, did you ask 'em?"

"No, I just wanted to see what they'd volunteer. I plan to circle back to that."

"Gotcha. Anything else come out of it?"

"The timeline. I did the math, and he definitely could have driven down to Florida. I asked his assistant where he kept his car and she told me. Place up on 96th Street. So I went there and found out he picked up the car about twenty hours before when Hawes estimated Jill was killed, then brought it back to the garage two days later."

"So, the timeline works," Ott said. "Even if he wasn't breaking any speed records, he had plenty of time."

"Exactly. Plus, something else important. I took a look at the security footage at his garage, and it clearly shows only Simpson in the car when he picked it up and him alone again when he brought it back."

"So, no girl?"

"Nope, and my sense from my first conversation with him was that he was saying she was with him when he came back from the lake."

"Implying he didn't drop her at her apartment before he dropped off the car?"

"Exactly. Then there's a third thing that I don't have an answer to yet."

"What's that?"

"His assistant mentioned he had just gotten the Mercedes back from its ten-thousand-mile check-up. So, when they did the check-up, they'd definitely clock his mileage."

"Oh, that's good, man. So, if the mileage was ten thousand when he took it to the dealer and it's twelve thousand five now, he's got a lot of explaining to do."

"Exactly. Where those twenty-five-hundred miles came from."

"Did the dealer tell you what the mileage was when Simpson dropped it off?"

"I haven't gotten a call back yet. What I'd really like is to get access to his car in the garage. Check its odometer. That's obviously key."

"You've gathered a hell of a lot of circumstantial evidence. You think it's enough to hang him?"

"I don't know. I gotta check with the prosecutor's office. Run it by them."

"Any idea when you'll be back?"

"At this point, no. I've got to find out when and where Jill's funeral will be."

"Okay, so what do you want me to do?"

"I've been thinking about that. Why don't you see if you can spot Simpson's car on any security footage down there? You know, coming up or going down South County, or maybe somewhere on Jungle. Also, see if you pick up anything on the tag readers at any of the three bridges. Black Mercedes, tag number ESX4311, big old yellow New York plate."

Ott noted the plate number. "Hm. I'd expect a guy like Simpson to have a vanity plate."

"You mean like DOC 1 or something?"

Ott laughed. "DICK 1 is more like it."

Crawford laughed. "Maybe you get some rookies to check the tag readers. It'll take you all day."

"Tag readers" were just what they sounded like, cameras mounted on the three bridges into Palm Beach, situated so they could read license plate numbers.

"Roger that. I'm gonna go read Hawes's report," Ott said. "See whether there's anything useful in it. Talk to the techs, too, in case they got any DNA."

"The problem is," Crawford said, "Simpson's DNA's gonna be all over the house."

"Yeah, I know. Who knows, though? Maybe someone helped him. Coulda hired somebody."

"I'm beginning to doubt that."

"Yeah, me too," Ott said. "We still haven't completely ruled out a burglary gone bad, have we?"

"No, not completely, but I'd give it a 20% shot."

"Yeah, probably about right," Ott said. "You gonna be staying with your friend in Brooklyn for the whole time you're there?"

"Yep, but I'm going over to Jill's mother's house for dinner tonight. That might get a little emotional."

"I'll be there in spirit, ol' buddy."

"I know you will," Crawford said. "And I appreciate it."

*****

Lucy Dellasandro had a three-bedroom co-op at 17 East 89th Street. It was where Jill and her sister, Jessie, had grown up, a mere block away from the Guggenheim Museum and Central Park. Before they got married, Crawford would swing by Jill's building, and they'd take a few laps around the reservoir in Central Park. Jill was fast and Crawford, jock that he was, had trouble keeping up with her.

Crawford arrived at the building with a bottle of Santa Margherita pinot grigio, which he remembered Lucy Dellasandro liked. Frank, the doorman, welcomed him exactly as he had six years before, the last time he was there. "I used to read about all your exploits in the *Daily News*," he said with a big toothy smile, "but I haven't read anything in a while."

"I moved down to Florida four and a half years ago."

"No wonder. Fighting crime down in the Sunshine State, huh?"

"Yeah, something like that," Crawford said. "Well, great seeing you again, Frank."

"Likewise."

There was something about a guy who responded with "likewise" that Crawford liked.

He took the elevator up to the twelfth floor, got out, and saw the open door to Lucy's apartment. She had always done that in the past: either opened the door a crack or waited in the doorway with a big welcoming smile.

"Lucy?" he said, as he pushed open the door and walked in.

She walked toward him with an ear-to-ear smile on her face, looking a little more hunched and grayer than the last time he'd seen her, but still a lovely older woman.

"Oh, Charlie, I am so glad you came—" then, ushering him in—"more handsome than ever."

He put his arms around her, and they hugged. "I wouldn't pass up your cooking for the world," he patted her shoulder. "Again, I am so sorry about Jill."

He didn't know two people who were closer than Jill and her mother. Well, in fact it was probably a tie—Jill and Jessie were extremely tight as well.

He handed her the bottle of wine. "You're still a Santa Margherita girl, right?"

"Yup, sure am. Thank you, Charlie. Always the thoughtful one," she said, kissing him on the cheek.

They didn't talk about Jill until after they finished dinner. Lucy suggested they hold off on it, said she wanted to first hear about Charlie's new life in Florida. They could get around to the inevitable conversation about Jill later.

"So you've told me about everything except the women in your life," Lucy said, halfway through dinner, "and I'm sure the list is long."

His old detective friend, Artie, had asked the same thing the night before. It wasn't a subject Crawford ever felt entirely comfortable with. He wasn't sure why, but he felt even less comfortable talking to Lucy Dellasandro about it. After all, her daughter had been his first love and only wife. Something told him Jill might always be his only wife. Even though…yes, he could picture a happy life with Dominica. Hell, maybe even Rose. But he had a pretty nice life now. Did he really want to mess with it?

"The list is actually very short," he told Lucy. "I'm so busy down there…actually busier than I was here."

He was hoping that was enough to get them off the subject of women in his life, but just to avoid any follow-up, he decided to say what he had always thought, but never said, about Jill. "Lucy, I just would like to tell you, you raised one of the best women in the universe. I mean, she had everything going for her. And there's no question in my mind that you and Tony had everything to do with it."

"Thank you, that is so nice of you to say—" he noticed her hands tremble and her eyes darken—"Oh, God, you don't know how it is, Charlie, the last thing a mother ever wants is to outlive her child."

Crawford nodded. "I understand. I definitely understand."

Lucy looked away. First, across the room, then out a window. "So tell me more about exactly what happened. You must have more details by now," she said with a deep sigh. "On the one hand, I don't want to know, on the other…I have to."

"She was strangled," he said simply and as unemotionally as he could. "We're not sure whether it was a burglar she caught in the act, a home invasion, or something else."

"You haven't caught anybody yet?"

"No, we haven't. My partner and I are focused on it exclusively. We'll catch whoever did it. Our first suspicion was that it was a burglar, but we're not so sure about that now."

"Well, at least I know I've got the best man on it."

"Thank you, Lucy. They don't get any better than my partner. Or our crime-scene people, for that matter."

"I'm sure. Just keep me informed, please."

"Oh, don't worry. Anything comes up, I'll let you know right away."

Lucy looked out the window again. "Jessie told me she told you about the marital problems between Jill and Giles. Well, more than marital problems, Jill was about to divorce the man."

Crawford nodded, wondering if Jessie had told her mother about his conversations with her, in which they had both voiced their suspicion that Giles might be the perp. He guessed not. It was something Jessie probably wanted to keep between them. At least for the time being.

"I was sorry it didn't work out between them," Crawford said.

Lucy cocked her head to one side. "What happened between you two? I always thought you were the perfect couple."

Crawford's first reaction was, *We were... until we weren't.* "You know, I think it was the classic: I spent too much time being a cop. Fact is, cops don't have the best record when it comes to marriage. There's the stress and the long, erratic hours. I think it just got too much for Jill, and I can't blame her."

"I always thought that having a child would be the answer. 'Course that was partly because I wanted so much to be a grandmother."

Crawford patted her hand and smiled. "Then along came Brian and Kelly." Jessie's son and daughter.

"Yes, but I was still hoping."

"We tried."

"I know you did," Lucy said, then paused a moment. "I don't think it was any secret that I liked you better than Giles. Or for that matter, Jill liked you better than Giles—" She paused again, as if unsure whether to share what she was thinking. "I have to tell you something you probably don't know. Jill came to me once after being married to Giles for about two years and told me she was thinking about getting in touch with you and seeing if you'd give it another try."

Crawford was dumbstruck. "You're kidding. You mean divorce him and—"

Lucy nodded. "Then, I don't know...I guess she just decided to work on her marriage harder. She never mentioned it again. When she first said it, I was secretly thinking 'great.'" She cocked her head. "I take it she never brought it up with you?"

"No, not a word."

"Something tells me that Giles might have found out that was what she was thinking."

"Why do you say that?"

"Because one time I was over at their house for dinner. Just the two of them and Jessie and Jack. Giles took me aside and started peppering me with all these questions about you. Where you lived down there? How much you made? Like I had a clue. And whether you had any intention of moving back here. I mean, it wasn't like you were a long-lost friend of his and he was curious what had become of you."

"Hardly. We met twice. And it was *not* love at first sight."

Lucy laughed.

"Have you and Jessie decided when the funeral's going to be?"

Lucy nodded. "I was just going to tell you. Day after tomorrow at Heavenly Rest."

The Church of Heavenly Rest was right around the corner: 90th Street and Fifth Avenue.

"If it was good enough for Gloria Swanson and Lillian Gish, I guess it's good enough for my girl," Lucy told him.

Crawford could tell she was struggling to be upbeat, but the trembling in her hands had gotten worse and her voice sounded reedier.

"I remember Jill was a big fan of Gloria Swanson," he recalled. "Loved a bunch of those old classics. She had this cassette of *Sunset Boulevard*. Played it all the time."

"*All right, Mr. De Mille, I'm ready for my close-up*," Lucy quoted.

"What's that?"

"Her famous line at the end."

"I've got to admit, I never quite got to the end."

"The woman was a great actress…not such a good wife."

"What do you mean?"

"She had six husbands."

Crawford shrugged. "Keep trying 'til you get it right, I guess."

"That woman *never* got it right," Lucy said. "So, I think it's going to be a pretty small funeral at Heavenly Rest."

"But Jill had a ton of friends," Crawford said, immediately realizing how the past tense sounded so sad and… final.

"I know, I just…because of the circumstances of her death…."

"I understand. I totally understand."

Lucy put her hand on his. "You'll go, right?"

"Of course. Do you even need to ask?" Crawford said. "I've got to invest in a suit, though."

And whatever the trigger was, Lucy Dellasandro broke down. The tears flowed, her body shook, and she was a wreck. Crawford simply put an arm around her and didn't say anything. What was there to say?

A minute or two later, she stopped crying but her chest continued heaving spasmodically until, after a minute or two, it tapered off.

"Well," she said. "I guess we've said all there is to say. She was a hell of a daughter."

"A hell of a wife. And sister, too."

"Well, we agree," Lucy said, her eye shining like wet steel. "Now go get the bastard who did it."

CHAPTER THIRTY-EIGHT

Crawford had just dropped in at the 10th Precinct, his former home as a cop.

The woman at the desk had no clue that he had been a highly decorated gold-shield detective there. Or that he had been awarded two Medals of Honor.

"Hi," Crawford said simply. "I used to be on the job here. Captain Visconti in?"

"Yes," she said. "Your name, please?"

"Charlie Crawford."

She nodded and dialed a number.

Two minutes later a beefy man with a shaved head and a big smile appeared. "Well, well, look what the cat dragged in."

Crawford gave Visconti a firm handshake. "That shiny head of yours is new. I mean, not that you weren't 90% bald already."

"Fuck off," Visconti said, under his breath. Then with a smile: "Come on back."

Crawford followed Visconti back to his office. There were pictures of kids all over and, on his desk, a pizza box.

"If I recall, that box was there five years ago," Crawford said.

"A guy's gotta have his nutrition," Visconti said, sitting down. "So what's new in the world of the rich and famous?"

Crawford shrugged. "Oh, you know, still not getting the invite to their fancy parties. How's everything with you and your crack team of detectives?"

Visconti sighed. "It's changed, Charlie. You were around in the good old days."

"I think I know what you mean, but what exactly's changed."

"That whole 'defund the police' thing back in 2020. *De-fang the police,* I call it. It's made us all too cautious, afraid of ending up on the

11 o'clock news. It's made good cops fearful cops. Cops getting charged with murder for doing their jobs."

"Yeah, but the cops who killed Eric Garner and that guy in Minnesota weren't exactly doing their jobs. They went way overboard."

"Jesus, Charlie, you turn into a liberal down there?"

Crawford shook his head. "Nah, just the way I feel—" change-of-subject time—"How's Julie?"

"We're still hangin' in there. Thanks for asking," Visconti said. "Hey, I was really sorry to hear about Jill, man."

"Thanks. Yeah, it happened in my own backyard."

"So, you caught the case?"

Crawford nodded. "That's what I'm doing here. Looking into a suspect." He didn't think it was wise to identify Giles Simpson yet.

"You need my help, let me know."

"Yeah, actually I do."

"What can I do for you?"

"Break into a suspect's car."

Visconti shot him a thumbs-up. "Child's play, my friend."

"But it needs to be done so there's no sign it happened."

"Not a problem. I got a ton of guys who can do that."

"The car's in a garage up on East 96th Street. Can I meet someone there—" he looked at his watch—"at, say, eleven today?"

"Yeah, sure, it's either gonna be a guy named Bisbee or Martino."

"Thanks, Cap. I really appreciate it."

"Hey, man, you did a lot to make us look good in your day. Not a lot of two-time Medal of Honor winners on the job now."

Crawford felt himself blushing a little. "Oh, while I'm asking, one more thing."

"Shoot."

"What's the procedure for a Florida cop to make an arrest here?"

"It's pretty simple. You just make the collar with one of my guys."

"Well, I hope it gets to that point," Crawford said, getting to his feet. "If it does, I'll take you to Peter Luger's for a big ol' rib-eye. On the Palm Beach Police Department."

"That'd beat the hell outta this shit," said Visconti, pointing at the pizza box. He stood, reached across his desk, and shook Crawford's hand. "You got a deal."

*****

Crawford's cell phone rang as he walked down the steps of the 10th Precinct building.

Ott's name and number were on the display.

"Hey, Mort, just came from where I used to work. The 10th."

"How was it?"

"I'd rather be down there with you."

"I'm touched. So, I may have found something good on Jill's murder."

"Let's hear."

"I went through every square inch of her house on Jungle and a guy named Crispin Baylis came up a few times."

"*Came up*…meaning?"

"Well, first in her address book, which had almost all women in it. Got me curious who he was."

"Keep goin'."

"Remember how we couldn't find her phone or her computer in the house the day we were there?"

"Ah-huh."

"So, I'm at the house with Shaw and Sanchez and I dial the phone number you gave me for her and walked all over the house, thinking maybe her phone's hidden somewhere and I'll hear it. Nothing. Meanwhile, Shaw's outside the house looking around. He comes running in holding a cell phone. He heard it ringing and found it in the bushes in back of the house. Clearly the killer had chucked it back there, figuring no one would ever find it."

"Good work, Mort. Any luck finding a computer?"

"No. I can only think the killer took it with him. So anyway, I looked at calls and emails on the phone and noticed a lot of calls to this one number. I went to the reverse directory and find it's this guy Crispin Baylis's number. Then I checked emails and see a bunch of emails to him and from him. Most of 'em were kinda cryptic, like shorthand, almost. Like she was afraid her husband might read 'em, maybe. But there were a few further back, like six to eight months ago, making plans to go out for dinner, plus a couple of references to a gallery. So I do a quick Google search of Crispin Baylis and find out he's an artist, had a show at a gallery on Broome Street, wherever that may be."

"SoHo," Crawford told him. "New York City."

"Okay. And the last email said, 'See you on the 24th.'"

"You mean, two days before Jill was killed."

"Exactly."

"Okay," Crawford said, sitting on a bench at a bus stop, taking it all in. "So maybe she's got something going with this Baylis guy, but nothing points to him having killed her, right?"

"Right. Just saying it maybe gives Simpson an additional motive to kill Jill. You know, if Simpson finds out his wife and Baylis had something going, plus he doesn't want to give her a bunch of money. I need to look into this guy further. I mean, for all I know, maybe he's got a motive too."

"Nice goin', Mort, that's good info. I can look into Baylis while I'm up here. You know where he lives or anything?"

"No, I don't, but I'll find out, then let you know."

*****

It was Bisbee, Todd Bisbee, who met Crawford outside the garage on East 96th Street.

Carrying a long black canvas case, Bisbee walked up to Crawford and nodded. "Visconti told me you were the greatest lawman since Wyatt Earp."

Crawford chuckled. "Well, yeah, next to Visconti himself."

Bisbee laughed. "So where's the car?" he asked, pointing at the garage. "In there?"

Crawford nodded. "Let's talk to the guy at the window. Find out exactly where it is."

Bisbee nodded.

"So I take it you got the tools of the trade in that bag?" Crawford said, pointing to Bisbee's case.

"Yeah. Should do the trick."

They walked up to the window and Bisbee flashed his badge. "We gotta check out one of your cars here."

"Okay, whose car?" the attendant asked.

Crawford stepped closer to the window. "Owned by Dr. Giles Simpson. Black Mercedes."

"Oh, yeah, the doc's got his own spot up on the second floor. Walk up there—" he pointed to a stairway—"and it's on the left. Along with all the other big shots' cars."

"Thanks," Crawford said, "we won't be long."

They walked up the steps, turned left, and saw a black Mercedes in between a Bentley and a shiny red Porsche.

"Wow, I might have to boost that Porsche," Bisbee said as they walked up to the Mercedes. He opened the case and took out three green tools. "Wedges," he explained, choosing one.

He put two back in the bag, took the third and shoved it into a spot above the driver's side door. "Mercedes are a little tougher than your basic Ford or Chevy," he said pushing it further in.

Once he had a crack, he reached into the case and pulled out an air pump connected to a rubber bladder and shoved the bladder into the crack the wedge had created. Then he started squeezing the pump, which inflated the bladder, widening the crack even further. After the crack had been forced even wider by the inflated bladder, he reached into the case and pulled out a long rod with a hook at the end.

Crawford was watching with interest. "What's that thing called?"

"A grabber," Bisbee said, as he put the tool through the crack and angled it down. It took him three tries, but he finally caught the lock with the hook and deftly raised it. There was a click and the door opened.

"Nice work," Crawford said, taking his iPhone out of his pocket. "Just going to take a couple of shots," he explained, opening the door and ducking his head into the front seat. He looked down at the odometer, aimed the iPhone camera, and took five shots at various angles. Then he pushed himself up and out of the car.

"That's all you need?" Bisbee asked.

Crawford nodded. "That oughta do it. Thank you, Todd…and your sidekick, the Grabber."

CHAPTER THIRTY-NINE

Ott dug further into Crispin Baylis and learned two things: one, he was an artist, and two, he had a record, having once been convicted of art forgery. Apparently, he painted quite convincing fakes of works by artists such as Vermeer, Dubuffet, and Matisse. A gallery owner in Boston who had been duped by Baylis and his fakes referred to him as a "charming rogue" who had taken him for hundreds of thousands of dollars. But ultimately Baylis had been caught and forced to relinquish what was left of the money, then spent ten months in prison.

After that he had gone back to his own paintings but apparently had had only modest success. Clearly, a fake Vermeer was a lot more valuable than an original Baylis. Ott had called the gallery, which had done a Baylis show a while back, to see if he could get the artist's phone number. After he identified himself as a detective, the man who answered at the gallery said: "I thought all that legal stuff was behind Crispy."

"This has nothing to do with that. I just need to talk to him," Ott said, thinking *Crispy* certainly fell squarely into the lame-nickname category.

There was a fair amount on Google about Baylis and one thing Ott found out was that the artist had actually spent three and a half years in prison instead of only the ten months he was sentenced to. Evidently, two violent incidents took place while Baylis was a prisoner. One involved a fight with another prisoner who became a paraplegic as a result. Another offense involved taking a swing at a prison guard...never a good idea. As a consequence of those two incidents, Baylis's jail time was extended to approximately four times the length of the original sentence.

Ott called the number the gallery owner had given him and left a message for Baylis to call him back. Then he gave Crawford a call and filled him in on what he had found out about the artist.

"So you still don't know if he's up here or down in Florida?" Crawford asked. "Right?"

"Or somewhere in between."

"Give me the name of the gallery. I'll drop by and see what I can find out."

"Yeah, those prison fights make me stand up and take notice. Seems we got a violent guy here."

"No doubt about it."

*****

Crawford's biggest question was how Jill had gotten mixed up with a guy like Crispin Baylis in the first place. He conjectured that, since she loved art and going to galleries, that must have been the connection. And a "charming rogue" artist combined with her own lousy marriage…he guessed that must've been enough.

The name of the gallery was the Ronald Freeman Gallery on Mercer Street and the owner introduced himself, not surprisingly, as Ronnie Freeman. Freeman was a gnome-like man who exuded nervous energy and couldn't stand still for more than a few seconds at a time. He didn't seem particularly nervous or put off, though, when Crawford introduced himself as a detective.

"You spoke to my partner earlier," Crawford said, after introducing himself. "Detective Ott."

"Oh, yes," Freeman said. "A very inquisitive fellow."

"Well, yes, that's his job. Mine, too. I want to know as much as you can tell me about Crispin Baylis. I know you recently had a show for him."

Freeman walked around in a circle and put his hand to his chin. "Yes, yes, I did. Very disappointing, actually. I sold three paintings and one of the buyer's checks bounced. Crispy—that's what I call him—is very lucky, though."

"Lucky? How so?"

"He's got a rich older woman who's his, ah, patron."

"Patron? Can you define that for me, please?"

"Benefactress. She loves his work, and he loves her money. She's also been very generous with my gallery. Buys paintings of his and several of my other artists. Between you and me, I think she's got more paintings than walls in her homes."

"What's her name and do you know where she lives?"

"Victoria Kelleher and she's got places in Westport, Connecticut, and Jupiter Island, Florida." Jupiter Island was only forty-five minutes north of Palm Beach—an hour if you caught a bridge in the up position.

"So I'm getting the impression there's more to their relationship than benefactress to artist," Crawford said.

"How perceptive of you, Detective," Freeman said, putting his hand on Crawford's shoulder. He had to reach pretty high up. "By the way, I want you to promise me this is all off the record. Wouldn't want to kill the golden goose."

"It's all off the record."

"Well, you might say that Victoria is the female version of a sugar daddy. She's very generous to Crispy in return for…well, I can only surmise."

"But you have a pretty good guess."

Ronnie Freeman winked at him. "Well, yes, I do."

"Something of an amorous nature?"

Freeman shuddered. "Ew, that's not a pretty image. She's old and squishy."

"So, this time of year, Ms. Kelleher's probably on Jupiter Island, right?"

"I think she is. She hasn't been to the gallery in a couple of months."

"Tell me about Crispin Baylis. What do you know about him besides he's a painter whose work doesn't sell very well?"

Freeman stroked his chin again. "Crispy? He can be devilishly charming one minute, but then…look out, he's got a nasty, nasty temper."

"What do you mean? What kind of things set him off?"

"Oh, God, you name it. I remember a little while back when his car was parked out front here and he saw a meter maid putting a ticket on his windshield. Flew out of here in a fury, after a few moments put his hands around the poor woman's neck and actually lifted her off the ground. She couldn't have weighed more than ninety pounds."

"Then what happened?"

"He let her down and came back in here. I guess she called for back-up, or whatever you call it. He raced out the back door and disappeared. Three cop cars showed up with their lights flashing, sirens going, guns drawn, but Crispy was gone. They impounded the car, but then I heard that Victoria bought him another one."

"A car?"

"Yes, not a new one, but still."

"Wow. That's quite a story."

"Isn't it?" Freeman said. "But you promise you won't—"

"Don't worry, I won't."

Crawford thanked Ronnie Freeman and asked that, if Baylis checked in, to try to find out where he was, then let Crawford know.

Something told him that wasn't likely to happen.

He called Ott back and told him that Baylis was gaining credibility by the minute as a suspect and man who might have something to do with Jill's death.

Only thing missing was neither he nor Ott had any clue what his motive might be.

CHAPTER FORTY

The next morning Ott was on his way up to Jupiter Island. At first, he thought about calling Victoria Kelleher and asking if he could drop by and ask her some questions, but then he thought if Crispin Baylis was staying there, and was his killer, he'd surely beat it out of the house, hop in his car, and head for parts unknown. So instead, he decided to just show up and get a read on things.

The only thing Ott knew about Jupiter Island was it was a place where athletes, specifically professional golfers, and a few celebrities lived. He knew Tiger Woods and Phil Michelson both lived there, along with golfers from the past like Greg Norman and Nick Price. He also remembered reading that older golfers, Lee Trevino and Gary Player, had once lived there. Through the grapevine he'd even learned that Venus Williams had recently bought a house on the island and that Celine Dion had sold one a while back. He wondered if some young entrepreneur was busy mapping out a celebrity-house tour on Jupiter Island...then guessed the insular little community would never let that happen.

He crossed the south bridge over to Jupiter Island, then headed north past a long row of six- and seven-story condo buildings that looked somewhere between expensive and *really* expensive. Past them, he saw the Martin County line with large, luxury houses on either side of the road. The ones on the right looked out over the ocean; most of the ones on the left fronted the Intracoastal.

He was looking for number 327 South Beach Road and could see the odd numbers were on the ocean side, the even numbers on the Intracoastal. Like Palm Beach, the landscaping on Jupiter Island was perfect—that was the only word for it—every square inch of the island, it seemed, designed by one of the notable landscape architects in the area. He had heard the name Mario Somebody a lot.

He saw the number 419. The numbers were going down. Then 393. He was close. Another half a mile and he saw 327 and turned in. You couldn't see the house from the road, which was true with most other houses along the way. He could tell that houses on Jupiter Island, for the most part, had quite a bit more land than those in Palm Beach. It was all relative as he thought about his little ranch on a postage stamp lot in West Palm.

He drove down the winding, chattahoochee pebble driveway until a big Mediterranean-style house loomed dead ahead. He got out of the Vic, which, if it had a mind, would have felt humbled and inferior in the shadow of the large, white Rolls Royce in the driveway.

Crawford walked over the crunching pebbles and up to the front porch of the house, hit the buzzer, and waited.

A black man in black pants, a black jacket, white shirt, and black tie answered the door bell. He looked Ott over warily. Like maybe he thought he was an encyclopedia salesman. "May I help you?"

Ott flashed him a quick, humorless smile. "My name is Mort Ott, Palm Beach Police Department. I'd like to ask Ms. Kelleher a few questions."

"I think she's napping at the moment."

Ott suppressed his first reaction: *Well, then, wake her the hell up.* "I've come quite a way and just have a few questions for Ms. Kelleher. Would you mind getting her, please?"

The man sighed deeply, then, as he walked away, ramped it up to full groan status.

If Crawford were with him, Ott would have said, *What a dick* under his breath, but he wasn't, so Ott remained silent.

A few moments later a short, round woman with white-rimmed glasses came to the door. She was wearing tight black Levis, a terrible fashion statement for a woman Ott figured to be in her late seventies or early eighties. She had a white poodle with a turquoise collar in her arms.

She looked Ott over, top to bottom. "Did I hear Maurice correctly? You're a detective?"

"Yes, ma'am, I am. Detective Ott, Palm Beach Police. I'd like to ask you some questions, please."

"About what?" she asked, imperiously.

"May I come in?" Ott asked. It was already up to eighty-five degrees, plus the last thing he needed was a sunburn on his mostly bald head.

"Of course you may," Victoria said with a smile, stepping to one side. "Come right in."

She led him into a den off the foyer. It had a lot of brightly colored, chintz-covered furniture, and strikingly vivid paintings. It contrasted mightily with her black jeans and dark, collared shirt. They sat facing each other.

"So what would you like to know, Detective?"

"You have a friend named Crispin Baylis, do you not?"

She smiled. "Well, let's just say I did."

He decided to not question the past tense right away, knowing it would soon come out.

"This concerns a murder that took place in Palm Beach four days ago. I'm sure you must have heard or read about it. The victim's name was Jill Simpson."

"Yes, I did. That was ghastly. The poor woman."

"Did you know her?"

"No, I didn't."

"Mrs. Kelleher, when was the last time you saw Crispin Baylis?"

"Last Thursday."

"So, five days ago?"

Victoria nodded.

"And where did you see him?"

"Right here."

"And why was he here?"

"Because I invited him."

"So he stayed here?"

"No."

Ott had pulled teeth before, but these were like deep-rooted wisdom teeth. "Mrs. Kelleher, I would really appreciate your help. The murder of Ms. Simpson was a brutal crime, and we are doing everything possible to solve it, but I need to know everything you know."

"Okay, then ask me a question."

"I have quite a few more. The first one is where is Crispin Baylis?"

"That I don't know."

"But he came to stay with you... here?"

"Yes, he came to stay with me here, but I didn't let him."

Ott shook his head and frowned. "Okay, now I'm confused. You invited him here and he came here... but you turned him away?"

Victoria took a deep breath and leaned forward in her chair. "Okay, I will endeavor to *un-confuse* you, Detective. I did invite Crispin here, and he did come here, but before he got here, I heard something very disturbing."

"And what was that?"

She exhaled and scratched her rouged cheek. "What happened was, a friend of mine told me, a few hours before Crispin was to arrive, that she saw him and this woman, Jill Simpson, at a restaurant having lunch. She said they were acting all lovey-dovey—" she fanned her face with her hand. "I was irate. I am considerably older than Crispin but he—" her voice cracked and got tremulous—"he said he…loved me and I…I, fool I was, believed him."

Ott's instinct was to pat the woman's arm consolingly, but he held back. "So, I'm guessing that when he arrived you told him what you had found out? What your friend told you?"

"Yes, I did," Victoria said, wiping away a tear. Then, she lowered her voice. "I really wanted to hurt the man for causing me such terrible pain. So I made up a story: I told Crispin that Jill Simpson had somehow found out he was coming to spend the weekend with me, and she called me, irate. Told me Crispin was her lover and he, obviously, was only interested in me for my money. Then, she said, 'Well, you can have the son of a bitch. If you see him, tell him to lose my phone number and never contact me again.'"

"But none of that was true, was it? Fact is, you never did have a conversation with Jill Simpson, did you?"

She shook her head. "No, I didn't. I made that up. I never met or spoke to the woman. My motive was to hurt Crispin as much as I possibly could. Make him think that he had gone from two-timing *two* women…to losing both of them."

Ott nodded slowly. It was a lot to absorb. If Crispin Baylis was the hothead people made him out to be, it was conceivable he might have gone straight to Palm Beach and taken out his wrath on Jill Simpson for ruining his relationship with sugar mama, Victoria Kelleher.

Baylis could well have seen his good life going up in smoke—having an older woman spoil him, buy him new cars, and cover her walls with his unremarkable art, but then ending his cavorting with the beautiful Jill Simpson. Victoria's lie might have turned him into a raging homicidal killer.

"So, after your confrontation with Baylis, he left, correct?"

"Yes, he left in a big huff."

I'll bet, Ott thought. "And you haven't seen or heard from him since?"

Victoria sat back in her chair. "No, actually, I have. He called and, in effect, pleaded with me to give him another chance."

"And?"

"The man can be so damned charming. But I suspected he had two-timed me in the past, so I just hung up on him. I didn't want to hear it."

"So you have no idea where he is? He has no Florida residence?"

Victoria shook her head. "Probably back at his fleabag on Grand Street."

"Is that in New York City?"

Victoria nodded. "The ugly part of New York City."

CHAPTER FORTY-ONE

"Know where Grand Street is, Charlie?" Ott asked.

"Sure, not far from my old stomping grounds. Why, what's there?"

"Maybe Crispin Baylis. S'posed to have an apartment there."

"Give me the number and I'll pay him a visit."

Ott filled him in on his conversation with Victoria Kelleher, along with Baylis's exact address, which was 111 Grand St.

"So, after talking to the old gal, what's your sense about him?" Crawford asked.

Ott thought for a few seconds. "I don't know. Making a guy a paraplegic. Attacking a guard in prison. Going after that poor meter maid. It adds up to a guy who's got a serious violent streak. I mean, he could have snapped when he thought he had no future with either woman and that Jill was the one who had caused it."

"Yeah, but what bothers me is that even if he went to Jill's house loaded for bear, Jill would have had time to deny ever calling Victoria Kelleher, right?"

"I thought about that. Maybe he just went in there in a blind rage and didn't care what she had to say. Just started choking her."

"Maybe."

*****

An hour after he hung up with Ott, Crawford called his old captain, Mike Visconti.

"What's doin', Charlie?" Visconti said.

"Hey, mind if I borrow Bisbee again?"

"Yeah, sure. What do you need him for this time?"

"My murder suspect lives in a four-story building on Grand Street." Crawford had driven down to the building and checked it out. "I want to go brace him, see if he's got an alibi for Jill's murder."

"You mean you want to rough him up a little? I can give you a guy who's more of a goombah."

Crawford laughed. "Hey, now, that ain't exactly my style. I just need a guy who can be out in the back of a building if my suspect makes a run for it."

"Oh, all right. Sure, Bisbee can handle that."

"Thanks. Is he on duty now?"

"I think so."

"Okay, can you ask him to meet me down 111 Grand Street at two this afternoon?"

"You got it," said Visconti. "If you don't hear back from me, he'll be there."

"Also, while I'm borrowing your guys, I might need to borrow a room."

"A room?"

"Yeah, at your precinct. That one with the three old chairs, that scratched-up metal desk, one-way mirror, and the camera to record confessions."

"You got it. How 'bout a jail cell, too?"

"Nah, if this is my guy, I'm gonna put him in the back of a rental car and drive him down to the Sunshine State. But thanks, anyway."

"You're welcome, Charlie. Sure you don't want your old job back?"

"Yeah, I'm sure.... I still hate dirty snow."

*****

Todd Bisbee showed up at a little past two in front of the four-story building on Grand Street. It had fire escapes on the upper three floors and the façade was thick with New York grime.

Bisbee gave Crawford a wave. "Something tells me this isn't the same guy who owns that Mercedes S."

Crawford nodded. "Two different guys, a Park Avenue doctor and a starving artist."

"So what did this guy do?"

"Suspect for a murder in Florida."

Bisbee nodded slowly. "So am I gonna need my piece?"

"I doubt it but keep it handy."

"I always do."

Crawford took a step closer to Bisbee. "All right, so I checked it out. My guy's got a loft on the second floor. I'm gonna hit the buzzer and when he asks who it is, I'm gonna say, 'Police, got a few questions for you.' He's gonna either come down or, more likely 'cause he's had trouble with the law before, try to beat it out the back."

"Where I'm gonna greet him," Bisbee said.

"Exactly," Crawford said. "What's your cell number?"

Bisbee gave it to him, and Crawford dialed the number. "Okay. We're connected." Crawford thought for a moment. "More I think about it, you probably should have your piece out."

"You think he'll have one?"

"I don't think so, but—"

"—I know, better safe than dead."

Crawford nodded. "Okay, let's do it."

Bisbee walked along the left side of the building as Crawford went inside and saw four buzzers. He pushed "Baylis C."

He waited and there was no answer for a few minutes. He pushed the buzzer again.

"Who is it?" the voice asked, in a tone that might be used on a collection agent.

"Police," Crawford said. "I need to ask you a few questions."

"What for?"

"Just let me in."

A long pause. "All right. Give me a few minutes."

"Okay."

One minute went by, then two, then three. Crawford hit the buzzer again. There was no response.

*****

Bisbee was in the back of the building, Glock in hand, behind an old pickup that had a flat tire. He saw a man in a black T-shirt, gray cargo shorts, and sneakers, no socks, come out of the back door and furtively look from side to side. "Got a guy coming out," he whispered. Then, "Hold it right there! Police!"

Baylis sprinted around one side of the building and Bisbee went after him. "Coming toward the front," he called loudly into his phone. "On the right side of the building."

*****

Crawford ran outside and to his left. He looked around the corner and saw Baylis twenty yards away, coming in his direction at full speed.

Baylis spotted Crawford and veered left. Crawford tried to cut him off, but Baylis squeezed past him and, not looking either way, sprinted across Grand Street, heading down a long alley dead ahead. Crawford raced across Grand a few feet ahead of a rumbling garbage truck and tried to call up his former college-football speed. He was gaining on Baylis as he saw the alley dead end fifty yards ahead. He tried to find another gear, now ten yards behind his suspect. At five yards, he gave it a final push, then dived at Baylis's legs. The man slammed into three tall metal garbage cans with Crawford hanging onto to him from behind. Baylis's cry of pain could be heard a block away.

From under Crawford, writhing in pain, he growled, "Son-of-a-bitch, the fuck's this all about?"

Crawford had his cuffs out and snapped one on Baylis's right wrist. "You're under arrest on suspicion of murder."

"What the hell are you talking about?" Baylis snapped.

Crawford pulled Baylis's arms together and slapped the other cuff on his left wrist as he heard footsteps behind him.

"I thought you were a halfback," Bisbee said a few feet away.

"What?" Crawford said, feeling sharp pain in his right knee where he had landed.

"Visconti said you were a star halfback in college…not a tackle."

CHAPTER FORTY-TWO

Crawford and Baylis were in Interview Room 2, Mike Visconti and Todd Bisbee watching through the one-way mirror. The interview was being recorded by a camera in the upper corner of the room.

Baylis had a large bandage on his chin, which had been deeply gouged by the edge of a garbage can. He had clammed up ever since Crawford had read him his Miranda rights. He hadn't said he wanted a lawyer; he just hadn't said a word.

They were seated in two wooden chairs facing each other. Between them was a gray metal table that had a few random scratches and a big bump in the middle. Crawford guessed maybe a suspect had slammed his fist down hard on it while denying a charge. Could have been a million things, though.

"So, Crispin, is it your intention not to say anything?" Crawford asked coolly.

"Hey, look, I don't know who you are or what this is about, but what I'm thinking is I'll get me a good ambulance-chaser lawyer and sue your asses off for police brutality. I keep reading how you guys been losing a lot of those cases lately. Defund the cops and all that shit."

"Okay, well, as I told you before, my name is Crawford and I'm a detective with the Palm Beach police, where you spent a little time recently."

"So what if I did?"

"Did you spend last Thursday and Friday at the home of Jill Simpson on Jungle Road?"

"So what if I did?"

"Is that a yes?"

"I heard what happened to her and I'm real sorry about it, but I don't know a thing about it," Baylis said, wiping his mouth with his hand.

"What did you hear happened to her?"

"She was killed."

"Yes, she was. When you were staying there."

"That's bullshit. When I left she was alive and just fine. Matter of fact, she gave me a nice, long kiss."

Crawford started to wince but stifled it. "Where'd you go, after you left?"

"Up to a friend's house."

"On Jupiter Island?"

Baylis leaned back and thrummed the desk. "If you know all the answers, why you asking me?"

"Then, when Victoria Kelleher told you that she got a call from Jill Simpson, who said she never wanted to see you again, what did you do? That was after Victoria told you to get the hell out of her house, if I'm not mistaken."

Baylis smiled, though it looked painful with the bandage on his chin and his badly bruised cheek. "There are lots of fish in the sea, my friend."

"Meaning what? You got women all over Florida?"

"Something like that."

"So, where'd you go?"

"Down to Boca."

"To do what?"

"See a woman."

"Give me a name."

"Petra."

"Last name?"

"Devere."

"Palm Beach is on the way to Boca. You stop by Jungle Road on the way there, by any chance?"

"Never stopped anywhere. Just flew into the waiting arms of Petra."

This time Crawford couldn't let it go. "You're a pig, you know?"

Baylis smiled. "I'll tell my lawyer you said that."

"Please do," Crawford said. "How long'd you stay in Boca?"

"Two nights, then flew back here."

Crawford looked around the room before he said anything. "Why'd you run when I came to your building?"

"Just not thrilled about cops coming to see me."

"I know why," Crawford said. "Probably figured I was coming after you for choking that ninety-pound meter maid. That's what it was, right?"

"I have no idea what you're talking about."

"I'm seeing a pattern here."

Baylis shrugged. "You're talking in riddles. What pattern?"

Crawford tapped the steel table. "You know, strangling women."

CHAPTER FORTY-THREE

Without a word, Crawford stood up and walked out of the interview room. He entered the room where Visconti and Bisbee were standing, watching through the 2-way mirror. "What do you think?" he asked.

"I don't know. Think you gotta talk to that woman, Petra," Visconti said. "But, man, what a dick the guy is."

"Yeah, no doubt about that," Crawford said. "Dick, yes. Murderer? I'm just not feeling it. Plus, I got a call from my partner, said he didn't find any tapes of the guy coming or going after he left on Saturday."

"You thinkin' it's the Mercedes guy, Charlie?" Bisbee asked, referring to their garage break-in.

"I don't know. I was sure it was…then Baylis came into the picture. Maybe someone else will, too."

"So what are we going to do with Baylis?" Visconti said. "We could get him for aggravated assault…the meter maid."

"Yeah, guy doesn't deserve to get off scot-free," Bisbee said.

"By the way, Charlie," Visconti said, "you ain't lost a step in there."

Crawford nodded. "Thanks, Cap. I'm not quite done with this clown." He turned and opened the door of interview room two and walked back in.

Baylis scowled at him as he walked in. "Got a new strategy?"

"So you're saying you never went back to Jill Simpson's house."

"Straight down to Boca. It was like a love triangle, you might say," Baylis said, with a vapid smile.

"What are you talking about?"

"Jill to Victoria to Petra."

Crawford shook his head. "Pretty pleased with yourself, aren't you?"

"What can I tell you, I'm a woman-pleaser."

Crawford so wanted to deck him. Right on his bandage, to inflict maximum pain.

"What kind of a car were you driving?" Crawford asked.

"3-series BMW."

"That's the small one, right?"

Baylis nodded.

"What color?"

"White. Well, actually mother-of-pearl white."

Crawford cocked his head. "Glad you clarified that," he said. "All right, you're going to be spending the night here…my friend."

Baylis straightened out as a frown cut across his face. "What the hell are you talking about. For what?"

"Assault. That ninety-pound meter maid," Crawford said with a smile. "That was one woman you didn't please at all."

CHAPTER FORTY-FOUR

Visconti clapped Crawford on the back. "I gotta remember that line when I tell the boys at the Rat Race." An old cop bar a few blocks from the 10th Precinct.

"What line?" Crawford asked.

Visconti got squinty-eyed. "'*That was one woman you didn't please at all,*' delivered just like fuckin' Clint Eastwood."

Crawford shook his head. "Big deal. Where'd it get me? He spends the night in jail, but I got nothin' on him."

"I think it's the Mercedes guy, Charlie," Bisbee said.

Crawford cocked his head. "Yeah, but what do you know? I didn't tell you anything about him."

Bisbee shrugged. "Something about the mileage on that Merc, though, right?"

Crawford nodded.

"Wanna catch an early dinner?" Visconti asked Crawford.

"No, thanks, man. Artie's old lady's whipping up some enchiladas or tacos or some damn thing."

"All right, well, good luck with the Mercedes guy," Visconti said. "Are you totally ruling out this guy here?"

"No, not at all. But something tells me his alibi, this Petra woman, is gonna clear him."

*****

Then, just like that, another suspect came out of nowhere, exactly as Crawford had guessed might happen.

Crawford was eating dinner and drinking a margarita at Artie Aguilar's house when he got a call from Ott.

"Where are you now?" Ott asked.

"Brooklyn, drinking margs. Envious?"

"Damn right I am. I'm at Good Sam, about to go into the room of our latest suspect in Jill's death."

Latest suspect? Good Samaritan was a hospital in West Palm Beach.

Crawford put his margarita down. "Oh, Christ, another one? They're comin' out of the woodwork." He stood up and walked into the foyer of the Aguilars' home.

"Yeah, this one apparently goes under the heading of a 'deathbed confession.'"

"Tell me about it."

"Well, it's a little sketchy at the moment. I'll know more after I talk to the guy. His name is Joey Gatto and I guess he's got something that's terminal. Anyway, here's what I know for sure: he asked his doc to contact the police so he could cop to something he supposedly did and wanted to get off his chest. So this uniform, Eddie Lambert, goes there and records the guy, who's apparently been in and out of the slammer his whole life. Guy said he read about the two burglaries in the Estate Section and decided to do a copycat."

"No shit, really?"

"Yeah, and supposedly Jill catches him in the act, and he panics and—" Ott lowered his voice— "you know the rest. So Lambert called me right away and told me about it."

"And you're at Good Sam now?"

"Just about to walk in."

"What did Lambert say about the guy? I mean, did he seem credible or could just be looking to make a headline?"

"I asked him, and he said seemed like Gatto, quote-unquote, 'Coulda did it.'"

"Grammar."

"Yeah, I know."

"So get back to me after you grill him."

"I will. You can go back to your tequila." Then Ott added: "Wish I was with you."

*****

The "deathbed confessor," as Ott had said, was named Joey Gatto– "just like the famous gangster," he told Ott, "except two T's instead of two L's."

"Officer Lambert told me what you told him, and I have a few more questions," Ott said, sitting on a chair next to Gatto's hospital bed. The self-professed gangster was hooked up to all kinds of tubes and wires: nose, wrists, chest.

"Ask away, chief," Gatto said.

"Okay, first, I need you to start from the beginning. Officer Lambert said you got the idea to burglarize a house in Palm Beach from stories in the papers or on TV news about the two break-ins near there."

Gatto smiled wide, revealing tiny yellow teeth. "Yeah. To quote the late Willie Sutton, *That's where the money is*, right?"

"I believe he was talking about banks."

"Well, I'm talking about Palm Beach."

"Okay," Ott said, with a nod. "So you went to the house on the night of January tenth. I forget, where was the house again?"

"You didn't forget. You know damn well. The house was on Jungle. 240 Jungle."

"Right. So you go there, where'd you park?"

"On the street."

"What kind of car?"

"Ford Taurus 2015."

"What color?"

"Black."

"Okay, and then what did you do?"

"Took my crowbar, went around the back of the house and jimmied the back door."

So far, his information was in all the newspaper and TV stories. But the big, black car checked out.

"Then what?"

"The house looked dark. Only one light was on when I cased it outside, so once I was in, I started walking around. Then I see this woman reading something, and she sees me. I think she's about to scream. So, well, I freaked out. Booked over to her and started choking her. I didn't plan to kill her, just...I don't know, make her pass out or something. Keep her quiet."

"So, she never screamed."

"She was about to. I stopped her."

Ott sighed. "Why are you making this confession, Joey?"

"I'm a good Catholic. I don't want to leave here with a guilty conscience."

"Here? You don't mean, the hospital?"

"Hell, no. I mean Earth, man."

Ott cupped his chin and looked into Gatto's eyes. "So, you think you're going to die… here."

"I know I am."

"So, to make sure I got this straight, you won't have a guilty conscience because you made this confession?"

Gatto nodded. "Correct."

"Let me ask you a few more things. What did you do with the stuff you took? The jewelry, the guns, and everything?"

"Don't forget the silverware."

"Yeah, all of it."

"Fenced most of it up in Riviera Beach and some here in West Palm."

"Where specifically? To who?"

"They're a bunch of street guys. Always got cash on 'em."

Ott nodded. "So, her computer, too?"

"Yup."

"What about her iPhone?"

No hesitation. "Chucked that out back somewhere. Into the bushes."

That information had *definitely* not been in any newspaper article or TV news.

Ott nodded, satisfied that Joey Gatto might indeed be his man. He reached for his handcuffs and took them off his belt.

Gatto looked surprised. "Whatcha gonna do with those?"

"You just confessed to murder. What if you make a remarkable recovery and want to get out of here?" Ott said, putting one of the cuffs around the bed frame, pulling up the bed covers and putting the other cuff around Joey Gatto's scrawny, slug-white ankle.

Then Ott stood up and looked down at Gatto. "I'm gonna go get your statement typed up. Then bring it back here for you to sign. You're not gonna go changing your story on me, are you?"

"Nah, what I told you is exactly how it went down."

Ott stared into Gatto's vacant eyes. There was something a little off about the man.

CHAPTER FORTY-FIVE

After interviewing Joey Gatto, Ott had an appointment to meet with Petra Devere in Boca Raton. He figured that, before reporting back to Crawford, it would be best to have spoken with both Devere and Joey Gatto. Petra lived in an apartment building that was not quite seedy but a far cry from fancy. She was on the first floor and had eye-level views of a public park that had two neglected-looking basketball courts and a rusty swing set that looked like it would snap if anyone over forty pounds sat in it.

Petra's apartment looked IKEA-generic, which was not unpleasant, but also not cozy or homey. Petra herself was attractive in a blonde, blue-eyed way but, Ott quickly noticed, had a lazy eye. The kind that makes sustained eye contact next to impossible. Nevertheless, Ott was making progress with her.

"So, you met him at that place you mentioned, the Art Students League in New York City," Ott said, "and you stayed in touch."

"Yes, that was like fifteen—no, closer to twenty years ago—but we'd talk every once in a while. Or he'd call when he was in the area and needed a bed."

"When would that be?"

"Well, like one time he had a show at a gallery in Deerfield Beach. Asked me if he could stay a couple of nights."

"And he did?"

"More like five," Petra said, with a smile. "Ate me out of house and home. Oh, but he did buy me a bottle of wine—" she laughed— "you know, from the five-dollar shelf at Piggly Wiggly."

Ott nodded. "So, I'm asking you to be as specific as possible. On January tenth, a week ago, do you know where Crispin was?"

"Why? Has he done something wrong?"

"I'm not saying that. This is all just part of an investigation, and I'm talking to a lot of different people."

"Okay, so he got here the night before. And in the morning, he got up late and we just talked most of the morning. He had coffee and a blueberry muffin and, like I said, we just talked. Then that afternoon—starting at about one—we went to the Art Museum—"

"Here in Boca?"

Petra nodded. "Then to a bunch of galleries. Some we just went in and went out of quickly, others we stayed for a while. Then we went down to the gallery in Deerfield where he had the show. He wanted to talk to the owner—something about a painting of his that the owner sold, and Crispin hadn't been paid for. It got a little heated between them."

"Heated. How so?"

"Well, Crispin accused him of holding out on him. Refusing to pay him what he was owed. Crispin has a temper, you see."

"So, then what?"

"We left after Crispin, in a huff, took three paintings of his off the wall of the gallery. He was mad. So was the owner, for that matter."

"Then where'd you go?"

"Crispin said he needed a drink, so we went to a bar. He had three drinks, I had one—" she rolled her eyes— "I know because I paid."

"What time was this?"

"I'd say we were at the bar for an hour, between five and six. Then we went back to my place and that was it."

"So he never left your place after that?"

"No, we watched something on Hulu and called it a night."

So that was it: Crispin Baylis was out, plain and simple. The whole day of Jill Simpson's death was accounted for. According to the detailed timeline, he was totally in the clear. Ott was convinced that Petra was telling the truth. He thanked her, left her apartment, got into his car, and called Crawford.

"Yeah, Mort, whatcha got?"

"First of all, we can rule out Crispin Baylis. I just left Petra Devere's place, and she gave me a whole timeline for the day Jill was killed. She was with the guy every minute of the day from the time he woke up to the time he went to bed. No way she was lying. No doubt whatsoever in my mind."

Crawford was silent for a few moments. "Okay, and what about the 'deathbed confessor'?"

"I was just going to tell you. He was every bit as convincing as Petra Devere, but there was something a little hinky about the guy."

"How do you mean?"

"I don't know exactly. Like the dude had a nowhere life of petty crime, in and out of jail, and he wanted to make the news."

"You mean commit a visible crime and have reporters and TV cameras all over him?"

"That's exactly what I mean. Front page news, his mug on TV, the whole nine," Ott said. "But here's the kicker: he walked me through the whole thing like he had read all the details in the *Post*. But then he said something that we never gave the papers or TV: where Jill's cell phone ended up."

"He knew *that*?"

"Yup, said he 'chucked' it in the bushes."

"Wow, that's key."

"I know," Ott said. "He also claimed he fenced all the stolen shit in West Palm and up in Riviera Beach."

"Did you believe him?"

"Yeah…I mean, I guess," Ott said. "Oh, also, he said he drove a black Taurus to Jungle."

"So that checks out," Crawford said. "What are you gonna do next?"

"I told him I wanted to go to his house and look around."

"What did he say?"

"He said that was no problem, so I got a key from him."

"Where's he live?"

"Lake Worth. I'm on my way there now. If I find a crowbar that I can match up to the busted back door, it might be case closed."

"I gotta tell you, Mort, you don't need me at all. You're a one-man crime buster."

"Well, thank you, Charlie. I just muddle along."

"Best damn muddler in the business."

"All right, I'll let you know what I find at Gatto's house. Talk later."

"Okay."

Twenty minutes later, Ott pulled up to one-story ranch house with peeling paint and a yard with grass up to his knees. There was a derelict sailboat rotting on a trailer off to one side of the backyard. The life of crime had clearly not worked out for Joey Gatto. The big heist…never happened. Next door to Gatto's house was the exact same house, yet neatly painted and with the grass recently mowed. In the driveway was a Palm Beach Police department cruiser.

Without a pause, Ott walked over to the house next door, up the steps to the front porch, and pressed the doorbell.

A man with a buzz cut, cargo pants, a tight T-shirt and flip-flops answered the door and smiled. "Well, well, if it isn't—"

"Don't recognize you out of uniform, Larry," Ott said.

Larry Bowles had been one of the two uniform cops first on scene at Jill Simpson's house the day her body was discovered.

"Why you slummin' in these parts, Mort?" Bowles asked.

"Checkin' out your next-door neighbor," Ott said, pointing at Gatto's house.

"Vernon Fleur?" Bowles asked.

"No. That dump over there," Ott said, still pointing. "A guy named Joey Gatto."

Bowles laughed and shook his head. "Oh, Christ, is he up to that shit again?"

"Up to what?"

"Playing mafioso dude. Just for the record, the guy's name is Vernon Fleur, not… whatever you said."

"Joey Gatto."

"Yeah, he was a small-time criminal who now works at a body shop," Bowles said. "He comes over once in a while and asks me about cases I've been working on."

A light bulb clicked on in Ott's head. "So, he's like a cop groupie?"

"Yup. I try to keep the chit-chat to a minimum. He can be pretty annoying."

Ott cut right to it. "So, I'm gonna take a wild guess that you told him about investigating the Jill Simpson case, specifically about finding her cell phone in the bushes behind her house on Jungle?"

Bowles dropped his head and lowered his voice. "Yeah, I guess maybe I might've."

Ott patted the cop on the shoulder. "Hey, don't worry about it, man. It didn't do any harm."

"That's good. So fill me in," Bowles said with a shrug. "Why are you looking at Vernon?"

"'Cause he's up at Good Sam. Terminal, supposedly. Told his doctor he killed someone and wanted to 'fess up before he died."

"Before he died?'" Bowles said, shaking his head. "Guy's as healthy as a horse. There's nothing wrong with him except he's a habitual liar."

"This has happened before?"

"Has it ever. Couple years ago, he pulled the same shit at the Delray Medical Center, I think it was. Told them he used to live up in D.C., killed that woman Chandra Levy in Rock Creek Park. Turned out he'd never been to D.C. in his life. Claimed he also killed some guy who Aileen Wuornos supposedly killed. Guy's like a professional confessor."

Ott exhaled long and loud. "Oh, Christ," he said. "So I'm back to square one again."

CHAPTER FORTY-SIX

"Shit," was Crawford's first reaction when Ott told him on the phone about Vernon Fleur. His second was, "Goddammit, that guy sounded good, too."

"I know," Ott said. "Had me fooled."

"All right, so unless some other suspect falls out of the sky, we're back to Giles Simpson, my vote all along."

"Yeah, but we need a smoking gun."

Crawford nodded. "Which we know is probably never gonna happen. Nor are we gonna get an eyewitness or him getting caught on a camera."

"So, what do we do now?"

"I don't really know. I've got Jill's funeral tomorrow; we'll see what comes out of that."

"So Simpson will be there… obviously?"

"Yup. Can't say I'm looking forward to seeing him again."

"Yeah, but at least your old sister-in-law and her husband will be there."

"It's going to be a pretty small funeral…."

"How is it staying at your old buddy's place?"

"Good. They're a nice couple. He and I stayed up until two o'clock telling war stories last night."

"All right, well, hope the funeral is nice. And that asshole Simpson isn't too big an asshole."

"Got a feeling he will be."

*****

Once again, Crawford called it.

Giles Simpson was acting as greeter for the forty-five to fifty people attending his wife's funeral at Heavenly Rest church at 90th and Fifth Avenue, when Crawford approached the front door.

A huge frown cut across Simpson's face when he saw Crawford. "What the hell are you doing here?"

"Lucy invited me," Crawford said. In fact, she had asked him to sit next to her.

Simpson shook his head and sneered. "It was such a nice little group until…"

Crawford just swept past him and went down the center aisle of the stately church, joining Jessie, Jack, and Lucy Dellasandro in the left front pew. He leaned over, kissed Lucy, and gave a little wave to Jessie and Jack.

"Did Giles give you a big hello?" Lucy whispered, rolling her eyes.

"Yes, like I was his long-lost brother."

*****

Lucy's few words in church about her daughter were poignant, affecting, and straight from the heart. Jessie's tribute was longer and more tearful but touching and eloquent in her expression of pure love for her elder sister. Giles Simpson started out with an anecdote, which he apparently felt was humorous, though it was more about him than his late wife. Then he went on to say how much he would miss his beautiful "soulmate" and how his life would never be the same without her. He ended it by saying, "Now, if you would all join me for lunch at the Union Club, where we can hoist a glass of Dom Perignon in honor of the memory of my dearest Jill."

With that, the service ended, and they all walked out.

"*His* dearest Jill," whispered Lucy. "Why couldn't he just say, *our dearest Jill*? And that thing about Dom Perignon, couldn't he just say *a glass of champagne*? He's always got to impress us with a name. *Pathetic*."

"Okay, Lucy, don't let it get you crazy," Crawford said in his most soothing tone as they walked outside. "After the reception, you'll never have to see him again."

Lucy nodded. "Just don't let me drink too much. You know how I get."

Crawford smiled at her. "I'll cut you off after two."

*****

The venerable Union Club, which had been in existence for close to two hundred years, was in a distinguished-looking limestone building on the corner of 69th Street and Park Avenue. During the cab ride to the Union Club, Lucy told Crawford that Giles had once regaled her—or as she said, "bored me stiff"—with a lengthy recitation of past members of *his* club, which included William Randolph Hearst and John Jacob Astor. She had burst Giles's balloon by asking, "So why'd they let you in? You only have two names…well, unless you count Doctor."

The small group was in a room that had a bar and two bartenders, and the champagne was flowing. Some were sitting at tables and others standing at the bar. Crawford heard the tinkling of a glass and turned around to see Giles Simpson tap his empty champagne glass with a spoon.

"Well, again, just a word or two more," Simpson said. "On behalf of my mother-in-law, Lucy, and my sister and brother-in-law, Jessie and Jack, I would like to thank you all for coming here on this sad, somber occasion." He signaled one of the bartenders to give him a refill. "It is with a very heavy heart that I say goodbye to my beloved wife, Jill. Jill, as you all know, was truly a one of a kind, with a huge heart, a fabulous personality, a kind, sweet nature, a frisky sense of humor—" Crawford glanced over and made eye contact with Lucy, who had a perplexed look, like what the hell did "frisky sense of humor" even mean? "She led a full life, had a million friends, and everybody who ever met her will never forget her."

Simpson had a full glass of champagne now—Crawford guessed his third—and was making eye contact with him. "I just noticed the presence of Jill's first husband, one Charlie Crawford, formerly a New York cop." *Uh-oh*, Crawford thought. *Where in God's name is this going to go?* "I'm not sure Charlie was invited, bu-ut here he is. My guess is he's the first cop to ever step into the hallowed halls of the Union Club…except maybe to issue a parking ticket to a double-parked member—" Simpson snickered, and it was now official: he was drunk and lacked a sense of humor—frisky or otherwise..

Jack Giordano took a quick step toward Simpson and said something only Simpson could hear.

"Well, my brother-in-law informs me that my time is up, so drink up, everyone…. You, too, Charlie. Hey, it's free."

Stunned silence.

It looked like Lucy was going to say something, but Jessie squeezed her hand.

Jack Giordano came over to Crawford and said under his breath. "Sorry, man. I tried to cut him off."

Crawford shrugged. "Don't worry about it."

Giordano shook his head. "The guy's just incredible... You know, for a smart woman, Jill had pretty shitty taste. With the exception of you, of course."

CHAPTER FORTY-SEVEN

Crawford didn't want to have a confrontation with Giles Simpson inside the Union Club, so he was waiting for him outside, leaning up against a black Range Rover with Connecticut plates. He had walked out of the club with Lucy, who said she wanted to walk the twenty blocks back to her co-op on East 89th Street and "clear her head." When they parted, Lucy urged him to stay in touch and said that if he came to New York again, he always had a bed at her place.

A half hour after Lucy left, Giles Simpson walked down the steps, a little shakily. He was with an attractive woman with a low-cut black dress that Crawford wasn't sure was appropriate for a funeral. Simpson saw him and scowled as Crawford walked toward them.

"Could I speak to you, Giles?" Then, to the woman, "Alone, please?"

"Oh, sure," said the woman. "Bye, Giles."

"Bye, darlin'," Simpson said, then to Crawford. "What are you gonna do, Crawford, give me a parking ticket?"

"I came up here looking into a couple of suspects in Jill's murder—" *and you're one of them,* he refrained from saying—"and I'm assuming you want to help me solve it."

"Yeah, but the whole thing's got nothing to do with me. I'm not a cop."

"But you do want the killer to be found, right?"

"Sure, but—"

"Your trip to Lake Waramaug, that's ninety-three miles from here."

"Yeah, so?"

"So that's a total of a hundred eighty-six miles round-trip."

Simpson chuckled. "You a math major, Charlie?"

"And you told me you didn't take the car on any other trips, right?"

"Yeah, yeah, right," Simpson said impatiently.

"So, the day before you went to Lake Waramaug, you picked up your car at the Mercedes dealership on Eleventh Avenue. When you brought it in, it had 10,512 miles on it—" his Perry Mason moment was almost here—"so, this seems curious…when you brought the car back to your garage on 96th Street, it had 13,070 miles on it. How do you explain that? The extra twenty-five-hundred miles, I mean."

Simpson shook his head in disgust. "Who the hell gives a damn?"

"I think a judge might. A jury might."

"Oh, Christ, Crawford. You're wearing me out with all this. I just had her funeral and—"

"Hey, look at it this way, I'm trying to find a way to rule you out, but you're not making it easy."

"From the get-go, you wanted to hang this on me."

Crawford didn't respond as a last straggler couple from the reception walked out of the Union Club and gave a wave and said goodbye to Simpson.

"Look," Simpson said, glancing down at the sidewalk, "here's what happened: Jill was having an affair with this guy. Maybe more than one, for all I know. So, I drove down there to catch her in the act."

"And did you?"

"No, she was all alone the night I got there."

"So what did you do?"

"Turned around and went back to New York."

"You went all that way and just turned around and went back."

"Yup."

"So, the Lake Waramaug thing was bullshit."

Simpson nodded. "Yeah. I'd gone up there about a month ago."

"To Lake Waramaug?"

Simpson nodded.

"With your woman friend?"

"Yes," Simpson said with heat. "Just for the record, I go *wherever* I want and do *whatever* I want with *whomever* I want."

Crawford cocked his head. "So, again, you drove twelve-hundred miles, said 'hi' and 'bye' to Jill, then got on the road and drove another twelve hundred miles back here."

Simpson smiled his smarmy smile. "I told you, yes."

"Really?"

"Hey, Jill and I were going forward with a divorce. She wasn't particularly keen on me staying in the same house with her. Especially since—" he did the quote thing with his raised fingers—"*the guy* might show up at any moment. By the way, I thought *the guy* might actually be you."

Crawford drilled in hard on Simpson's eyes. "I don't have anything to do with married women, or women going through divorce."

Simpson shook his head. "Holier-than-thou Charlie. Poor bastard. You miss out on all the fun."

"I guess one man's fun is another man's taboo."

CHAPTER FORTY-EIGHT

Crawford had to face the fact that all that he had was circumstantial evidence. He took a flight out the next morning after breakfast at Artie's in Brooklyn. At two that afternoon, he and Ott had a meeting with Norm Rutledge to bring him up to speed on the investigation and what he had discovered in New York.

Rutledge, as always, was wearing a spiffy brown suit. This one, with a snappy white chalk stripe, was complimented by a burgundy bow tie.

"I didn't know you were a bow-tie guy, Norm," Ott said. "It gives you an air of distinction."

"Thanks, Ott," Rutledge said. "Coming from you, a man with an air of bullshit, I'm not flattered."

"Never learned how to tie one of those suckers," Ott mused.

Rutledge turned to Crawford. "So, whatcha got? Besides probably a pricey expense report."

"What are you talking about? I took the subway everywhere and my friend fed me."

"Good man. So, come on, let's hear."

And for the next forty minutes, Crawford caught them both up on his trip.

"So, that's it?" Rutledge said, raising his arms. "Is this going to be the first case you two don't clear? When you claim to know who *did* it?"

"What do you expect us to do? We got nothing but circumstantial evidence on the guy," Crawford said.

Rutledge leaned back in his chair, crossed his arms on his chest. "This is usually the point at which you boys do something outside-the-box to nail the perp."

"Like what?" Ott said. "What do you recommend?"

"I don't know. Can't you discover Simpson's DNA under Jill's fingernails or something?"

Ott shook his head in shock. "Jesus, Norm, you're suggesting we tamper with evidence? Is that it?"

"Yeah, evidence we don't even have," Crawford said, displaying a little shock.

"Just trying to be helpful," Rutledge said. "Hey, this is your department."

Ott laughed. "No, actually it's your department, we just work here."

*****

At the end of the conversation, Rutledge made a suggestion they weren't expecting at all. "So, how 'bout this: Maybe it's time you two took a vacation? I get the sense you're a little burned out."

Crawford and Ott looked at each other, aghast.

"That's so unlike you," Ott said. "You usually like us working our fingers to the bone, twenty-four/seven."

"Yeah, but you need to recharge your batteries. I can see this thing has taken it out of both of you," Rutledge said, glancing at Crawford. "Especially you, Crawford."

"Yeah, you might be right about that," Crawford acknowledged.

Rutledge nodded. "I get it. Something as close to home as this is to you? It's bound to drain the hell out of you."

Crawford tapped on Rutledge's desk. "Yeah, I guess maybe it has."

"You come back rested, you can dive right back into it. Keep your record intact."

Ott turned to Crawford. "Where do you think you'd go?"

Crawford shrugged. "I don't know. I've had about thirty seconds to think about it. How 'bout you?"

Ott glanced out the window. "I don't know, this may sound kinda weird, but I was thinkin' about maybe visiting the birthplaces of some of my favorite country-western singers."

"More than weird," Rutledge said, nodding. "But who's surprised?"

Ott shrugged. "Hey, just 'cause the only place you ever go is Disney World."

"It's the number-one attraction in America," Rutledge said. "Which is exactly the problem."

Rutledge shook his head slowly. "You know, Ott, sometimes I wonder about you." He paused. "No, actually I *always* wonder about you."

CHAPTER FORTY-NINE

Crawford wasted no time in paying a visit to the cubicle of Dominica McCarthy in the crime-scene techs' area. He glanced around and saw that she was the only one around. Dominica had her feet up on her desk and her MacBook Air in her lap. She looked up and gave Crawford a smile. "Hello, Charlie."

Dominica's tawny dark hair was the first thing you noticed—well, after her incredibly curvaceous body—followed by her luminous emerald-green eyes, followed by her shapely red lips. To Crawford, she had gotten even better-looking in the four years since he had known her. That no doubt had a lot to do with the present state of their relationship, which for the last year could best be described as happily stable, with moments of wild passion. An accurate description for the two years preceding would have been on again/off again or, as Dominica had once described it to a friend, "rocky," which their relationship had been at its low point. But in the last twelve months, it hadn't even been close to rocky. The opposite, in fact.

"Hey. What's new in the world of latent prints and hair follicles?"

Dominica laughed. "Exciting as ever," she said, then turned serious. "Anything new on Jill's case?"

He shook his head. "Nah, wish there was…hey, you got any vacation time coming?"

"Yes, why?"

"Because I'd like to take you on a little trip I've been thinking about."

"You can do that with the case not solved?"

He nodded. "Rutledge actually suggested it. Said we needed to get our—" he did the finger-quote thing— "batteries recharged. I guess he's gotten used to the fact that we never solve 'em in the first forty-eight, but eventually we catch our man."

"So this little trip of yours, tell me what you're thinking."

"Well, it's only for a week so we can't go racing off to the Dalmatian coast or the beaches of Thailand."

"So wine-tasting in the Loire Valley is out?"

"Sorry, you need at least two weeks for that. I'm thinking of something I've dubbed *Charlie's Magical History Tour*."

"Oh, wow, that sounds…impressive?"

"It starts in the ancient city of St. Augustine."

"It's ancient?"

"By American standards, it is. Oldest city in the country. In fact, it was there before there was any U.S. of A. at all."

"And then where?"

"Two hours north to Savannah."

She pumped her fist. "All right! I've always wanted to go there. Supposed to be a very cool town."

Crawford nodded. "Then on to the Holy City."

"Rome?"

Crawford laughed. "Charleston. Beloved for its amazing restaurants and beautiful old houses and lots of churches. And you know how much I love churches."

"Oh, yeah, you're a real holy-roller. So I've never been to either Savannah or Charleston," Dominica said. "When do we go?"

"How long's it gonna take you to pack?"

"I've got to finish up some things today, but I can be ready first thing tomorrow."

Crawford gave her a fist pump. "Let's do it."

*****

Crawford had recently traded in his Camry for a three-year-old gray Lexus ES350 with relatively low mileage. He picked Dominica up the next morning at her apartment in a high-rise on North Flagler Drive in West Palm. She was waiting for him in her lobby with a large duffle bag and a backpack.

"Wow, what are you gonna do, change clothes every hour?" Crawford asked as he grabbed her duffle bag.

"I'm a girl, Charlie. We don't travel as light as guys."

"You're not bringing golf clubs?"

"Should I?"

"Nah, no need. I brought mine. If we ever want to play, we can both use 'em."

Crawford put her duffle in the trunk, they climbed into the car, and headed to I-95.

On the on-ramp to 95, Dominica turned to Crawford. "How far is it?"

"About two hundred fifty miles. We'll do it in a little less than four hours."

"Florida is a very long state."

"Sure is. About five hundred miles top to bottom," Crawford said. "But nothing compared to California, which is eight hundred."

"I always liked a man who knew his geography."

"I know state capitals, too."

"Wyoming?"

"Cheyenne."

"Nebraska?"

"Lincoln"

"South Dakota?"

"... Bismarck?"

"Sorry, that's *North* Dakota. Pierre."

*****

It was 7:15 p.m. and, since arriving in St. Augustine at a little past noon, they'd had an active day. They were having dinner now at a little place called Collage on Hypolita Street, just off of St. George in the heart of the historic district. Dominica took a sip of her white wine and set the glass down and smiled at Crawford. "This place is kind of romantic, Charlie."

"I agree," he said, reaching for her hand under the table. "Play your cards right, you might get lucky tonight."

"Does that mean I have to beg?"

She ordered sautéed escargot wrapped in a delicate puff pastry and he ordered the grouper, cooked with parmesan cheese, pecan, and brown sugar, and they shared a bottle of chardonnay.

"I don't know which I liked best, the old fort or the alligator farm."

"How about the museum?" Dominica asked.

"Beautiful old buildings," Crawford said and smiled, "and I'm always a sucker for shrunken heads."

Crawford had Googled *Things to do in St. Augustine* and had come up with a list of eight favorites. On it were an old Spanish fort called Castillo de San Marcos, built before the United States *was* the United States, back in 1672. The guide told them that though the Spanish maintained control of the Castillo de San Marcos for most of its military life, it was used by the British during the American Revolution and by Confederate soldiers during the Civil War. The Lightener Museum, described as "eclectic," was also near the historic district. It was formerly the Alcazar Hotel and had been built by Henry Flagler, who had left his mark in both St. Augustine and Palm Beach, not to mention many other places throughout the state. Its collections included paintings, furniture, sculpture, glass, and porcelain dating back to the Gilded Age, between 1870 and 1900. Also, on display were a few odd items like shrunken heads and old cigar labels.

"The only problem with the alligator farm was all the gators were all just lying around, all over each other. Like all day was one long siesta," Dominica said.

"What did you want them to be doing? Attacking children and small dogs?"

"I don't know. Swimming maybe? Something. Anything. They were just a bunch of slugs. On top of each other, never moving. It reminded me of one of those places where old tires are all piled up."

Crawford laughed. "Except you don't have to pay twenty-five bucks to look at old tires."

"Well, yeah, there's that," Dominica said. "I did like the fort, though."

"Yeah, cool old cannons."

Dominica laughed.

"What?"

"Guys and their guns."

*****

They were finishing up the last of the chardonnay before they headed back to the place where they were staying, a bed and breakfast called At Journey's End.

Crawford had balked at the idea of a bed and breakfast because he was not keen on striking up a conversation with total strangers at breakfast, particularly before he'd had his coffee. But Dominica had talked him into it. "You're too much of a hermit," she had said. "You need some new friends."

"I got you, Ott, and Rose. Isn't that enough?"

"For a golf foursome, maybe."

"Except Rose doesn't play," Crawford noted. "Hey, speaking of which, you have any interest in the World Golf Hall of Fame? That's around here somewhere."

"Sure. If we can go to Ponce de Leon's Fountain of Youth first," Dominica had told him, pointing to the side of her eye. "I'm getting crow's feet."

"Deal," Crawford said, giving her a fist bump. "And, by the way, your wrinkles? They're invisible."

The waiter dropped off the check and Crawford paid it. "That was pretty good, didn't you think?"

"Really good," Dominica said, then a little yawn. "But I'm pretty sleepy now."

"Sleepy?" Crawford asked.

"Well, you know," she said with a smile.

Crawford smiled back at her. "I think I do."

*****

They were sitting on a side porch of At Journey's End in a not-very-comfortable wicker couch. Crawford was sipping port that the night manager had offered.

"Since when are you a port drinker?" Dominica asked.

"Since it's on the house," he said, raising the glass to his lips.

It was 9:45 and no one else was in sight. Crawford put the port glass down, put his arm around Dominica and kissed her. She responded with alacrity.

Just as it started to get passionate, they heard footsteps. They looked up and quickly put a few inches between themselves as an older couple approached. Seeing Crawford and Dominica, the couple turned and walked away.

Crawford smiled as he got to his feet. "Come on, girl, beddy-bye."

"I'm right behind you."

They resumed the kissing just inside the door of their bedroom. After a long, heated session, they started stripping each other's clothes off. Dominica slid into bed with her panties on; Crawford was in such a hurry, he still had one sock on. He flashed back to the night after he saw Jill's body, when he'd had way too much to drink. He managed to slide Dominica out of her panties but couldn't be bothered with the sock.

CHAPTER FIFTY

Breakfast with four perfect strangers wasn't bad, but not particularly good either. The conversation was mostly about what people had seen or were about to see in the old city or where in the country they had come from.

Later that morning, Crawford and Dominica set out for the Old Jail, which was also built by Henry Flagler. The man clearly got around. It was built in 1891 and featured a distinctive Romanesque Revival-style architecture. In 1987, it had been added to the National Register of Historic Places.

After an hour at the jail, they went to find Ponce de Leon's Fountain of Youth, but, rather than locating a bubbling spring, as they'd expected, found only a plaque.

"Well, where is it?" Dominica asked, reading the inscription.

"The fountain?"

"Yeah, the fountain," Dominica said. "I want to lose five years."

"Well, just for the record, you're perfect the way you are."

"Thanks, Charlie," Dominica said, looking around for a spring or any other source of special water, then shrugged. "Didn't you think there was going to be a fountain here?"

Crawford shook his head. "See, I Googled it earlier. Here's the deal: Ponce de Leon was looking for it, but never found it. In fact, some of the Native Americans told him it was in Bimini."

Dominica smiled. "Bimini? Well, hell, what are we waiting for? Let's go to Bimini."

He patted her on the shoulder. "Not this trip."

Dominica put her arm around Crawford's waist as they walked away from the plaque. "I wonder why some young hustler hasn't figured out a way to install a spring around here, put up a sign, and sell water for five bucks a glass." She winked at Charlie. "I'd pay."

*****

Their next stop was the Pirate and Treasure Museum. Any place that had Blackbeard's blunderbuss—defined as "a firearm with a short, large caliber barrel that is flared at the muzzle and used with shot and other projectiles of relevant quantity or caliber"— was going to be a hit with Crawford. Dominica, not so much. She found the pieces of gold retrieved from Blackbeard's warship, *Queen Anne's Revenge*, far more interesting. There were 800 pirate artifacts in the museum, which kept them occupied for well over an hour.

Since they were eager to get up to Savannah, they decided to skip the World Golf Hall of Fame. They figured they could always catch it on the way back down to Palm Beach since it was just off of 1-95. They wanted to get to Savannah to take a carriage tour around the city while it was still light. A friend of Dominica's had recommended the ride as something that shouldn't be missed.

They checked into the Perry Lane Hotel on Perry Street. It was a splurge for Crawford because the Perry Lane was on the expensive end of the lodging spectrum. What won him over was a photo of a rooftop bar that seemed to have an extraordinary view of Savannah and was next to a sparkling pool where young hardbodies sunbathed and splashed around.

Their room, dominated by soothing beige and gray colors, was large and nicely furnished with comfortable-looking modern furniture. The bed was luxurious and inviting. They dropped their bags, grabbed a couple of bottles of water, and walked to where the carriage rides originated at 2 West Bay Street.

Dominica was patting the head of a black horse—one of two that would haul them around the historic district of Savannah.

"Old dude's got some mileage on him," Crawford said, coming up behind Dominica and the horse after paying for the trip.

Dominica patted the horse's nose. "But look at that beautiful face."

Crawford did. "Think he's due for his annual teeth cleaning."

Dominica laughed. "You're terrible. Come on, let's get in."

They climbed aboard the carriage behind the black horse and a white one. Their guide and driver was an older man wearing a ratty-looking Confederate hat and red, white, and blue suspenders.

"So where you folks hail from?" the driver, who had introduced himself as Silas, asked, turning back to them.

"Florida," Dominica said. "West Palm Beach area."

"Well, welcome to Savannah," and they were off on a scenic tour of Savannah's historic squares, one of which dated back to 1733, followed by the beautiful 30-acre Forsyth Park, featuring a huge, elegant two-tiered fountain made of white cast iron. They clattered along cobble-stone streets with moss-laden oaks as an alluring backdrop, listening as Silas described the old city's history and intriguing lore. They rumbled past the Telfair Museum, a distinguished old art museum; the imposing Cathedral of St. John the Baptist, the oldest Catholic church in Georgia; and alongside the Savannah River. They asked a lot of questions and learned a lot about the historic old city, that— thankfully—the Union's General Sherman had spared his Civil War torch.

"You getting hungry?" Dominica leaned close to Crawford and asked after they had been in the carriage for an hour and a half.

"Was it my stomach rumble that gave it away?"

*****

They had made a dinner reservation for 7:30 at a well-reviewed restaurant called Husk. They had a drink at the stylish Husk bar, which had twenty-foot ceilings and elaborate, old-world chandeliers, then enjoyed a long, slow dinner in one of several smaller, private, dining areas. Afterward, they walked the short four-block walk back to the Perry Lane in a light drizzle.

Two minutes after unlocking their hotel door after dinner, they were making love. It was long, languorous, and intensely passionate and left them both breathing heavily.

"I meant to ask," Dominica said between pants. "Did you intentionally have every aphrodisiac known to man for dinner?"

Crawford cocked his head. "What do you mean?"

"Well, let's see...you had avocado, oysters, salmon, and to top it all off, that heavenly chocolate pudding."

"Are those all supposed to be aphrodisiacs?"

"Let's just say they have a reputation for getting one in the mood."

He laughed. "You didn't have any of 'em, I noticed, but you were definitely 'in the mood.'"

"Two other ones are asparagus and ginger."

"Oh, well, there you go. That explains it."

CHAPTER FIFTY-ONE

They were having breakfast at the hotel. Crawford had just downed a slice of bacon.

"Is bacon an aphrodisiac?" he asked.

Dominica laughed. "You know, maybe we're overdoing the sex thing. I mean, if that's all we planned to do, we could have just holed up in your condo."

"What are you talking about? So far we've seen one fort, one jail, one shrunken head museum, one pirate museum, a million gators—"

"One Fountain of Youth...*not*!"

"One nice ride around this beautiful city taking in all the historical and cultural sights."

"I loved that."

He smiled and picked up another strip of bacon. "Okay, so on the docket today we have another couple of forts, the Bonaventure cemetery, Wormsloe Plantation—"

"Plus shopping, a manicure...do we really need to go to another fort?"

"You mean, if you've seen one fort, you've seen 'em all?

"Something like that."

"Okay, ix-nay on the fort then. How about a round of golf?"

"Where?"

"I told you. That friend of mine who lives out on Skidaway Island. They've got six courses there. I've got a standing invitation."

"Sure. Late afternoon maybe?"

"Yes, and if he doesn't already have plans, let's have dinner with him and his wife afterward."

Dominica nodded. "Sounds good. What are their names?"

"Tim and Ellen Pitts. You'll really like 'em."

"Better call him up. See if it works for them."

*****

Tim and Ellen Pitts were their hosts for eighteen holes at a course in the Landings, an upscale development twenty minutes from downtown Savannah.

Crawford and Dominica were sharing clubs from his bag, and he was carrying it.

They were on the thirteenth hole on a course in a section of the Landings called Oakridge. It was a par 5 with water running along both sides of the fairway. Crawford's friend, Tim, was a good player and his wife even better. But Crawford's real competition was Dominica, who was an eight handicap and also an inveterate bettor.

"Okay, Charlie," Dominica said, as he was teeing up his ball. "Ten bucks on this one. And because of your hook—" his habit of driving the ball way to the left—"and your tendency to drown balls, I'm going to give you one stroke."

Crawford looked off at the distant green. "That's very generous of you, Dominica. But my plan's to get on in two. Birdie it."

Tim perked up. "I want in on the action. I'll give you ten to one that says you don't birdie it, Charlie. And five to one you don't even par it."

Crawford turned to Pitts and smiled. "Thanks, old buddy. Always good to have you in my corner. I'll take the par bet. A fiver?"

Pitts nodded.

"I bet you can do it, Charlie," Ellen said. "But you gotta drive it straight."

"No problem."

Big problem, Dominica mouthed to Pitts.

Crawford took a practice swing and launched his drive 250 yards down the fairway. Straight and—incredibly— dead in the middle of the fairway.

"Nice one," Dominica said, clapping.

"Thanks. I'm over halfway home... not to mention, dry."

They walked up to the women's tee and Dominica borrowed Ellen's driver. She took a practice swing, waggled the club, and crushed her drive. It bounced a couple of times, then rolled a few feet past Crawford's ball.

"Jesus!" Crawford said, in awe.

Dominica turned to him and smiled. "That's all you have to say?"

"Jesus Christ!"

They walked down the fairway. First, Ellen hit a three-wood just to the right of a sand trap. Then, Tim sliced a three-iron, but it stayed in the fairway.

Then, it was Crawford's turn. He looked longingly at the green 220 yards away, then glanced over at Dominica and smiled.

"You're going to go for it, aren't you?" Dominica said.

He shrugged. "Hey, live dangerously," he said pulling out his three-wood.

"Good luck," said Dominica.

He took two practice swings this time, inhaled deeply, and stepped up to the ball.

He struck the ball with a long, fluid swing. But his hook was back... back with a vengeance. There were houses that ran along the left side of the fairway where the water formed a pond. Crawford's ball was heading toward a house that had a long row of sliding glass doors in back. Crawford prepared himself for the sound of glass shattering, but instead his ball hit the roof of a one-story house and plunged into a nearby lagoon.

"Oops," said Dominica.

"Boy, I really suck," Crawford said with a groan, as he pulled another ball out of his pocket.

He decided not to go for the green this time and laid up, hitting a nice, conservative shot seventy-five yards short of the green.

"Think I should go for it, Charlie?" Dominica asked, taking a practice swing.

"I always go for it...that's my problem."

"I think I'm gonna give it a shot. What the hell."

"It's two hundred and ten yards."

"So, I'll just hit Ellen's driver again," she said, turning to Ellen.

"Really? Off the grass?" Crawford asked.

"You mind?" Dominica asked Ellen.

"Not at all. Go for it," she said, handing Dominica her driver.

"Just so you know, there's water short of the hole," she advised. "You can't see it from here. Just don't be short."

Dominica nodded, took another practice swing, and took a hard cut at her ball. It rose up high, and it looked like the wind was going to catch it but landed on the near edge of the green.

Tim gave her a thumbs up. "Cleared the water by just a few feet," he said. "Helluva shot."

Crawford took out his wallet and handed Dominica a ten. "You could four-putt from there and still win."

"Thank you, Charlie. Pleasure doing business with you."

He shook his head. "I hate losing to you."

*****

They went to a restaurant not far from the Landings called Jalapeñas?

All four of them were on their second margarita. They were strong and Tim cautioned that if you had three, more than likely, you'd crawl out of the place.

"Working on any good cases?" Tim asked Crawford.

"That's why I'm up here. Taking a break from one."

"Charlie always gets his man," Dominica said.

"Eventually," he said.

"What about you," Crawford asked Tim, "you still writing?"

"Oh, God, it's like squeezing blood out of a stone," Tim said, shaking his head. "Or whatever that cliché is."

Dominica turned to Ellen. "Charlie told me you're a painter?"

"A damn good painter," Tim said.

Ellen smiled. "A loyal husband."

They settled up a little later, no one wanting to get anywhere near a third margarita. The four said goodbye in the parking lot and Crawford and Dominica got in the Lexus.

They looked at each other and smiled.

"So," Crawford said. "I know one thing that's an indisputable fact."

"Oh-oh. And what's that?"

"Margaritas are 100% an aphrodisiac."

CHAPTER FIFTY-TWO

It was ten-thirty and Crawford was on the edge of falling asleep when his cell phone rang. He assumed it was Ott, maybe with a break in the case. But then he remembered, no, Ott was roaming the hills of Alabama or Mississippi, or wherever it was, visiting the birthplaces and graves of his fallen country-western music heroes.

It was a 917 number on his screen. "Hello?"

"That neck of Jill's," said a hideously distorted voice, "it was so nice and…and *oh so* fragile."

The caller clicked off before Crawford could respond.

He took a deep breath and sat back, replaying the call. He had no doubt about it—it had been Giles Simpson on the line, using a voice disguising app.

Dominica, reading a travel book about Charleston, glanced over. "Who was that?"

He didn't want to spoil their trip. "Wrong number."

It took him three hours to fall asleep and he slept fitfully until he got out of bed at 7:00 a.m. Dominica wasn't awake, so he left her a note, dressed and went down to have breakfast and think. He was the only one in the small, but tastefully designed, breakfast room.

Forty-five minutes later, Dominica appeared in short shorts, sandals, and a light blue, collared shirt. Crawford was on his third cup of coffee.

"Hello, beautiful," he said as she came up to the table.

She kissed him on the cheek. "You all right? You were tossing and turning all night."

"The margaritas maybe."

"You haven't ordered yet?"

"Nah, not really hungry. I know…not like me, is it?"

"Totally unlike you," she said as a waitress came up with a pot of coffee.

"Coffee?" the waitress asked Dominica.

"Love some, thanks."

"So it's about a two-hour drive to Charleston," he said. "You got our day planned?"

"There's so much to do there."

"Yeah, I know. So what's on your list?"

"Just so happens," Dominica said, reaching into her handbag, "I wrote a few things down: I want to go see Middleton Place, Drayton Hall, and walk 'til I drop. Seems like so many cool old houses all over the city to see."

"Yeah, I know. That's all?"

"Oh, God, no. I want to see the Angel Oak Tree—"

Crawford gave her a fist bump. "I'm with you on that."

"And do the Ghosts of Charleston Walking Tour, some shopping on King Street, and go see Mrs. Whaley's garden."

"What's that?"

"Well, see, I read this book last year that came out, um, maybe twenty or twenty-five years ago called *Mrs. Whaley and her Charleston Garden*, and even though I'm not much of a gardener, I decided one day I was going to go see it."

"And that day has come, huh?"

Dominica nodded. "What about you? What's on your list?"

"Well, as you may have guessed, a fort. Fort Sumter, in this case."

"I'll go see that with you. That one's famous. What else?"

"That tree you mentioned."

"The Angel Oak. Supposedly the oldest live oak east of the Mississippi. Between three hundred and four hundred years old."

"I love how the branches go in all different directions."

"And how some of the lower ones actually rest on the ground. Okay, so one fort and one old tree. What else?"

He raised his hand to the waitress. He was finally ready for eggs and bacon. She came over, he ordered, then he turned back to Dominica. "So, about twenty years ago they found this old submarine called the *H. L. Hunley*, which was built for the Confederate Army back in 1863. A year later it was lost at sea until they found it a hundred fifty years later, restored it, and now it's at the Charleston Naval Base. I want to see it."

"Perfect. When I'm shopping on King Street you can go there."

Crawford chuckled. "Somehow I figured an old sub wasn't going to do much for you. But sticking with the nautical theme, I booked us on a 'sunset cruise' on this four-masted schooner called the *Schooner Pride*."

Dominica smiled. "When you say 'sunset cruise,' is that anything like a 'booze cruise'?"

Crawford nodded and smiled. "Could be, but we've got to bring our own."

"Okay, I'll take care of that. So how big a boat is it?"

"It can accommodate like fifty people."

"We can make some new friends, huh?" She winked.

"Yup. I'll bet we'll see some pretty amazing views too. I've got two other places I'd like to squeeze in while you're on King Street."

"Called?"

"Well, one's called the Striped Pig Distillery and the other, the Frothy Beard Brewery."

Dominica laughed. "And they give out free samples, I'm guessing?"

"I hope so."

The waitress brought Crawford's bacon and eggs.

"All right, well, eat up, I'm dying to get to Charleston," Dominica said, standing up. "I'm going to pack."

As soon as Dominica walked away, Crawford dialed his cell phone.

"Hey, Charlie," Mort Ott said, "how goes the vacay?"

"It was going fine until I got a call from Giles Simpson. He was using one of those voice disguising apps, but it definitely was him."

"What the hell did he want?"

Crawford thought for a second. "Verbatim: *That neck of Jill's, it was so nice and... and oh so fragile.*"

"What a sick bastard," Ott said, slowly and deliberately. "Sure as hell sounds like a confession to me."

"Yeah, well, he'll just deny it was him, of course."

Ott didn't say anything right away. Then, "What the hell's he trying to do?"

"I don't know. But it reminded me of when Ward Jaynes confessed that he killed that kid, Darryl Bill. Remember?"

"Yeah, I sure do."

Crawford was referring to the first murder case they had in Palm Beach. The killer was an arrogant billionaire hedge-fund manager who they finally put away for life after a long, often frustrating pursuit.

"You suppose he just wants to torture you?" Ott asked.

"Sure as hell looks that way."

"But why?"

Crawford thought for a few moments. "I told you about having dinner with my mother-in-law when I was in New York for the funeral. She told me how Giles was jealous of me because even though he was Jill's husband and I was her ex-husband, the family apparently liked me better. They thought he was a cheating prick—" he laughed—"I guess they just thought I was a negligent husband. Jessie's husband Jack never wanted to have anything to do with Simpson."

"So what do we do?"

"Enjoy our vacations. When we get back we'll figure out how to get the bastard. Where are you now?"

"Well, this'll take some explaining, but I'm in Mississippi. Remember that old song by Bobbie Gentry, *Ode to Billie Joe?*"

"Kinda. Was he the guy that jumped off the whatever-it-was bridge?"

"Yeah, exactly the Tallahatchie, up near Choctaw Ridge. So, I always liked the song and I just wanted to go visit where it all took place."

"Not exactly normal, but okay."

"Normal's boring, Charlie. Get this: the Tallahatchie Bridge is no more than ten feet above the muddy, slow-moving Tallahatchie River."

"So?"

"Well, I always pictured Billie Joe jumping off this really tall bridge—"

"You mean, like the Golden Gate or something?"

"Exactly. But this would have been a short jump and I don't see how it would kill him. Unless maybe he drank the water or something."

Crawford exhaled and thought for a moment. "I don't know. You're a detective, figure it out. Or maybe you're going to have to track down Bobbie Gentry and ask her."

"I thought about that, asked around. Nobody seems to know where she ended up."

CHAPTER FIFTY-THREE

The entire drive up to Charleston, Crawford thought about Giles Simpson and his disturbing words from the night before. He considered mentioning it to Dominica, but she was deep in her Lonely Planet Charleston & Savannah travel book, reading up on even more things to do in Charleston.

"What's the name of the place you booked?" Crawford asked.

"It's called the Mills House on Meeting Street," Dominica said, reading about the hotel in her book. "24/7 gym, pool, multilingual staff.'"

"That's important."

"Yeah, in case I want to break into Spanish," said Dominica, who had some Spanish lineage in her family tree.

Crawford kept wondering why Giles Simpson would, in effect, confess to killing Jill. At the end of the two-hour drive, he thought he knew the answer. Like Crawford's first murderer in Palm Beach, Ward Jaynes, Giles Simpson had a massive ego and was about as arrogant as any man Crawford had ever met. Maybe it was the scourge of self-important Park Avenue surgeons, he theorized. In Crawford's experience, men with the supreme conviction that they are the smartest man in the room also believed they were bulletproof and could get away with anything. Because all their lives they were used to outsmarting the competition and, as the cliché went— *getting away with murder*.

They were on Savannah Highway, ten miles from the bridge to Charleston, when Crawford's cell phone rang. It was a number Crawford recognized. Chief Norm Rutledge.

"Hey, Norm," he said. "What's up?"

"Charlie, you're not going to like what I'm about to tell you."

"All right," Crawford said, "Well, tell me anyway."

"I've gotten two calls in the last eight hours. Let's call them, for lack of a better phrase, *good citizen* calls."

"Go on."

"The first one was the cleaning lady at your ex-wife's house. Told me she's been wrestling with her conscience about certain information she has. Said she saw you at Jill's house the morning she was killed. Coming out of Jill's bedroom, in fact. In a bathrobe."

Crawford smacked his steering wheel in shock and anger. "That's total bullshit, Norm—" Dominica looked up in surprise—"I never saw Jill once in Palm Beach… except, of course, when I went to the scene."

"You have any idea why this woman would make this up, out of whole cloth?"

"I have a theory," Crawford said, hitting speakerphone so Dominica could hear.

"Well, hold off on telling me. Then this guy called this morning. Said he recognized you from the investigation. A photo in the *Post* of you at the scene, he said. Guy turns out to be a bartender and told me he remembered you being with a woman who he recognized from her picture as Jill. At his bar."

Crawford sighed as Dominica watched him. "So here's what those two have in common: Giles Simpson. He obviously got to those two with a couple envelopes full of cash and told them exactly what to say. This is a frame-up if I ever saw one."

Rutledge was silent. "It's gonna be tough to prove they're lying. So why's Simpson doing this?"

"I can't think of anything but the obvious."

"To divert attention away from himself."

Crawford nodded. "Couldn't be anything but that. Plus he's not a big fan of me."

"When you gonna get back?"

"Jesus, Norm, I just left."

"Yeah, but this is serious. I'm gonna do my damnedest to keep a lid on it. Keep it out of the papers. And TV."

"Good luck."

"I'll need it," Rutledge said. "Talk later."

"Okay," and Crawford clicked off and glanced at Dominica.

"This guy Simpson seems like real bad news," Dominica said

He shook his head slowly. "You believe that?"

"You want to head back to Palm Beach, Charlie?"

"And miss the sunset cruise and that four-hundred-year-old live oak? No chance in hell."

"But, seriously, you might have to do some damage control."

He patted her arm. "There's no damage. It's just a lame effort to frame me. You've never seen me in a room with a lying witness. I'm pretty good at getting them to change their tune."

"So I've heard," Dominica said, patting his arm as they went over the bridge from West Ashley into Charleston.

"I mean it," Crawford said. "Let's just forget about this thing for the next few days and have a good time."

CHAPTER FIFTY-FOUR

They were on the *Schooner Pride,* having just pulled out of the Harbor Walk dock near the Charleston Aquarium. Primarily, the passengers were couples of all ages—20s to 60s—plus a few families. Turned out the *Pride* was a reproduction of an 18th-century schooner, and the crew was young, enthusiastic, and capable of answering even the most obscure questions. The *Pride* was a graceful ship with a wooden mast, leather-buffered joints, and a well-maintained rigging.

Dominica broke out a bottle of rosé and two plastic wine glasses from her Yeti cooler after they had been out on the water for a half hour.

It was a twist-off and Crawford poured two glasses.

"Look, look," Dominica said, pointing at a pair of dolphins that swam under the schooner and surfaced on the other side.

"Flipper and friend," Crawford said, observing the two dolphins. "It almost looks like they're smiling."

Dominica tapped her wine glass to his and looked back at the Charleston skyline. "Really beautiful," she said. "I like how they restricted the heights of all the buildings here. And I love all those church steeples.

"They don't call it the Holy City for nothing."

Dominica nodded as she shaded her eyes.

"So I don't know about you," Crawford said, "but my legs are sore as hell. Walking around looking at all those old houses."

"Yeah, me too. I'm not sure which was my favorite street, Legare or Church. I think maybe Church just because Mrs. Whaley's Garden was there."

Mrs. Whaley's Garden at 58 Church Street even brought a smile to Crawford's face. "Place was really beautiful. And it smelled so nice."

"I loved the roses and hydrangeas and daisies in front of all those azaleas and camellia bushes."

Crawford nodded. "Not sure what any of those are, but it was really beautiful."

"I read somewhere that the garden has like twenty thousand visitors a year."

"I believe it."

"But Legare Street was pretty amazing too. Actually, all those streets south of Broad were."

"Yeah, I really liked Rainbow Row," Crawford said, referring to thirteen houses in a row swathed in a rainbow of vibrant colors on East Bay Street. "Especially the pink, lavender, and turquoise ones."

She clicked his wine glass again and looked him in the eyes. "The sensitive, aesthetic side of Charlie Crawford."

"Well, thanks for noticing."

She gave him a kiss on the cheek. "I've always noticed, Charlie."

CHAPTER FIFTY-FIVE

The next day they visited—separately or together: the ancient Angel Oak Tree; Drayton Hall, one of the oldest surviving plantation houses in the south; the *H. L. Hunley* submarine; Middleton Place, home to some of the most breathtakingly beautiful gardens in the south; Fort Sumter, where the first shot of the Civil War was fired; and at the end of the day, for Crawford, a stop and a pint at the Frothy Beard Brewery.

At seven-thirty they were sitting at a table at a restaurant called Revival on Bay Street, re-hashing their respective days.

"Catchy name," Dominica said about the brewery Crawford had visited.

"Yeah, they had this one stout called Cluster Shuck that they added oyster juice to."

Dominica frowned. "Ew, gross. Another catchy name, though."

"Oh, also," Crawford said, reaching into a bag on the floor next to him, "I got presents for Ott and Rutledge."

"Oh yeah, what?"

"Look away, for a second," Crawford said.

"Okay," Dominica said, turning her head.

"Okay," Crawford said. "You can look now."

Dominica looked back at him and burst out laughing.

He was wearing a Donald Trump mask.

"Love the hair," Dominica said.

"Ott and Rutledge had the mother of all political debates a while back," Crawford said, taking off the Trump mask and putting on a Joe Biden one. "It got pretty heated."

"I remember hearing about it," Dominica said.

"I found these in this little knickknack shop," Crawford said, taking the Biden mask off.

"I'm sure the boys'll love them."

"They better. The things cost me big bucks," Crawford said, putting the masks back in the bag. "So what was your favorite of all?"

"Hm. I'd say… Middleton Place. It has all these beautiful gardens. The whole place was kind of… *Gone with The Wind*- ish."

Crawford's cell phone rang. He looked down at the screen. It said Paul Beal.

"Ever heard of someone named Paul Beal?" he asked.

"Nope."

He decided to answer. "Hello?"

"Charlie Crawford?"

"Yes."

"My name's Paul Beal, reporter at the *Palm Beach Post*—" reporters' calls were never something Crawford welcomed—"I have a few questions for you."

"I'm right in the middle of dinner. How 'bout calling back tomorrow morning?"

"It can't wait. First question is, did you kill Jill Simpson?"

"It *can* wait 'til tomorrow morning," Crawford said, hitting the red button.

Dominica saw his expression. "What's wrong?"

"Guy was a reporter. His first question was, 'Did you kill Jill Simpson?'"

Dominica put her hand on his. "I'm sorry, Charlie."

He exhaled. "We might have to go back. I don't think I can shove this under the rug any longer."

"I understand. Well, it's been fun. A lot of fun," she said, squeezing his hand. "We can always come back."

CHAPTER FIFTY-SIX

Before they got on the road back to Palm Beach, Crawford had a breakfast meeting with a Charleston detective. The backstory was that his Palm Beach friend, David Balfour, had gone through a devastating divorce a year before. At the heart of it was that his wife of a short-lived marriage had concocted a complex scheme with her artist lover to substitute fake paintings for some of Balfour's extremely valuable paintings. Ones by Franz Kline, David Hockney, and Wayne Thibaud. The plot unraveled, as did Balfour's marriage, but the artist of the fake paintings had made his escape, reportedly to Charleston.

In wanting to do all he possibly could for his friend Balfour, devastated first by his wife's adultery, then her participation in the art scam, Crawford went after the man, named Roy Jenkins, with all he had. He contacted the Charleston Police Department and was put in touch with a detective. The detective looked into Jenkins but was unable to locate him. Then the detective made the rounds of Charleston art galleries and finally found an artist fitting Jenkins's description exhibiting at a Broad Street gallery. But apparently Jenkins had somehow gotten wind that the detective was searching for him and had never returned to the exhibition. Even to retrieve his paintings.

The detective had reported back to Crawford and brought him up to speed six months back. A few days ago, when Crawford and Dominica first decided to put Charleston on their itinerary, Crawford had called the detective and offered to buy him breakfast to meet, discuss, and thank him for his efforts.

Crawford and the detective met at 7:30 a.m at a restaurant on Market Street called Another Broken Egg Café. Crawford ordered a local favorite, shrimp and grits, and the detective ordered a tall stack of pancakes with a side of sausages.

Dominica had decided she was going to get a little extra sleep that morning, maybe order up a room-service breakfast.

Crawford and the detective were facing each other sipping coffee.

"So the guy just disappeared?" Crawford asked.

"Yeah, poof, gone," the detective, Nick Janzek, said. "But a friend of mine who's an artist told me he was spotted in a gallery on Sullivan's Island. That's just over the bridge from here. I went there and nosed around but couldn't find him."

"I'd really like to track him down. He and this woman—as I told you, my friend's ex-wife—did a real number on my friend."

Janzek nodded. "Well, I can promise you, I'll keep checking my sources. Not that I have a ton of them in the art world."

"I really appreciate it, man."

Right after Crawford's shrimp and grits arrived at the table, his cell phone rang.

Paul Beal, it said on his display.

"This won't take long," Crawford said to Janzek. "Yeah, Paul, what do you want?"

"For starters, tell me if you killed your ex-wife."

"No, Paul, I didn't. Next question."

"There are two eyewitnesses who say they place you at the scene."

"I wasn't there, Paul. I haven't seen my ex-wife in almost five years. End of story, my friend."

"Can I ask you where you are, Detective?"

"On vacation."

"In the middle of a high-profile murder investigation?"

"Listen, Paul, what I'm right in the middle of, is breakfast. Maybe when I get back we can sit down and talk."

"But—"

"Bye."

Janzek cocked his head. "What's that all about?"

"Aw, nothin' much. Seems I'm the prime suspect in my latest murder investigation."

CHAPTER FIFTY-SEVEN

After the call from Paul Beal, Crawford and Janzek had a relaxing breakfast together and talked about their former gigs, in New York and Boston respectively, and how they didn't miss snow and cold weather but did miss the Yankees and the Red Sox. Janzek said he'd keep an eye out for Roy Jenkins and let Crawford know if the artist surfaced. Crawford thanked him, paid the check, and headed back to the Mills House.

Dominica was sitting at the end of the bed wearing a long-sleeved shirt of Crawford's. She had a tray in her lap with a plate that had a few crusts of toast on it.

"Did you have a nice breakfast with the detective?"

"Janzek. And yes, I did. But it didn't get me any closer to the art forger."

"That's too bad. I know David would love it if you found him."

"Yeah, well, guess it's just gotta wait," he said, looking at her plate. "Your usual? Two eggs, over easy?"

"Yup. Delicious."

Crawford smiled just as his cell phone rang. He looked down at the caller. Malcolm Chase.

"Oh, Christ," he said. "If you got a call from the mayor of Palm Beach, what would you do?"

"Not answer it."

Crawford nodded, letting the call go to voicemail.

"Why do you suppose *he's* calling?" Dominica asked.

"He wants to know why a detective of his is being talked about in the press as a murder suspect," Crawford said. "Can't say I blame him."

"So are you going to call him back?"

"Eventually," Crawford said as his cell phone rang for the third time in an hour. It was Norm Rutledge.

"Hey, Norm."

"So I got the *Palm Beach Post* in my lap, Charlie, and it's making for some interesting, but very disturbing, reading," Rutledge said. "You need to hear it."

Long exhale. "Okay... go ahead."

"*Charlie Crawford, known to some as the Playboy Detective—*"

"Where the hell'd that bullshit come from? No one's ever called me that!"

"*—has some explaining to do. Several witnesses have allegedly placed him at the scene of the murder of his former wife, Jill Simpson, on the day it took place.*"

"Norm, are you reading this just to piss me off, or is there a good reason for making me hear it?"

"No, I have no interest in pissing you off, Charlie. Just want you to know what we're up against here while you're off on vacation."

"You'll be happy to know the vacation is over and we're heading back—" He stopped, realizing that using the plural "we" had been a mistake.

"*We?*"

"I'll be in your office in seven hours. Six, if I push it."

"Push it," Rutledge said. "Mal Chace wants to talk to you, too."

"Okay, Norm, I got it." He clicked off.

Shaking his head, he turned to Dominica. "Sorry, babe, vacation's officially been cut short."

She nodded, like she knew it was coming. "What was it he said that 'no one's ever called you'?"

"Never mind. It's not important."

*****

He wanted to change his clothes before going to the station and stopped off at his building, the Trianon. There was a white van parked out front of the building with a big WPEC logo that said Channel 12 News. Beside it was a man with a camera and a woman with a microphone. She was a perky blonde news reporter he had seen on TV a few times. He U-turned and figured he'd have to make do with dirty clothes.

"Jesus, Charlie," Dominica said, "I'm sorry you have to go through all this."

He nodded and patted her arm. "Sorry for you, too," he said, checking his rearview mirror to see if he was being followed.

"I'm sure once you get in a room with those alleged *eyewitnesses* you can make it all go away."

"I sure as hell hope so. I wonder how much Giles Simpson paid 'em," Crawford said, pulling his car over. "Do me a favor. You mind driving? Think I'm gonna duck down in the passenger's seat."

"Sure, no problem," Dominica said with a nod.

They changed seats.

It was the same thing at the Palm Beach police station on South County, except this time there were three vans parked there. Fox, NBC, and ABC, with cameramen and male and female news reporters clearly champing at the bit to get interviews and live footage.

With Crawford ducked down, Dominica hung a left into the police station and went all the way to the end where only police vehicles were allowed.

"I'll go in first," Crawford said. "Rutledge will be eager to see me. Why don't you wait a few minutes, then go in—" he looked around to see if anyone was nearby, then kissed her. "I had a really good time. We'll do it again…next time, longer and with no interruptions."

"It was the best," she said, and kissed him again. "Sorry it got cut short."

*****

"Well, well, Charlie," Rutledge said, as Crawford walked into his office, "the wayward son."

"Hey, Norm, let me remind you again…you're the one who suggested I take a vacation."

"Yeah, yeah, I know. I just didn't know all this would blow up right after you took off," Rutledge said, dialing his desk phone. "Hey, Mal, Crawford just walked in…okay."

He clicked off and smiled. "Well, at least you look well-rested anyway."

Crawford had no time for small talk. "So sum it all up, will ya?" he said, impatiently.

"Sure, as I told you, we first got calls from the two supposed eyewitnesses, then all hell broke loose with the media—TV news, the papers. Then Mal called in a panic and wanted to know what it was all about."

"What did you tell him?"

"I told him I thought it seemed like a frame-up. Probably by the guy who killed Jill."

"What did he say?"

"Something like, 'Well, I know Crawford's sure as hell no murderer—'"

"Well, gee, thanks for that vote of confidence, Mr. Mayor."

And at that point, Mal Chace walked in. He went over to Crawford and shook his hand. "Hey, Charlie. Glad you're back. We're in a big mess of shit here."

"I know. I plan to have a little Q & A with those eyewitnesses as soon as I leave here."

Chase cocked his head and squinted. "You really think that's a good idea?" he asked. "I mean, the prosecutor in a trial could later make a claim that was witness tampering."

Crawford held up his hands and shook his head. "Whoa, whoa, whoa. A trial? There's never going to be a trial. This thing is going to fall apart way before there's anything even *close* to a trial. I mean, first of all, has anyone even speculated about what my motive might have been?"

He thought about telling them about Giles Simpson's call but didn't know how it would help.

"Look, Charlie," Chace said. "I know you didn't do it. Okay? I know this is just a big smokescreen made by the guy who really did do it, but we've got to be cautious how we proceed."

"Yeah, yeah, I know that. So what are you suggesting?"

"That Ott question those two so-called witnesses. He's a pretty damn good interrogator."

Crawford shrugged. "Hey, I'm fine with that. But he's off in hillbilly heaven at the moment."

Rutledge shook his head. "He's due back any minute," he said. "I reeled him back in too."

"Bet he was pissed about that."

"He said, *For Charlie, anything.*"

"Aw. What a pal."

As if on cue, in walked Ott. He was wearing blue jeans, cowboy boots, and a black T-shirt that said *Waylon* on the front. "Hello, boys," he said with a smile. "Mr. Mayor."

"Hey," Crawford said with a smile. "Nice shirt."

"Thanks," Ott said, going over to a chair facing Rutledge and sitting down. "So you fella's makin' a plan without me?"

"Never," Crawford said. "How would you feel about talking to the guy who said he saw me in the bar with Jill and the cleaning lady who claimed I was at Jill's house?"

"You mean, the two fuckin' liars," Ott said.

Mal Chace cringed.

"Sorry, Mal."

"I think you've got to be careful how you deal with those two," Chace said.

"Don't worry," Ott said. "I'm a little more subtle than that."

"I know," said Chace. "And you do need to poke holes in everything these people are claiming."

"And we can't think of anyone more capable of doing that than you," Rutledge added.

Ott grinned at Rutledge. "Well, thank you, Norm. It's not that often when you sing my praises. Give me their names and numbers and I'll get on it."

*****

Later that afternoon Mort Ott went to the bar where one of the newly minted eyewitnesses, Gene Rossiter, was bartending. It was just past five. Ott figured there wouldn't be many people in the bar, and he was right. Rossiter had a droopy handlebar mustache and reddish-brown hair that was combed straight back. He looked like a guy from Mississippi or Alabama, where Ott had just come from.

Ott introduced himself as a detective from the Palm Beach Police Department, which brought a barely disguised frown to Rossiter's face. "What can I do for you, Detective?"

"So I looked you up, my friend, and guess what? I found you had a *sheet*. That's a phrase we use in law enforcement to mean someone with a history of criminal behavior."

"What are you talking about? Just a couple minor things."

"Passing a bad check, beating up your ex-wife, assault in a strip joint in Miami, pistol whipping the owner of a pawn shop, shoplifting at a Walmart… you want me to go on, Gene? 'Cause there's more."

"What do you want with me?"

"The truth, old buddy," Ott said, sliding two photos out of his jeans pocket. The first was Crawford. "You've never seen this guy before in person, have you?" Then he showed him a picture of Jill. "Or this woman. No offense, Gene, but these two would never patronize a dump like this."

"They were in here. A couple weeks back," Rossiter protested lamely.

"No, they weren't," Ott said. "Know what else I found? An outstanding warrant for you. For beating up *another* woman. A hooker, in this case. With all your priors, you'll probably get a year or two for that last one. But I'm prepared to let that slide…*if* you quit bullshitting me and tell me you never saw either of those two."

Rossiter let out a long sigh and his eyes darted from side to side. Like he'd much rather be mixing a drink for someone. In the next county.

"Make up your mind, Gene. Jail or the truth?"

"Okay. So if I tell you what you want to hear, that warrant goes away?"

"No and no. One, you tell me the truth, not 'what I want to hear.' And two, I can't make that warrant go away. I'm just not going to take you in for it now."

"But some other cop—"

Ott put up his hands. "I can't control what some other cop's gonna do."

"But you're not gonna tell another cop to go and arrest me."

Ott shook his head. "No, I'm not."

Rossiter had another think. "All right," he said slowly, "this guy put me up to it."

"'This guy'? Come on, Gene. Details? What did *this guy* tell you to say? How much did he pay you? And what's his name?"

"Never told me his name," Rossiter said. "Told me to say I saw that detective and the woman who got killed in here the night before her murder. That I saw a photo of her on the news and a newsreel of Crawford investigating the murder at her house the day they found her."

"But you've never seen either one of them before. Ever?"

Rossiter exhaled deeply. "No, never have."

'And, this guy, the guy who put you up to it, what did he look like?"

"No clue. It was all done by phone."

Ott almost asked for the caller's number, then figured Giles Simpson would have been smart enough to use a burner phone.

"And the money?"

"A messenger brought it to me."

"How much?"

"Three thousand in cash."

Ott nodded slowly. "Okay, don't you feel better now?"

"What do you mean?"

"Well, you got that off your chest," Ott said, "and you know what they say, Gene: the truth'll set you free."

CHAPTER FIFTY-EIGHT

The cleaning lady turned out to be a well-dressed black woman with red-dyed hair. Ott had gotten her number from Rutledge, called her, and asked her to come into the station. She sashayed back into Ott's cubicle wearing a cream-colored skirt, a silk polka-dot collared top, and a bright red scarf around her neck. Ott stood and motioned to the chair next to his.

"Thanks for coming in, Pearline," Ott said, sitting down, and leaning back in his chair.

"Anything to help the po-lice," she said.

"Well, that's exactly what I want to talk to you about," Ott said. "What you've done is just the opposite. You harmed the police. One, in particular."

"I'm not quite sure I—"

"Let me make it clear to you. You claimed you saw a man where you worked as a housekeeper, at the Simpsons' house on Jungle. That man is my partner, Detective Crawford, who's never been to that house on Jungle except to investigate Ms. Simpson's murder." Ott fished the photo of Crawford out of his jacket pocket. "This is Detective Crawford, a man you've never seen before except maybe on TV news."

"He's a handsome man," Pearline said.

"I'll tell him you said that," Ott said. "So now let's talk about you retracting what you said about seeing him at Ms. Simpson's house. No, let's *first* talk about what could happen to you for committing perjury—" he was winging it now—"a crime punishable by up to five years in federal prison. You ever been to federal prison, Pearline?"

She shook her head.

"No, of course you haven't. Trust me, you wouldn't like it there. But that's where you're headed if you don't tell me what really happened."

"But... that man might do something to me if—"

"No, Pearline. If *that man's* in jail, he can't do a damn thing to you."

She was silent for a few long moments, then nervously, she scratched the side of her face.

"Well, there *was* a man there," she protested weakly.

Ott thrust the photo of Crawford in her face again. "This man?"

"Well, ah, no," she said, her voice just barely above a whisper.

"How 'bout this man?" Ott said, showing her a photo Crawford had taken of Crispin Baylis.

Pearline shook her head. "No, I never seen him before in my life."

Ott handed her another photo. It was of Giles Simpson, taken from the website of his orthopedic practice. "How 'bout him?"

"That's Dr. Simpson," she said.

"I know. The man who put you up to this. Told you to say you saw Detective Crawford here and gave you the five grand."

Pearline shifted from one leg to the other. "You know, actually he said the five thousand was pay in advance."

Ott's eyes seem to darken. "What are you saying? 'Pay in advance.'"

"For cleaning. He said it 'cause Mrs. Simpson and he weren't gonna be around that much. You know, 'cause they'd be up in New York. So he'd just pay me in advance."

"And you just remembered that?"

"Yes... yes, I did."

The guy was slick, Ott realized, very slick. Covered his ass nicely.

"Did you *forget* anything else, Pearline?" Ott asked.

"I don't think so."

"But Mr. Simpson definitely told you to say you saw Detective Crawford here?"

"Yes, he did."

"Why do you think he'd ask you to say that when he knew it wasn't true?"

Pearline glanced away from Ott's riveting stare. "I—I don't know."

Ott decided he was going to ask Simpson himself.

"Okay, Pearline, you're free to go. I may need you to come back in and sign a sworn statement attesting to what we just discussed."

Pearline's eyes nervously raked the room. "Oh, o-kay."

"And the last thing you want to do is lie again." Ott said and caught her eyes flitting away from his. "Or else, what?"

"Ah, I might be sentenced to five years in federal prison for perjury."

"No, Pearline, not *you might*, you *will* be sentenced to five years in federal prison for perjury."

CHAPTER FIFTY-NINE

Crawford was in his office, fidgeting with a few bills he needed to pay and wondering how Ott was faring, when his cell phone rang.

He looked down at the iPhone display. It said UNKNOWN, as it had the time Simpson called before. "What do you want, Simpson?"

"The name is Beelzebub," the disturbingly bizarre voice cackled, almost as if he was channeling Boris Karloff in an echo chamber.

"Oh Christ, Simpson, how hokey can you get?"

"I just want to share a few memories with you, Charlie. I don't know about you, but I love it when they fight."

"What the hell are you talking about?"

"Oh, she was a wild one, Charlie. That last time I saw her. It's so much fun when they're biting and kicking and trying to scratch your eyeballs out. Trying to scream, but they can't 'cause you got your hand over their mouth. Man, I tell ya, it was a hell of a rush, Charlie, a *real* turn-on."

Crawford was seething. "You raped her, didn't you? Before you killed her, you raped her," he finished, his throat dry.

"I'm not the kind of man who kisses and tells, Charlie."

"You're a pig. A total fuckin' pig."

"Okay, Charlie, calm down. It was just the heat of passion. Two people who—"

Crawford hung up. His whole body was shaking. If Giles Simpson was there, he would have broken every bone in his body.

Ott walked in just as Crawford was about to hurl his lamp across the room.

"Whoa," Ott said, seeing the look in his partner's eyes, "you okay, bro?"

"I just had a conversation with that scumbag, Simpson. He told me about raping Jill before he killed her. How it was such…" He couldn't finish.

"Like I said, he's one sick bastard, man."

"Yeah, problem is, he's twelve hundred miles away and we got nothing but a Mercedes odometer on him," Crawford said, his hand still gripping his lamp like he was going to crush it. "You talk to those two?"

"Yeah, you're in the clear. They admitted to being *mistaken* in their identification of you. I saw that reporter, Sue Bonner, outside the building. She's gonna go interview them."

Crawford stood up and bought his arm around Ott's shoulder. "Thanks, man. I really appreciate it."

"No problem," Ott said. "So back to Simpson, I asked you this before, is he just trying to torture you? I mean, what is the deal?"

Crawford shrugged. "You know pretty much everything I do. Except there was one thing Jill's mother told me."

"What was that?"

"Jill asked her once what she thought of the idea of seeing if I had any interest in getting back together."

"You mean, divorcing Simpson and re-marrying you?"

"Yeah, that was the gist of it."

Ott shrugged. "So there it is: Simpson thought she was down here so she could get back together with you."

"Yeah, but there're three problems with that: It was Simpson who wanted to buy the house here, not Jill. At least that was what it sounded like to me. And two, in the entire time she was here, she never once tried to come see me or get together. You know, never said, 'Hey, let's have drinks or dinner' or something."

"So? Maybe she was planning to. Or, at least, Simpson thought she was going to."

"Maybe. Or she just changed her mind about trying to get back together. Don't forget Crispin Baylis was also in the picture."

Ott nodded. "Yeah, that's true. But seems like Simpson might have found out about Jill thinking of asking you to get back together at some point anyway."

"I guess," Crawford said, "but hang on: Number three is they were getting divorced anyway."

"That's easy," Ott said. "Money. You said she had a good prenup. But kill her and she gets nada."

"Yeah, I know, but it falls short of actual proof," Crawford said and exhaled. "All right, you got me *off* the hook, Mort. Question is, how are we gonna get Simpson *on* it?"

Ott tapped the side of his chair. "I don't know, man, as I said before, this case reminds me so much of Ward Jaynes."

"Who we knew did it early on. I was thinking the same thing. Big difference is Ward Jaynes actually confessed."

"Yeah, just to bait you," Ott said. "But sounds like Simpson has, too."

Crawford nodded very slowly. "I don't know what we can do at this point, I just don't know."

Ott nodded. "It feels like we've never been at this point before. A dead end, I mean."

Crawford leaned back, closed his eyes, and nodded.

CHAPTER SIXTY

Ott got Giles Simpson's number from Crawford and went back to his cubicle and dialed him on his cell.

Simpson answered right away. "Hello."

"Simpson, it's Mort Ott, Palm Beach Police."

"Why, yes, Mort. To what do I owe the pleasure?"

"Calling about you trying to frame my partner for the murder of your wife."

"I have absolutely no idea what you're talking about."

"Pearline, your cleaning lady, said she never saw Charlie Crawford at your house. Told me you paid her five grand to say you did."

No hesitation. "The only five grand Pearline White ever got from me was what I paid in advance to clean my house for a year."

"Her accusation was that she saw Crawford in your house the day Jill was killed."

A slight hesitation. "Okay, so I bent the truth a little. So shoot me—" he laughed—"Better not say that, you just might."

"Why'd you tell her to say that?"

"Well, I'll tell you why, Mort. See, I wanted to make a case for my divorce that Jill was cheating on me. 'Cause she was. There was some artist, and I'm pretty sure Crawford, too."

"You're dead wrong about that, Simpson. That's not Charlie's style."

"That's your story."

"Good-bye."

As Ott had figured out long before, the guy was slick. Very slick.

*****

Later that day, Crawford got a call from Mike Visconti, his old boss in New York.

It was just past five in the afternoon.

"Got something for you, Charlie," Visconti said. "That guy Simpson—"

Crawford jumped almost like someone had goosed him. "Yeah?"

"A woman filed an assault charge against him."

"Jesus. When? Where?"

"Last night. Her place down on Bank Street in the West Village. Said he beat her up. Accused her of two-timing him or some shit. She called it in after he left. Said when he took off, he told her, 'Do it again and you might end up like my wife.'"

"Sounds just like the guy," Crawford said. "So where's Bank Street, the 5th Precinct?"

"Yeah, the guy investigating filled me in on the whole thing."

"I can't thank you enough, man," Crawford said. "So one more thing I need—"

"Sharon Hufty." Visconti followed with the woman's phone number.

"Thanks, man, always one step ahead of me," Crawford said. "So was Simpson arrested?"

"He would have been if they found him," Visconti said. "They tried his co-op up on Park Avenue and his office, but nada. Office said they were expecting him first thing in the morning for a procedure, but he was a no-show."

"Really?"

Crawford's mind went racing ahead. So if Simpson were trying to avoid arrest in New York, Crawford thought, where would he go? His house in Palm Beach was a good choice. New York cops weren't likely to pursue a first-time assault suspect all the way to Florida.

"Anyway, I knew you'd want to know," Visconti said.

"Damn right. Hey, thanks a million. You hear anything else—"

"You'll be the first to know."

"Cool. Stay well."

"You got it," Visconti said and clicked off.

Crawford called the garage in New York that he had visited the week before with Officer Bisbee. It turned out that Giles Simpson had gone there and picked up his car the night before at 8:48 p.m.. Probably not long after beating up Sharon Hufty.

He could already be in Palm Beach. Or soon to arrive.

*****

He went straight to Ott's cubicle and told him about the conversation with Visconti. He had a burning question for Ott. "How do I get into the evidence room?"

"You don't know?"

"No, I've never had to get anything from there."

"Just so happens, I got a key," Ott said, waggling his heavy brows.

"I thought you couldn't go in there without a tech."

Ott tapped a pen on his desk. "Yeah, but what have I always told you, Charlie?"

"I don't know, lots of stuff."

"Yeah, exactly, and high on the list is the memorable 'Rules are meant to be broken.'"

Crawford signaled with his hand. "Come on, then. I need to check Jill's locker. Is it gonna be locked?"

"Yeah, and there's a camera there. But that's no problem."

"Why do you say that?"

"'Cause, like I said, I got a key and can block the camera with either my meaty hand or my substantial body."

They walked down to the evidence room, which was in the basement of the station house. Ott reached into his pocket, pulled out his key chain, selected a large silver key and opened the gray metal door.

Crawford smiled broadly. "You da man."

"What specifically are you looking for?"

Crawford looked him in the eyes. "You don't need to know."

Ott frowned. "You mean, you and I've got secrets now?"

"Just *a* secret," Crawford said, spotting what he was looking for.

He pointed across the room. "Look away," he said.

"What?"

"Look over there."

Ott did as he was told, and Crawford quickly picked up something and slipped it into his pocket.

"What did you do?" Ott asked, still looking away.

"That's the secret."

"Oh, Christ, Charlie," Ott said, then he looked down at his watch. "Hey, it's seven o'clock, time to go get a pop at Mookie's. I'm buyin' and, hell, I'll throw in dinner, too."

"At Mookie's?"

"No, man, the shit there's inedible. Maybe go to Duffy's, get a bite, catch a game on the tube?"

"Thanks, but I got an errand to run."

"Well, then, after that."

"Nah, sorry, might take a while."

Ott scratched his chin. "You're being awfully mysterious."

Crawford nodded. "What do you expect? We're in the mystery business."

CHAPTER SIXTY-ONE

Crawford took a right onto Jungle Road in his Lexus a little later. If Giles Simpson was at his house the last thing Crawford wanted him to see was his Crown Vic. A vehicle that screamed Palm Beach Police. He didn't slow down as he passed Simpson's house or even look to his side. But his peripheral vision saw nothing in the driveway.

An hour later, he came back. Nothing again.

Then at just past 8:00, he pulled into Jungle again, and this time there it was: a shiny, black Mercedes with New York plates. He imagined the dead bugs on the front windshield from the long drive down. He drove to the end of the street, then turned around and kept going past Simpson's house.

Crawford went back to his office and made two calls.

The first was to the woman who had been assaulted by Giles Simpson.

Sharon Hufty sounded vengeful, like she wanted to do whatever possible to put Simpson behind bars. "This was actually the second time. The first time he just slapped me, but really hard."

"But this time," Crawford said, "as I understand it, it was a number of blows."

"Blows? How about really hard punches, with his fist closed?" Sharon said. "I mean, he was just out of control. Like some kind of switch had been flipped. He's a very dangerous man, Detective."

"I know that," Crawford said, deciding not to tell her what his relationship with Jill was. "Well, thank you very much. If we need you to testify in our case in Florida against him, would you?"

"In a heartbeat," Sharon said. "That monster needs to be put away."

His next call was to the ADA who would serve as prosecuting attorney on the Jill Simpson case, when and if, they had enough evidence to move forward. Crawford was optimistic the prosecutor would decide the case had enough merit to pursue it now, particularly after he told him about the Sharon Hufty assault in New York.

He was wrong.

"I mean, what do you want me to say, Charlie?" the prosecutor said after he told Crawford there was not enough there.

Crawford raised his hands. "That it's a clear pattern: the guy habitually beats up women and one time he killed one," he said, vehemently.

"Okay, that all may be true," the prosecutor said, "but it's still not enough to pin premeditated murder on him. I just can't make that stick. Not only that, but from what you've told me about the guy, he's got the means to hire the best defense lawyer around."

"So?"

"So, we'd lose."

Crawford kept insisting until he plainly saw he wasn't getting anywhere, then thanked the prosecutor, clicked off, and let out a long, harrowing sigh.

Then he reached into his desk drawer for the bag of things he'd bought in Charleston.

*****

Giles Simpson's Mercedes was not in his driveway on Jungle Road at just past 9:00 p.m. Crawford drove past the house again and this time parked at the end of the street. He just sat for a few moments and thought. Then he got out of his Lexus, walked up to Simpson's house, put on his vinyl gloves, took out the key he had filched from the evidence locker, unlocked the front door, and walked into the house.

In the foyer was a coat closet where he first thought about hiding. But then he walked into the living room and saw thick silk floor-to-ceiling curtains on all four bay windows. Even better. He got behind one and put on the mask.

He had no idea how long a wait he'd have. For all he knew it might be a late one. Knowing what he knew about Simpson, the man might have a girlfriend in Palm Beach he was wining and dining. Nothing would surprise Crawford about the man. It had gotten very personal.

He looked at his watch a little later. 9:35 p.m.

He rehearsed his hastily conceived plan. There was not much to it. He remembered back to the next-to-last time he saw Jill; it was a few days before he left New York for good. He reminisced a little and saw her beautiful, smiling face. The one that Giles Simpson had…

He looked at his watch again. 10:05 p.m.

Then he heard the crunching of car tires on the chattahoochee pebble driveway.

A few moments later he heard a key in the front door, then the door opened, and he heard footsteps on the hardwood floor in the foyer. God, what if he had a woman with him! But he heard no voices. He just heard the click of a light switch and footsteps coming into the living room. He rushed out from behind the curtain, his right fist raised.

Before Simpson could react, Crawford landed a ferocious punch on Simpson's cheekbone.

Then another, then another, then he missed with one, then landed an uppercut to Simpson's chin. Simpson straightened and Crawford drew back his left hand and smashed his fist into Simpson's nose. The distinct cracking sound and Simpson's loud cry of pain told Crawford he had broken it.

But he was only warming up. He charged the wobbly Simpson and head-butted him, again on the chin. Simpson's howl was so loud, Crawford worried it would wake the neighbors. If so, he only had five minutes until one of his fellow cops could come barreling into the driveway.

Simpson was shaky now, barely standing. Crawford swung hard and connected with the side of his head.

Simpson went down on the hard wood floor with a thud.

Crawford lined up a kick and swung away. It was a direct hit, smack into Simpson's ribs. He reared back his leg and kicked again. A loud guttural *uhhh* came out of the body below him.

`Finally a muffled, "Jesus, stop, please stop!"

But Crawford, remembering Simpson's phone calls, kicked him again with his right foot. Even harder. Then he drew his left foot back aiming for Simpson's head. But he stopped, thinking he might kill the man.

Simpson's eyes were shut now, and he was breathing in heavy spasms. He seemed to be out cold. For one moment, Crawford pictured Jill's face, then kicked the doctor once more, for good measure. Really hard.

He listened for a few more moments. Nothing.

Giles Simpson, dressed in khakis and a dark pull-over sweater, was lying on the white herringbone hardwood floor, his head off to one side like a rag doll, blood streaming out of his nose and mouth.

Crawford took silent satisfaction that Simpson looked worse than Jill had, lying on the same floor several weeks before.

He looked at his hands, expecting to see that the vinyl gloves were ripped on the knuckles. But, surprising, they weren't. Just bloody as hell.

He started to walk away but had a quick flash. He took two steps over to Simpson's prostrate body and, with all he could muster, stomped down hard on one hand of Simpson's. It made a sickly crackling sound. Then he did the same to the other one. He almost wanted to say aloud, 'okay, Giles, how you plan on operating now with busted up hands like those?' but kept it to himself.

Then he had another thought... a sinister, ungodly one. With his right foot he viciously booted Simpson in the groin. Again. And again. And, what the hell... one last time just as hard as he possibly could.

Then he walked to the far wall, reached up, and lifted a Matisse painting of two dancers dressed in red off the wall. He walked through the living room into the foyer and on his way out caught a glimpse of himself in a gold-framed mirror.

Bad hair and all, Donald Trump seemed to be flashing a smile of contentment.

CHAPTER SIXTY-TWO

He got to Ott's house in West Palm at a little before 11:15 and walked in the open door.

He knew Ott never got to bed much before midnight. Ott, beer in hand, was watching Jimmy Kimmel do his opening monologue.

"Hey, Charlie," Ott said. "Grab a beer."

Crawford was already in Ott's kitchen. "Finished up my errand and just thought we'd have a pop and shoot the shit a little."

It was not that unusual for Ott to show up out of the blue at Crawford's apartment or Crawford to drop by Ott's house, where they'd talk about their latest case or just shoot the breeze.

"Everything go okay?" Ott asked.

Crawford thought for a second. "Oh, my errand. Yeah, just fine."

Ott nodded and looked back at the TV.

"By the way, I got here at around eight o'clock tonight," Crawford said. "Refresh my memory, what did we watch on the tube?"

Ott smiled. "Well, we caught the second half of *The Resident* on Fox, which kinda sucked, followed by *NCIS*, which was okay, then a little local news," he said, pointing at his Samsung. "And now, my man Jimmy."

Crawford asked Ott to walk him through what happened in each of the shows and Ott gave him basic plot summaries.

Crawford nodded when he was done. "And don't forget, I brought over a sausage, pepperoni, and onion pie I had in my freezer," he told his partner.

"Yeah, which also kinda sucked," Ott said, with a smile. "Tasted like goddamn cardboard."

"I thought it was pretty tasty," Crawford said.

He could see the look on Ott's face he had seen so many times before. His partner was dying to know what he'd really been up to.

CHAPTER SIXTY-THREE

Ott figured out what his partner's "errand" had been when Pearline, the housekeeper at the Simpson house on Jungle Road, called Palm Beach police to report the theft of a small, but very valuable, Matisse painting. This was the morning after Giles Simpson had been taken to Good Samaritan hospital in an ambulance with a wailing siren so loud it woke the neighbors on Jungle.

He and Crawford didn't catch the Giles Simpson assault case for the simple reason that it wasn't a homicide. Pretty close, though.

Turned out that Simpson had thirty-five stitches in his mouth, nose, and right cheek, a broken left arm, internal bleeding, a concussion, and five broken ribs. Crawford wished it had been worse but didn't choose to share that sentiment with anyone.

Upon hearing about the incident, Rutledge called Crawford and Ott into his office. He was wearing the brown suit with what looked like an old mustard stain on it.

"Did you wear that to a baseball game, Norm?" Ott asked, pointing to the stain.

Rutledge looked down at it. "I don't know where that came from," he said, then turned all-business. "All right, so what do you guys know about Giles Simpson?"

Crawford shrugged. "Only what I read in the paper."

"Yeah, poor bastard got the shit beat out of him," Ott said.

Rutledge pointedly turned to Crawford. "Yeah, he sure did, didn't he? I heard his hands got really destroyed."

"I don't know, Netzker's the one you should be talking to," Crawford said, referring to the head burglary detective. "It's his case."

"Sounds like the burglar went back for a second dip," Ott said. "Simpson should never have told that reporter he was lucky the burglar didn't take his Matisse."

Rutledge nodded. "Yeah, guess that was an invitation for the guy to go back a second time." He laced his fingers together behind his head. "So, looks like you boys are going 9 and 1."

"What?" said Crawford, then he got it: he and Ott had together solved 9 murders, but not their 10th.

"Hey, Norm, relax," Ott said, "sucker's not even in the cold-case file yet. We'll get the guy."

Crawford still hadn't figured out what he was going to do with the Matisse. It would look awfully good in his living room at the Trianon. He could say it was a Crispin Baylis knock-off. But finally, he decided he was going to drop it off in some public place, like the library on Clematis or maybe the Norton Art Museum. That would be fitting.

It would be discovered and whoever found it would know right away it was the stolen Matisse that had been in the news. Netzker and his men in burglary would probably assume that the burglar couldn't unload the painting because it was too hot. Then Giles Simpson could come and pick it up when he got out of the hospital.

"Where is Simpson, anyway?" Rutledge asked. "What hospital, I mean?"

"Good Sam," said Ott.

"I heard he's gonna be there for like two weeks or more," Rutledge said.

Crawford nodded. "Yeah, he's got all kinds of nasty bumps and bruises."

Rutledge put his feet up on his desk. "Aw... the poor baby," he said, turning to Crawford. "I'm thinkin' you really oughta send him a get-well-soon card. You know, we all sign it."

"Yeah, and I could swing by Publix," said Ott, "pick him up one of those nice twelve-dollar carnation bouquets they got there."

THE END

DYING FOR A COCKTAIL

Exclusive sample from Savannah Sleuth Sisters Murder Mysteries Book 3

CHAPTER ONE

Ryder Farrell, who could be very convincing when she wanted to be, was trying as hard as she could to talk her sister, Jackie, into opening a satellite office of Savannah Investigations in Charleston, South Carolina. She started working on Jackie after they'd both had had a couple of Texas Margarita's at Jalapenas in Sandfly outside of Savannah.

Ryder knew from experience that after a few stiff Marg's under her belt, Jackie was more apt to say yes to things that she might balk at if she was stone-cold sober. Case in point, Jackie had agreed to give her sister a raise after Happy Hour at Jalapenas. Then, a few months later, after the two knocked back a jeroboam of Whispering Angel celebrating Jackie's thirty-first, Ryder had talked her sister into buying new furniture for what they laughingly called their Savannah "world headquarters". It was long overdue because when Jackie had started out on a shoestring it was furnished with scratch 'n dent specials from Haverty's and a few homely gems from the Salvation Army.

"It' like... you know how doctors have a few different offices— like in Pooler, Richmond Hill, Garden City. Thunderbolt—"

"Thunderbolt? Where the hell's that?"

Ryder shrugged. "I don't really know. Around here somewhere. Anyway, you get the concept, right? A satellite office."

Jackie nodded. "Yeah. Where are you going with this?"

Ryder took a prodigious pull on her Texas Margarita.

"I told you, I think we should open a branch of Savannah Investigations in Charleston."

"Charleston? It's two hours away. Why?"

"For one thing, we'd have double the number of homicides."

Jackie smiled knowingly. "And for another, Beau is there."

"Well, yeah, but…"

"But what?"

Ryder shrugged. "Who knows whether that's gonna last or not."

"Why wouldn't it?"

"'Cause the guy's the biggest flirt I've ever met," Ryder said, putting up a hand. "Don't try to change the subject. See, the main reason would be so we could work on murder exclusively instead of taking on cheating husband cases, or missing persons, stuff that neither of us wants to do."

Jackie squinted and didn't say anything.

Ryder kept going, figuring the hook was at least half in. "Plus, I don't know about you, but I think they're more things to do up in Charleston. Better restaurants, museums, you know, *cult-chah*. We both could use a little culture."

"Has Beau been introducing you to this *cult-chah*?"

"The only culture Beau knows about is in the bedroom."

Jackie held up her hands. "Okay, okay, TMI."

"Sorry," Ryder said. "So, what do you think?"

"I think I'll think about it."

*****

And she had, and miraculously, she agreed to opening a Charleston office. Savannah would still be the main office, but one or both would go up to Charleston occasionally. Specifically, when they landed a homicide. They both agreed that they would turn down jobs that were not murder cases, which would eliminate a fair amount of the previous year's income. They figured if it didn't work out and there wasn't enough murder to pay the rent and allow them to eat, they could always go back to chasing cheating husbands to no-tell motels. Then, when they got no calls for a solid two weeks, they decided that in addition to homicides, they would at least consider the occasional missing person case.

The office they settled on in Charleston was dingy and had low ceilings, and with it, they inherited furniture from Habitat for Humanity and a Calhoun Street tag sale. So, they ordered a 30-yard dumpster, chucked everything, and spent half a day up in North Charleston outfitting their new space with furniture from two stores called Celadon and At Home. Fashion-forward it was not; functional it was.

Speaking of which, though the office had a King Street address, it was not the chic part of King Street, but a mile or two north of where the Charleston debs and fashionista's shop and strut their stuff.

Their three-room office was on the second floor of a loft building, and Jackie's office was almost double the size of her sister's, which got Ryder bellyaching from the git-go, but Jackie was, theoretically, the boss and, in fact, the one who paid the bills. The third room served as a waiting area, which had a telephone booth-sized reception space manned by a natty, two-hundred-fifty-pound black man by the name of Wendell (pronounced wen- DEL,) whose shoulders practically touched the walls on either side of him.

It was just past ten in the morning, a week after C.I. hung out its shingle, when the front door opened, and Wendell glanced up at a well-dressed woman. Things were slow, which was to say murder-free in Savannah at the moment, so both Jackie and Ryder were in the Charleston office, looking for something to do.

The woman, in her mid-forties, was wearing a stylish, cream-colored pencil skirt, a blue silk blouse, and Tory Burch flats.

"Mrs. Roberts?" Wendell asked.

The woman nodded. "Yes, here to see Jackie Farrell," she said.

"I'll let her know you're here," Wendell said.

The woman frowned. "*Her?*"

"Yes," Wendell said, "you'll be meeting with Jackie and her associate, Ryder."

The frown was still there. "I just assumed Jackie was a man."

"Nope."

Mrs. Roberts nodded, apparently satisfied that at least Ryder was a man.

Wendell got up and went and knocked on the door to Jackie's office.

"Yes, Wendell."

The big man opened the door. "Mrs. Roberts is here," he said, then lowering his voice. "You being of the female persuasion got what I'd call a negative reaction."

Jackie pinched off a smile and stood up.

"Tell Ryder, will you."

Wendell nodded.

"Thanks," Jackie said, going through her door into the waiting room. "Hello, Mrs. Roberts, I'm Jackie Farrell."

Jessica Roberts looked up from the waiting room's *Garden & Gun* magazine and rebooted her frown. Clearly, she didn't expect anybody so pretty and well-dressed to be a private investigator.

"Would you follow me back to my office, please?" Jackie asked.

"Sure," said Jessica.

"We're going to be joined by my associate," Jackie said, holding the door for Jessica.

"So I understand," Jessica said, taking in Jackie's office, which had three framed posters from old Gary Cooper movies on the walls that gave it some pizazz.

Ryder walked in wearing blue jeans with a tear in the right mid-thigh, electric lime Nikes, and a white T-shirt so snug it looked like it made breathing a challenge.

Jessica Roberts didn't look impressed with her wardrobe or her gender.

"Mrs. Roberts, this is my associate, Ryder," Jackie said.

"So, you're not only a female," Jessica said to Ryder, "but a teenager at that."

Ryder extended her hand and stifled a sigh. "That's flattering, Mrs. Roberts, but I'm twenty-six," she said, going for a world-weary tone she felt appropriate for a PI.

Jessica Roberts just nodded and eyeballed the rip in Ryder's blue jeans.

"When I called here and spoke to—I guess, that gentleman out front—I wasn't expecting, the Number 1 Ladies Detective Agency," Jessica said.

"The what?" Ryder asked.

Jackie smiled. "Mrs. Roberts is referring to a book about a woman who started a detective agency in Uganda," she said. "They made a movie of it, too."

"Oh, right," Ryder said, vaguely remembering it.

"It was Botswana, actually," Jessica said.

"My error," Jackie said. "So, Mrs. Roberts, clearly, we're both women...does that disqualify us from being of service to you."

Jessica shook her head, emphatically, like she didn't want to be accused of being a traitor to her sex. "Oh, no, not at all. I just didn't know, is all."

"I mean, there are other investigation companies which employ men," Jackie had the rap down. "In fact, most of them do... if that's what you want."

It came off as, 'if you want to stoop so low.'

"No, no," Jessica said, "let's just get past this and talk about why I came?"

"Oh course," Jackie said, "we're all ears."

"Okay," Jessica said, "are you familiar with the name Roland Roberts, my late husband?"

Ryder shook her head.

Jackie nodded. "Yes, I am, I didn't make the connection."

She had read about his murder when she was in Savannah. It was front-page news for close to a week.

"No reason why you would," Jessica said, turning to Ryder. "My husband was murdered six months ago. The police haven't found the killer. It's now a 'cold case,' though they don't officially call it that. They tell me it's still active, but, in reality, I'm convinced they're not really working on it."

"He was shot in his office, as I recall," Jackie said. "On Broad Street. Three shots from a semi-automatic, wasn't it?"

"Four, actually," Jessica said. "He was working late. It happened around eight at night."

Jackie remembered reading that a tipped-over bottle of bourbon with three glasses was found on Roberts' desk when the homicide detectives got there.

"I remember it pretty well," Jackie said. "Your husband was a very prominent real estate developer. As I recall, he had just been found innocent in a hit-and-run?"

Jessica frowned. "It wasn't a hit-and-run. Roland turned himself in right after it happened—" Jackie seemed to remember it was more like three or four hours later—"and the main suspect in Roland's murder was the father of the girl who was killed."

"Because he threatened to kill your husband. In court, right? After the innocent verdict was announced?" Jackie asked.

Jessica nodded. "And a week later Roland was dead. Come to your own conclusion."

"So, are you saying you think the father did it?"

"Actually, I don't really know," Mrs. Roberts said. "At first, I figured who else could it be? But the lead detective told me he was almost positive it wasn't him."

"The father's last name was something like Jennings, wasn't it?" Jackie asked.

"You have a good memory," Jessica said. "Jenner. Charles Jenner."

"So, what exactly would you like us to do that the police haven't?" Jackie asked, glancing over at Ryder whose foot was tapping restlessly.

"I'd like you to solve it," Jessica said. "Just like that case I read about on your website. That soap opera star who was killed up in New York."

They had gotten a lot of mileage out of the Philomena Soames murder.

"Well, of course, if we take it, our objective would be to solve it. We just need to be convinced that we can bring something to the table that the Charleston homicide detectives couldn't," Jackie said, suddenly conscious of the 'are you eff-ing kidding me?' look her sister was drilling into her. She knew Ryder was thinking, *come on, girl, lose the 'if we take it' BS. We need the damned work!*

"The detectives just came up with the one suspect," Jessica said. "Then when they couldn't get anything on him, they just kind of ran out of steam."

"In fairness to the police department here, they're usually pretty dogged," Jackie said. It was a pure guess. "Tell us about your husband, will you?"

"Well, as you said, Roland was a prominent real estate developer," Jessica said, "Also, very active with a lot of charities, not to mention an alderman at our church."

Jackie nodded. Ryder yawned.

"But what was he *like*?" Ryder suddenly piped in.

The question jolted Jackie because she had told Ryder before the meeting to just listen and observe, since this was their first meeting with a prospective client in Charleston and her sister could sometimes—no, frequently— be a bit of a loose cannon. She knew, though, that Ryder couldn't stay quiet for long.

"Well, for starters, Roland was an extremely intelligent man," Jessica said. "Like number three in his class at Carolina. He worked hard and became very successful. Roland was also starting half back on the Gamecocks football team for three years and used to love to hunt and fish, too. I don't know what else you want to know?"

"What a Gamecock is?" Ryder blurted.

Jackie wanted to jam a tube sock in her sister's mouth.

Jessica looked at Ryder in disbelief but didn't say anything.

"Ryder moved down here just a little while back," Jackie explained. "Used to be with our New York affiliate—" then to Ryder— "a Gamecock is the mascot for the University of South Carolina football team."

Ryder was undeterred. "Mrs. Roberts, let me ask you a question, is it possible that your husband might have been involved in an extra marital affair?"

Jesus... where in God's name did that come from? Jackie had forgotten just *how much* of a loose cannon her sister could be.

But Jessica took the question in stride. Like she might have been asked it before.

"Possibly," she said. "We were married for twenty-one years. He was away a fair amount and clearly... women found him attractive."

"Did it occur to you that if your husband *was* having an affair, that the boyfriend or husband of the woman he was having the affair with... would be a logical suspect?" Ryder shrugged. "I mean, it happens quite often."

Like she had any firsthand knowledge whatsoever about what she was talking about, thought Jackie. She knew where it came from, though. When Ryder had first started out, less than a year ago, Jackie had recommended that Ryder read a few detective novels— instead of her usual chick-lit trash— as part of her on-the-job-training. Sure, it was just fiction, but at least it was a good intro to the vernacular. Turned out Ryder blew through everything by Michael Connelly, most of James Lee Burke and half of Elmore Leonard in a few weeks. It was safe to say, she had lots of plots dancing in her head. And a whole new vocabulary. Some of it a little dated, though.

"I guess that makes sense," Jessica said, nodding. "That it could be a boyfriend or a husband... if Roland actually was seeing someone."

"And if he *was* seeing someone, do you have any idea who it might be?" Ryder asked.

"No."

Jackie had her mouth open ready to speak but Ryder cut her off.

"Did you ever find any evidence at all that indicated your husband might, in fact, be having an affair?" Ryder asked. "You know, an email maybe? A whiff of perfume? A receipt from a hotel? Anything at all like that?"

"No," Jessica said.

Jackie wanted the floor back and opened her mouth again—

"That strikes me as a tentative 'no', Mrs. Roberts," Ryder said.

"A no is a no."

"You're sure?"

Jackie put up a hand to her sister and clawed her way back into the conversation. "Hang on a second. You understand, Mrs. Roberts, that my associate is simply pursuing one of the most common scenarios. A spouse being killed by the other spouse's—"

"I get that," Jessica said, turning to Jackie. "Now, let me ask you a question."

"Sure," Jackie said, "go right ahead."

"You keep referring to Ryder as your 'associate,'" Mrs Roberts said. "Isn't she actually... your sister?"

"How do you know that?" Jackie asked, feeling a sudden urge to deny it.

"Well, for starters, you both have the same eyes," Jessica said. "And also, you both seem a little..."

"What?"

"I don't know.... intense maybe."

CHAPTER TWO

Intense was not quite accurate but not way off the mark either. In Jackie's case, more like determined and persistent, but balanced by a distinct soft and feminine side. Ryder, unquestionably, was a woman with strong opinions, and never timid about voicing them. So, intense was pretty close. When it came to looks— except for the eyes— the two couldn't be more different. Ryder was a stunning five foot eight, though she looked taller, and had long mahogany brown hair, high cheekbones, and a laugh you could hear across the street. Not to mention a mouth on her that sometimes made her sister cringe. Jackie was a pretty five-two, with dirty blonde hair and an unblinking, watchful gaze.

Using her sister's middle name was actually Jackie's idea. They were born Jacqueline Nichols Farrell and Alexandra Ryder Farrell, but Jackie didn't think Savannah—and now Charleston— was ready for a private investigation firm whose PI's had names that sounded like they were interior decorators. Or ladies who lunched.

Jackie also pointed out to Ryder that "half the women in the south" had last names for first names anyway. Ryder said, oh, yeah, like who? Jackie had to think for a second, but—English major she was— came up with Harper Lee and Flannery O'Connor.

In any case, Jessica Roberts retained Charleston Investigations to find her husband's killer. What clinched it was when she asked Jackie a question about the Philomena Soames murder case that she had read about on the Charleston Investigations website. That was the reason why she had called CI in the first place and was apparently impressed by how Jackie had handled and, ultimately, solved the case.

"So, anyway, Mrs. Roberts," Jackie said, "I bill out at a hundred dollars an hour, my associate—" she flipped her hand at Ryder— "seventy-five. Plus fifty cents a mile in car fare. Just so you know, the competition charges seventy to eighty an hour and forty-five cents a mile. We will need a three-thousand-dollar retainer, none of which is refundable. I'm from the school of, 'you get what you pay for,' but, of course, you'll come to your own conclusion."

Jessica Roberts nodded. "I'm from the same school," she said. "And your terms are acceptable. But I'm still curious... why you came here from Charleston?"

Jackie chuckled. "Ask my sister."

"Well, I met a man... who turned out to be a douche," Ryder said.

Jackie wanted to bitch slap her. "I apologize for my associate's unprofessionalism, Mrs. Roberts. Now if you would write us a check we can get started right away."

Jessica wrote a check, shook their hands, and left.

Standing in the Charleston Investigations reception area, Ryder said. "I like this new office. I think it's gonna be fun here."

"Ryder," Jackie said, "let me point out a few things. First, it's just a job, not something that's supposed to be fun."

"Well, aren't some jobs fun?" Ryder asked. "Not that I'd know, since that ad agency job of mine was the most *un-fun* thing I've ever done in my short, boring life."

"There you go," Jackie said. "Second thing, let me ask most of the questions and make comments with the clients. You've still got a lot to learn about this business in general and, for that matter, the South Carolina football team."

Ryder exhaled dramatically.

"Gimme a break," she said. "The Gamecocks. Are you *fucking* kidding me? That's really their name?"

"Watch it, girl, they're the local religion down here," Jackie said. "And just for the record, most people call 'em the 'Cocks."

Ryder laughed. "Of course they do."

"And third of all, try reading something other than Elmore Leonard and Michael Connelly once in a while," Jackie said.

"What are you talking about?"

"Well, like that book she mentioned, *The Number 1 Ladies Detective Agency*," Jackie said. "It was a huge best seller."

"Hey, bro, if it ain't Elmore, Mike or chick lit... it ain't," Ryder said.

"You're scary, you know that," Farrell said. "And don't call me 'bro? I'm your damn sister."

"You don't want me to call you 'sis' do you?"

"No, why not just call me my name?"

"Yes... Jackie. But, I still like 'bro,'" Ryder said. "It's got kind of a refreshing contrariness to it."

Jackie shook her head. "Whatever... and do you have to use words like 'douche' with prospective clients we've just met for the first time?"

"How 'bout 'dick?' Is that better?"

"Oh, for God sake, you're out of control."

"Mrs. Roberts said 'intense.'"

"Yeah, I didn't know whether she meant that as good or bad."

"I thought good."

"Why?"

"'Cause the opposite of intense is weak... namby-pamby maybe."

Jackie got up, figuring the conversation had run its course.

"Where you going?" Ryder asked.

"We still have to finish up that cheating spouse case," Jackie said. "'Member? The one we were working on before we decided to go all-homicide, all the time."

"I like that, *all-homicide, all the time.* Good motto," Ryder said, "Where we goin'?"

"A cozy little, no-tell motel out in West Ashley."

CHAPTER THREE

The no-tell-motel actually turned out to be a perfectly nice Comfort Inn.

"How do you know this is where our two love birds went?" Ryder asked as they pulled into the motel's parking lot in Farrell's Ford Escape.

"Because I stuck a GPS on the guy's bumper," Jackie said. "And in South Carolina a GPS is a legal means of tracking an adulterer or adulteress."

"I see," Ryder said, "but doesn't adulterer cover both sexes?"

"Don't be a know-it-all. You were a college drop-out, remember?"

"Yeah, 'cause you remind me daily. So, you put a magnetized GPS on the bumper?"

Jackie nodded.

Ryder patted her on the shoulder. "Very good. Harry Bosch always does that."

Jackie looked blank.

"Come on, where you been?" said Ryder. "Michael Connelly's hero. You never saw the TV show? So, what exactly's the game plan here?"

"Okay, here's the deal. Our client, Francie Heyburn—the woman who suspects her husband of cheating—is worth a small fortune. Her husband, a charmer by the name of Tim Heyburn, is a serial cheater and Francie is *so* done with him. In South Carolina there are five grounds for divorce and the only one this guy is guilty of is infidelity, but he's very slippery, and she hasn't been able to get the goods on him yet."

"So, he's just hangin' in there 'cause of the money?"

"Yup, and she wants to cut him loose for once and for all. She's had it with the lowlife."

"Okay, so what are we gonna do?"

"Simple," Jackie said, turning off the car's engine. "We go see the desk clerk and flash some cash—" Jackie pulled her wallet out of her purse, reached in and lifted out five crisp hundred-dollar bills— "then I tell him or her I want to go say hello to the couple who just checked in—Mr. and Mrs. Smith, ninety per cent of the time—then he slides me a plastic card that opens the door."

"You don't think that just three of those Ben Franklin's would be enough?"

"Don't worry, it's in the budget."

"But can't the clerk get fired," Ryder asked, "if he or she gets caught giving you the plastic card?"

"Theoretically," Jackie said. "But what cheating guest's ever gonna go to the hotel manager and complain. They're in too big a hurry gettin' the hell out of Dodge."

Ryder hesitated, then nodded. "I still think that's too much to give the guy. I mean that's like a week's salary. I forget, how much do we get for a gig like this?"

"We get a flat rate for a money shot," Farrell said. "Three thousand."

"Money shot?"

"Yeah, that's what it's known as in the trade."

"Well, come on then," Ryder said, "let's go get our money shot."

*****

The only problem was that when Farrell put the plastic card in the lock and opened it, the couple was having drinks. The man was sitting on the side of a built-in desk looking down at the woman who was sitting in the desk chair. Worse, they both had their clothes on.

Jackie snapped off four quick shots with her phone camera anyway.

By that time, the man was getting aggressive and hurling epithets chocked full of four-letter words.

Jackie and Ryder beat it out of there exactly twenty seconds after Jackie first opened the door.

"So, is that enough evidence for our client to get her divorce?" Ryder asked, out of breath, as they got back into the Escape.

"I don't really know, depends on the judge. It definitely would have been better if there was some boffing going on," Jackie said, turning the ignition key.

Ryder laughed. "'Boffing? Jesus Jack, what century are you from?"

Jackie ignored her. "I'd say it was pretty incriminating, though. I mean a guy in a motel with a woman. What's he gonna say, they went there to play chess?"

Ryder thought a moment. "Hmm, naked chess maybe… that actually might be a lot of fun."

TO KEEP READING VISIT:
https://amzn.to/3JAo9ag

Audio Books

Many of Tom's books are also available in Audio...

Listen to masterful narrator Phil Thron and feel like you're right there in Palm Beach with Charlie, Mort and Dominica!

Audio books available include:
Palm Beach Nasty
Palm Beach Poison
Palm Beach Deadly
Palm Beach Bones
Palm Beach Pretenders
Palm Beach Predator
Charlie Crawford Box Set (Books 1-3)
Killing Time in Charleston
Charleston Buzz Kill
Charleston Noir
The Savannah Madam

About the Author

A native New Englander, Tom Turner dropped out of college and ran a Vermont bar. Limping back a few years later to get his sheepskin, he went on to become an advertising copywriter, first in Boston, then New York. After 10 years of post-Mad Men life, he made both a career and geography change and ended up in Palm Beach, renovating houses and collecting raw materials for his novels. After stints in Charleston, then Skidaway Island, outside of Savannah, Tom recently moved to Delray Beach, where he's busy writing about passion and murder among his neighbors. To date Tom has written eighteen crime thrillers and mysteries and is probably best known for his Charlie Crawford series set in Palm Beach.

Learn more about Tom's books at:
www.tomturnerbooks.com

Made in United States
Orlando, FL
27 December 2024